T0156696

The Abandonment of Me

The Abandonment of Me

CATHERINE M. CLIFTON

 iUniverse®

THE ABANDONMENT OF ME

iUniverse books may be ordered through booksellers or by contacting:

iUniverse
1663 Liberty Drive
Bloomington, IN 47403
www.iuniverse.com
1-800-Authors (1-800-288-4677)

Because of the dynamic nature of the Internet, any web addresses or links contained in this book may have changed since publication and may no longer be valid. The views expressed in this work are solely those of the author and do not necessarily reflect the views of the publisher, and the publisher hereby disclaims any responsibility for them.

Any people depicted in stock imagery provided by Thinkstock are models, and such images are being used for illustrative purposes only.
Certain stock imagery © Thinkstock.

ISBN: 978-1-4917-9032-8 (sc)
ISBN: 978-1-4917-9033-5 (e)

Library of Congress Control Number: 2016904506

Print information available on the last page.

iUniverse rev. date: 03/13/2018

Contents

Part
I

Eyes Of Deceit

Whenever you have to ask the question,

"Is this really love,"

Take a step back and carefully

observe your situation.

Sometime we will substitute what we feel

for what we desire.

Keep in mind, once you commit
yourself to a relationship,

You're also committing to the love, wishes,

and desires of someone else.

So remember, when in love;

Every action, intentional or
not, requires a reaction.

Prologue

The infatuation of love broke my heart while deceiving my mind in the process. I wanted to forget, but the ramifications of betrayal was haunting my every thought. How do you force yourself to get up, when the depth of your fall causes all of your emotions to collapse? I didn't want to be alone nor did I want my heart to be broken; but when you entrust your future to manipulative men, the outcome you seek will never be the one that you receive. I had hoped that I would be different. That my virtue would somehow lead me to the right guy, but I was wrong. In the end, I played the fool, not once, but twice.

My breathing intensified as I tried to calm myself down. I sat in silence trying to clear my head. I felt like the most naive person in the world. How could I have been so foolish? I applaud whomever came up with the statement, "love is blind," because they were right on the mark. I was so blinded by love that I had allowed myself to overlook suspicious behaviors, incomplete timelines, and a lot of too good to be true moments. I sat on the couch obsessing over what to do next. How do I utter out loud what I allowed myself to fall victim to once again.

Tears began to fall, but I quickly wiped them away. I didn't know what I was doing wrong. Maybe I was too trusting when it came to men, or maybe I was too eager to be in a relationship, but one thing was certain, I was done with dating for a while. I couldn't deal with my heart being broken over and over again by men whom I trusted. In time, I would eventually meet the right guy; or at least that's what I had hoped, but one thing was certain. I was in no hurry in becoming another man's fool.

Chapter 1

Sweet Tooth

The hotel was buzzing with excitement and many of the guests were starting to mingle amongst themselves. It was a big night for me, because I was catering my largest celebrity party yet. I could overhear a lot of the guests raving over the desserts that were being served throughout the night. All of my hard work had finally paid off, and a chill ran through my body as I reminisced on the journey it took for me to get to this point.

I was young and determined to make a name for myself, so I took a leap of faith and opened my first bakery in downtown Atlanta, Georgia. Ten years later and twenty five shops under my belt, Davenport's Sweet Cakes had become a household name, and were labeled the best bakeries in the eastern region. I'd put so much time and dedication into my shops that it left no time for a personal life. On one hand, my career had blossomed into a great success, but on the other, my love life was drowning in a sea of nonexistence.

While wearing my chef's whites, I mingled in the crowd, and posed in pictures with celebrities as the night commenced. The evening was going well and I decided to slip into the kitchen to take a break, but before I could make a move, someone in the crowd stopped me.

"Excuse me."

When I turned around, all I could do was stare. It was a guy I'd seen many times before. I would spot him with a different woman various nights of the week, whenever I was out making deliveries. He was tall, handsome, had caramel skin, gorgeous eyes, and was wearing a killer suit. I didn't want him to think that I was gawking at him, so I immediately snapped out of my trance.

"Yes. How can I help you?"

"Hi. Do you happen to know what type of cake this is?"

I looked down in his hands and he was holding my famous chocolate cherry cake.

"Yes, it's called a Cherry Bomb. It's flavored like the chocolate covered cherry candy that's usually bought during Christmas, and it's drizzled in a semi-sweet chocolate glaze."

"Well, it's delicious. Would you happen to know who made this?"

I was trying not to smile.

"Yes. I made it. To be honest, it's one of my favorites."

"Well, it's becoming one of my favorites as well. Forgive me…I know this may not be the right time to do this, but my brother owns a restaurant downtown and he's looking for a new pastry chef. . ."

"I'm sorry but…"

"Wait, wait. Hear me out. His restaurant is well-known. Maybe you've heard of it…Fosters?"

"Fosters. Yes, I've heard of it. It's off of Peachtree Street. A very classy place, but what would your brother need with another pastry chef? Doesn't Felipe work there? He's very good. . ."

"And he's gone. Come on, my brother could really use your help. All I'm asking you to do is think about it."

I knew I had no time to take on another restaurant, but I was incapable of saying no.

"Okay. I'll think about it."

As I began to walk off, I was stopped once again.

"Wait. I'm sorry. Do you have a business card?"

"Sure." I reached down into my jacket pocket, and handed the gentleman a card. "Here you go."

"Thanks again."

"Anytime."

I proceeded to walk away, but before I could take a step, the gentleman stopped me once more.

"Wait a minute. You're Jeremiah Davenport - the Jeremiah Davenport, who owns Davenport's Sweet Cakes."

"Yes. That's me."

"This is crazy! My brother is going to flip. You have to give him a chance. We love your desserts. Hell, I didn't realize I had a sweet tooth until the day I tasted your famous peach cobbler."

"Thanks. That one usually hooks a lot of people. How about this? Tell your brother to give me a call, and I'll see what I can do. So what's your brother's name?"

"Brandon. Brandon Foster and I'm Julian, by the way."

"Well, Julian, it was nice meeting you, and tell Brandon I'll be awaiting his call."

I smiled and walked off. I didn't have time for another client, but I was willing to give Brandon a chance. Besides, if he looked as good as Julian, then I was going to be the one suffering from a sweet tooth.

Later on that night before heading home, I decided to stop by and visit my father, William Davenport, to tell him all about the event. My father suffers from dementia, which was hard to digest, considering he used to be known as one of the most influential judges in Atlanta, Georgia. Now he sits at home all day too afraid to leave the house. I promised him a long time ago that I would never put him in a Senior Care Facility, regardless of the severity of his illness. Instead, I hired a nurse to take care of him at home so he'd be surrounded by some sort of familiarity. Some days were better than others. And then there were days when I would look into his eyes and wonder if he recognized me…or, if I was lost to him forever.

I walked into the house, and Mary, my father's nurse, was sitting in the living room watching television with him. It was late, but he loved his late night television shows. I walked over and gave him a kiss on the forehead.

"So, how was he today," I asked Mary as I pulled up a chair beside my father's recliner.

"He was okay. He's been a bit moody lately, but that's to be expected."

I laid my hand upon my father's hand, and he pulled his away as if I was a stranger he didn't want touching him.

"Dad. It's me, Maya. Dad?" My father fanned me away as if I was interrupting his television show. I walked over to the fireplace's mantel and picked up a family portrait of us to see if he could recognize me. "Dad. See. Maya." My father glanced at the picture, and then he stared at me. "It's me, dad. Maya."

"Patricia," my father said as if he called out the right name.

"No, dad. Patricia was your wife. I'm your daughter, Maya." I continued to show my father the picture, nevertheless, he insisted I was Patricia. Eventually I gave up. "Yes. It's Patricia. So, guess what happened to me tonight?"

"What happened?" My father asked in an inquisitive voice.

"I catered my largest celebrity party yet."

"That's good, Patricia. Did you bake them your famous sour cream pound cake? That's my favorite."

"No, I didn't serve any pound cake because that's just for you and me." I reached into my bag and pulled out two slices of pound cake. My father's eyes gleamed with excitement when he saw the plates.

"You brought me pound cake!"

"Yes, I did. You know I couldn't forget about you. Do you want some milk with it?"

"Yes. Thank you."

It broke my heart to see my father in such a helpless state. I walked into the kitchen and poured him a glass of milk. We sat in front of the television and talked about his shows while eating cake.

The next day, I woke up feeling groggy with a headache. After I left my father's, I stopped by a bar for a couple of drinks hoping the alcohol would numb the pain, but it didn't. I got up and made a cup of coffee and decided to watch some television. Saturday was my only day off, and Allison, my assistant, managed the shop for me, which gave me time to think and create new recipes.

Allison and I knew each other from college. We were the best of friends, and then we met Charlie and our duo turned into a trio. Allison dreamed of becoming a famous fashion designer, our friend Charlie, wanted a career in Human Relations, and my dream was to become the lawyer who represented them both. Although law was not my ideal dream job, I knew it would make my father happy. Our plans were working out for the most part, then my interest changed, and our dreams collapsed before they could take off. After a big fight, I stopped all communication with Charlie, but Allison was persistent in getting the group back together. Her efforts were quickly undermined when I decided to ditch law school for culinary school. Allison, however was determined to follow her own dreams, with or without me by her side. She opened a shop in Manhattan, New York, but within a year, it closed. I reached out to Allison, and offered her a job at the bakery until she was able to get back on her feet. Years passed, and Allison never made an advancement to reopen her shop. I tried offering her assistance in rebranding her name, but she wanted nothing more to do with her company. Instead, she decided to give up on her enterprise in order to help me flourish in mine. From that point on, I never questioned Allison about her decision to stay, and in return, she promised not to harass me about reconnecting with Charlie.

I dragged myself to the kitchen and stared at the pantry trying to think of various flavors I could pair together. While in mid thought, I caught myself fantasizing about Julian, who I knew was off limits. He was obviously a player, and I didn't have time for men like him. My job was very demanding and what little time I did have to spare, I wanted to spend it with someone who was only interested in me.

Frustrated, I decided to get dress and go shopping. I headed to the farmers market to check on some fresh fruit and berries I could use in my recipes. While chatting with one of the local vendors, my phone rang. I looked down at the unknown number, and decided to let it go to voicemail. As I continued to shop, my phone rang again. It was the same number, so I answered.

"Hello."

"Hi, my name is Brandon Foster. My brother, Julian gave me your card, and told me to give you a call."

"Brandon, yes. Julian told me you were looking for a new pastry chef, and I explained to him that I would consider you as a new client if I was able to fit you in."

"Well, I was hoping you would give me a chance. I could really use your business right now if you're available. My current chef took another job without any warning. Now I'm left with no pastry chef or desserts to offer my guests."

I felt bad for Brandon. In our line of work, if one person quits, then it can disrupt your entire business.

"I understand what you're going through…trust me I do. I don't want to get your hopes up, so let me see what I can do."

"Great!" I could hear the excitement in Brandon's voice. "I know you're a busy person, so whenever you're free, you can stop by the restaurant at any time and we can discuss different business options. If that's alright with you?"

"Sounds great. How's today?"

"Today?" I could sense that my request may have taken Brandon off guard.

"Yes, today. If you're serious about my business, then let's set up a meeting for today. If that's alright with you."

"Today is fine. How does one o'clock sound?"

"One o'clock is perfect. I'll see you then."

I only had two hours to make it home, change, and try to put together a great presentation. I changed into my business attire and stopped by the bakery to pick up some samples. I grabbed my portfolio and business calendar, then darted for the door. When I arrived at Fosters, I took a deep breath and walked inside. I loved the atmosphere of the restaurant. It was chic, cozy, and very inviting. The lights were dimmed and jazz music played throughout the corridor. The seating inside the restaurant was very intimate. There were bamboo tables with white wrap around booth seating, and colorful art décor dressed the walls. I greeted the hostess and asked for Brandon. Before long I was being escorted towards the back of the restaurant. While walking, I could feel the items in my hands slowly slipping away from me. As I leaned forward to place my basket of samples on the table, it began to fall; but luckily, there was a mysterious guy there to catch it. I looked up and our eyes met.

"Thank you."

"No problem."

"I'm Maya by the way," I said while extending out my hand.

"I'm Brandon, and it's so nice to finally meet you." Brandon was as handsome as his brother. Same caramel skin, gorgeous eyes, and killer smile. Boy, was I in trouble. He placed the basket on his desk while trying to compose himself. "I'm such a big fan of your desserts."

"And I'm a huge fan of your restaurant." I looked up, and before we could get started, the door opened and Julian walked in.

"You remember my brother, Julian?"

"Yes, I remember. It's good to see you again." I shook his hand and sat back down.

"Well, I hope you don't mind Julian being here. He may be my older brother, but he's also my lawyer."

"Oh, so you're a lawyer. Well, that's good to know." At that moment, I turned my sites back toward Brandon. "So, do I need to call *my* lawyer, because I thought this was just a simple business meeting?"

"It is, but just in case we come to an agreement, I want to have Julian look over everything to ensure we're both getting a fair deal."

"I understand, but know if a deal is reached, I'll have my own lawyer look over the contract, if that's alright with you."

Julian stood back and acknowledged my request as Brandon and I discussed a suitable arrangement regarding my service. I advised him there would be no staff working on site, but we could provide him with whatever type of desserts he desired. Then I pulled out some of the shop's favorites. The "Roger Rabbit" carrot cake, Chocolate Thunder fudge cake, The Sweet Heart raspberry tart, the

Double Dutch cupcakes, and my famous peach cobbler. Brandon was in heaven sampling all of the cakes, but Julian kept to his favorite, the peach cobbler.

"So what do you think?"

"Everything tastes good, but I wonder…will the same desserts be in rotation or will there be a monthly variation?"

"Once Kyle overlooks the contract…"

"Who's Kyle?" Brandon asked.

"I'm sorry. Kyle is *my* lawyer. Once he overlooks the contract, and if I decide to move forward with the deal, then you'll be given a list of all the desserts we have on menu. At that point, it'll be up to you to let us know what you would like to have on a weekly basis. We're constantly adding new items to the menu, so whenever you see something you like, all you'd have to do is let us know."

The office door opened, and a tall slender woman with long dark brown hair came walking in. Her rich brown complexion made her red lipstick pop, and her hazel eyes took center stage.

"Angela. Come in." Brandon met her at the door and gave her a kiss on the lips. "Maya, this is my girlfriend, Angela."

Girlfriend? Well, that's one brother who's now off-limits. Angela walked over to me and shook my hand.

"It's so nice to meet you. Brandon has been going on and on about you and your desserts."

"No. I think it was the other way around. She's had to adjust her workout routines every week because she can't stay away from your shops." Brandon joked with Angela.

"In my defense, it's hard to say no to white chocolate. And Maya, your gingerbread spice cake dipped in white chocolate is one of my all-time favorites.

"Alright, you guys know that buttering me up isn't going to persuade me one way or another…but it doesn't hurt either."

We all started to laugh.

"Well, Maya, I want to thank you again for considering my restaurant as a possibility. I know that I'm asking a lot from you, but hopefully you'll decide to do business with us. Now, I'll leave you in the hands of Julian, and it was nice meeting you."

"It was nice meeting you guys as well."

We shook hands and Brandon and Angela left the room. I began to pack up and placed the contract in my brief case.

"My brother really appreciates what you're doing for him. After Felipe quit, let's just say that Brandon wasn't prepared for his leaving.

"I understand. In our line of work untimely things can easily happen." I started to clear away the food that was left on the desk. "Once Kyle reviews the contract, I'll be sure to give you a call."

I began to pack up the desserts while placing them evenly in the picnic basket.

"Wait." Julian placed his hands over the peach cobbler. "Do you think you can leave the cobbler?"

I started to smile. "Sure, I can leave the cobbler. But be careful. Don't let your sweet tooth get you into trouble." Julian and I reached for the picnic basket at the same time and our hands touched.

"I'm sorry." I swiftly moved my hands away from his.

"There's nothing to be sorry about." Julian handed me the basket and I proceeded towards the door.

"So, Maya, tell me something. Are you busy tomorrow night?"

I turned around and before I knew it, I could feel the warmness in my cheeks. "I don't know. It depends."

"Depends on what?"

"On why you're asking?"

"Well, if you're not busy, I'd like to take you out to dinner."

"Dinner?" I stood in shock. I couldn't believe Julian was asking me out. "I'm sorry, but I have plans. Maybe next time."

"What about Monday?"

"Busy."

"Tuesday?"

"Busy."

"Wednesday, Thursday, Friday?"

"Busy, busy, busy. Look Julian, you seem like a nice guy, but I'm not going out on a date with you."

"And why not? I'm not crazy. I have all my teeth and I'm very fun to be around. But most importantly, I find you very attractive. So what do you say...Maya? Are you willing to turn that no into a yes?"

Julian seemed like the type of man who was always use to getting what he wanted, but he was about to find out that I wasn't as easily moved as other women. "No, I'm sorry Julian, but you're just not my type." I smiled, as I walked towards the door. "Goodbye, Mr. Foster."

A date with Julian would've been nice, but he was a player, and I didn't have time for games. The right guy for me was out there and sooner or later, we were going to meet.

I took the contract to Kyle for his review. He spent an hour scrutinizing it, but finally concluded it was a fair deal. I went back to the bakery to inform Allison that Fosters were going to be one of our new clients. Afterwards, I stopped by my father's and sat with him for a while. By the time I made it home, my Saturday was gone. I was beat and all I wanted to do was lie down. I passed out on the couch, but before I could get comfortable, my doorbell rang. I looked at the clock because it was late.

"Who is it?"

"It's Julian."

Julian! What did he want and why was he at my door? More importantly, how did he know where I lived? I opened the door.

"Hi. Did I forget something?"

"Yes. My number." Julian handed me his business card.

"And why would I need your number?"

"So you can call me once you've signed the contract. Remember?"

"And what makes you so certain that I'll sign the contract?"

"Well, I could see it in your eyes. You don't want to let my brother down, so that's how I know you're going to sign the contract." Julian continued to inch closer to the door as if he wanted me to let him in, but that wasn't about to happen.

"Really? You got all that from looking into my eyes. Don't you know the eyes can be deceiving?"

"Yes, but you look trustworthy."

"Trustworthy." I began to laugh. "So tell me something, Honest Abe: how did you get my address?"

"Well, to be honest it was quite easy. I Googled you."

"Really? Try again, because my address isn't listed online. So how did you get it?"

"I. . ." Julian seemed as though he was at a loss for words.

"Come on. Tell me."

"I'd rather not say." All he could do was smile.

"Okay. Well, let me guess…Allison? Am I right?"

"Look, don't be mad at her. I pressured her into giving me your address."

"How? Because Allison is a vault. She wouldn't just give you my address."

"She would if I told her it was an emergency. You see, I convinced her that the contract was missing some very critical information and we couldn't close the deal unless it was addressed tonight."

"And she believed you?"

"Yes. I can be quite convincing."

"No. You didn't convince her of anything. You lied to her. There's a difference."

"I wouldn't call it lying. I was just stretching the truth, because technically you can't call me about the contract unless you have my number."

"Well, technically I could have Googled you and got your number." Both of us started to laugh. I looked at the business card and motioned as if I was about to close the door. "Well, I have your number and if I decide to sign the contract, I'll give you a call. Good night, Julian." As I pushed the door, Julian blocked it with his hand.

"Wait."

"Yes?"

"Are you sure I can't convince you into going out on a date with me?"

"Oh, I'm sure. Goodnight."

"Okay, so what is it? Why won't you go out with me?"

"I told you why."

"Yeah. I'm not your type, but I'm not buying that. So what's the real reason?"

"Look, Julian, there's no conspiracy. You're just not my type; and I'm not trying to put myself down or anything, but I'm not your type either. So go home. It's late."

"And how do you know what my type is? You know something that I don't?"

"Let's just say, I've seen you around the way and the type of women you've been with. I think it's safe to say that I'm not your type. So, goodnight."

"See, that's where you're wrong because I don't have a type."

I smiled. Julian was quite charming, but there was no way I was going out on a date with him.

"Goodnight, Julian."

I closed the door and placed the card on the table. Going on a date with Julian would've been a nice distraction, but I was looking for something long term - not just an easy fix. If I was truly honest with myself, then maybe I would have said yes and took a chance for once. I had everything going for me. A great business, good friends...but no love life. I needed to take myself down off the pedestal and loosen up a little. I knew Julian wasn't the relationship type, but in a way, neither was I. My business would always be my first love and that would never change. So, if it was meant for us to ever go out on a date, then eventually it would happen. However, I was in no hurry in becoming one of Julian's latest victims.

Chapter 2

❧

Why Not

A couple of months passed and my arrangement with Brandon was working out quite well. He would select the desserts he wanted for the week, and Allison and I dropped them off every Sunday like clockwork. His staff was always fascinated to see which desserts Brandon had chosen for the week. I think his employees were more excited about the desserts than their actual customers. And sadly enough, I continued to see Julian along my delivery routes, seducing a different woman various days of the week. Occasionally, I'd glance at him, shaking my head in disappointment, and he wondered why I wouldn't go out on a date with him.

One Sunday evening, after the deliveries were complete, Allison and I ventured back to the shop. It was late, and everyone was cleaning up and preparing to head home. As I walked through the door, there sat Matthew Coleman waiting for me in my office. Matt had dark brown hair, a fit body because he loved to work out, and oh could he wear a suit! He was a white male who could easily turn the head of any woman, regardless of race - which spoke volumes considering my shop was centrally located in the urban distract. Matt worked for Jackson & Murray, a large lucrative law firm that has been trying to buy me out for the past four years. Each time he came around, my answer was always no, but that never stopped Matt from periodically popping up at the shop trying to persuade me to sell. His name should have been Matthew Persistence, because he didn't know how to take no for an answer.

"Matt. So what can I do for you?"

"Well, Maya. You know the routine. I ask if I can I buy you out, you say no, and we continue on with this charade month after month, but you know I have to ask."

"I know you do and my answer is still no. Sorry, Matt."

"No need to apologize. One day I'm going to stop by and your answer is going to be yes. I can feel it."

"Keep feeling yourself, Matt, because that's never going to happen." I sat down at my desk and poured myself a glass of wine. "Join me."

"No, I can't. I'm still on the clock."

"You're always on the clock. Drink with me."

Matt sat down and I poured him a glass of wine. Even though I viewed him as the enemy, our monthly encounters had somehow transformed into a cordial friendship.

"So are you ready for this beat down on Friday?" Matt asked as he sipped on his wine.

"Beat down? Really? I don't quite remember it that way because last I checked, your team lost!"

"Only because your team cheated!"

Matt and I played with a very competitive softball league. It was usually the lawyers against the shop owners, which worked to the lawyer's advantage. Some shop owners were somewhat hesitate about selling their business, but the league allowed both sides to see each other in a different light. The lawyers were able to see the owners with their families, which made them adjust their terms when it came to buying them out. It became a win-win for both sides.

"Really? And how did we do that? Last time I checked you made it very clear that your team was made up of softball professionals and we were nothing more than just a bunch of girls trying to play ball. Remember?"

"All girls. Some pretending to be girls. It doesn't matter. Your team cheated, but we're not holding back this game. It's on!"

"Bring it, Matt, because we're not afraid of you or your professional team. Ha!"

Matt's phone began to ring. He checked it then placed it back in his jacket pocket.

"Well, Maya. This was fun but I have to go."

"I don't know how you do it. There has to be a cut off time when it comes to work."

"And there is, but that wasn't work. That was Amy. I'm late for our date."

"Amy? Wait a minute. What happened to Samantha?"

"Samantha who?"

"Don't play coy with me, Matt. Hell, less than a year ago, you two were so in love that you couldn't live without each other. So, what happened?"

"I grew up, plain and simple. I realized I was ready to settle down and she wasn't."

"Settle? Is that word even in your vocabulary?"

"I get it, Maya. I know it's hard to believe but some of us do change."

"And some of us are good at pretending. But if settling down makes you happy, then I'm happy for you."

"And I'll be happy for you too, once you decide to stop lying to yourself and start dating."

Really. Matt didn't just come at me. He decided to hit me below the belt. "What did you say?"

"Look, I'm telling you this as a friend. In the four years I've known you, I can always count on you to be in here on a Sunday night. That's not good, Maya. You need to start dating."

"No. What I need is a friend who doesn't lecture me about my love life."

"FYI, you don't have a love life, you're not in a relationship, and the last time I checked, you didn't have a man either. You're living in denial and it's time you woke up." Matt could tell that I was bothered by his comment. "Goodnight." He kissed me on the cheek and walked out the door. I was hurt because Matt was right. I didn't have a man nor was I in any type of relationship. All I had was my business. I had to put aside this fantasy of the perfect guy and start dating before I grew into an old, lonely, and bitter woman.

The next day I decided to get up early and head to the farmer's market. Since I was putting myself back into the dating pool, I was going to need food to feed this so-called man I was destined to meet. While out shopping I felt a tap on the shoulder. I turned around and there stood Brandon.

"Good morning, Brandon."

"Morning. You're just the person I needed to see." Brandon gave me a hug.

"Oh really? So what's up?"

"Well, as you know, your desserts have become a hit at the restaurant, so I wanted to know if you would like to partner up with my catering company, and make this a permanent deal."

"Partner up in what way? We're already in a binding contract?"

"Yes, with the restaurant, but not with my catering company.

I thought about it and realized our partnership could be huge. Everyone loves your desserts, so if I attach Davenport's Sweet Cakes to my catering menu, then…"

"Okay, slow down for a minute. I already have a catering company. So what's in it for me if I sign with your business?"

"This." Brandon reached into his backpack and handed me a printout of our company's annual revenue and a projection of what we could earn if our businesses merged. "All I'm saying is think about it."

"So, how were you able to come up with *my* revenue?"

"I had Julian do some digging for me. I hope you don't mind, but I needed to show you just how much of an opportunity this could be for the both of us."

I was seriously considering the proposal . . . and the extra money could allow me to open up another shop if I played my hand right.

"Are you sure about this? I mean Fosters is your baby, and…"

"And I want you to be a part of it. Face it Maya, Davenport's Sweet Cakes is a staple, and I'd be a fool not to pursue a merger."

"Okay. Let me get with Kyle and I'll get back to you. No promises."

"Great! You won't regret this. I promise!"

Brandon looked like a kid who was given a free pass at the candy store. All I could do was smile. I headed home, and before I could pull into the driveway, I spotted Julian standing at my front door. I could feel my body jump with excitement, but I had to check myself. Julian was not my man, even though I had envisioned him so many times in many compromising positions that he could've been; but only in my thoughts. I grabbed the groceries from the car and headed towards the house.

"Hi, and what do I owe this visit?"

"I just spoke with Brandon, and he told me he pitched you the deal about the catering venture."

"He did." Julian took the bags out of my hands as I opened the door.

"Well, I wanted to know straight from you if you think this could be plausible? I know my brother, and he gets excited over a lot of things, but this is different for him. He truly believes in this collaboration."

Julian placed the bags on the kitchen counter and I began to unpack the groceries.

"Look Julian. I get that Brandon is excited. I could see the enthusiasm on his face when we discussed the deal, but what I don't get is why you feel the need to show up every time a pitch is made? You know your presence doesn't have an effect on my decisions… right."

"I know, but I like being here." Julian began to unpack some of the groceries.

"And that would be okay if you were invited. But you weren't. So, is there any other business you came over here to discuss?" I began to take items away from Julian and put them away in the refrigerator and kitchen cabinets.

"Yes. I wanted to know if you have given any more consideration to my last proposal."

"And what proposal was that?"

"Oh, you know what proposal I'm talking about."

I could feel myself smiling on the inside but prayed the emotions I was feeling weren't resonating on my face.

"A date?"

"Yes, I knew you remembered."

"But why me? I see you out all the time with different women. So why would going out on a date with me be any different?"

"Because you're different."

"I'm not different? I'm about as ordinary as ordinary gets. So tell me, what's the real reason behind this stalker-like vibe you have going on?"

"Stalker? I don't think so, but I am curious about you. That's why I want to take you out on a date."

"Curious? Really? So, what would happen if I were to tell you no again? Would you come back later on or show up on my doorstep in the middle of the night again?"

"No, and despite what you may think about me, I know how to take rejection. So the next time you say no, I'll stop by your shop to harass you." I started to laugh. Julian was smart, funny, and very sexy. Three things I knew could get me into trouble.

"Fine. You win. I'll go on a date with you, but after you hear my list of rules, you might change your mind."

"Bring it. I've heard them all. So what are they? You don't have sex on the first date, or no PDA, or no feeling on your booty. Give it to me. I can take it."

I was trying my best not to laugh.

"Okay, but I warned you. The first rule is, when you take me out on a date, we're only to do fun things. Nothing serious like candle lit dinners. Boring. Next, cell phones have to be off for the duration of the date. If we're talking, I don't need a phone call interrupting our conversation. And last, since I really don't know you that well, kisses only. I figure no harm ever came from kissing, but that's it. So, after hearing all that, do you still want to go on a date with me?"

"So, let me get this straight. We are only to do fun things, no cell phones allowed, and if we like each other, all we can do is kiss. Is that about right?"

"You got it. So what do you say? Deal or no deal?"

"Well, for starters, I think you're a little crazy but that's beside the point. So deal. Once I figure out where we're going, I'll give you a call with a date and time."

"That sounds like a plan."

Julian took a muffin off the kitchen counter and walked out. I couldn't believe it. I was going out on a date...with Julian. I just pray my emotions remain calm and his charm and swagger doesn't lure me into bed.

I went to the shop and Allison was bagging a big order.

"I see you're busy."

"Yes. Regina is coming by to pick up the treats for the kids."

Regina was a local school teacher who would splurge on her kids every other week, by buying them various treats off the menu. Even though her students were teenagers, she still liked rewarding them with something special.

"Do you need any help?" I could feel myself smiling.

"Sure."

I glanced at Allison and I noticed her glaring at me.

"What? And why are you staring at me?"

"I don't know. Maybe I'm trying to figure out why you have a big grin plastered across your face. So what's up? What has you in such a good mood?"

"It's nothing."

I went into the kitchen and Allison followed.

"Why are you lying to me? You forget that I know you Maya, so spill. What's up?"

"Well, if you must know, someone asked me out on a date."

Allison looked as though she wanted to say something, but all she could do was stare at me in shock.

"Are you serious? Miss I'm not having sex until I'm married and there are no good men left, is going out on a date?"

"Yes. Can you believe it?"

"So what happened? Scratch that. Who's the lucky guy?"

"Well, if you must know, it's Julian Foster."

"Julian? The same Julian who you've been labeling as a whore since the day you met him; Julian?"

"Yep! That would be the one."

"So what happened? You swore me up and down that you would never go out on a date with him? So what made you change your mind?"

"I don't know. Maybe I'm just tired of being alone."

"So you decide to give in to Julian? Come on Maya. He's not relationship material and you know it. Once he gets what he wants, he's gone."

"Who said I was planning on giving him anything? I know what type of man Julian is, and I know he likes to use women. So my question is…why can't I use him?"

"Use him how?"

"Julian thinks that eventually I'm going to sleep with him, but I'm curious to see how long he's willing to stick around, before he realizes that's not going to happen."

"You know what you're doing is risky, right? Do you even trust yourself enough to play this type of game with him?"

"Yes, and why would you ask that? I've been doing this for years and haven't caved in before; so why would I start now?"

"Because you've never dated anyone like Julian. Superficially, he's everything you want in a man…but he's every woman's man. He doesn't know how to be with just one woman."

"I know this, Allison. Besides, I'm not looking to marry the guy. I just want to have some fun. That's all. Am I not allowed to have any fun?"

"You're allowed to have fun, but know you're playing with fire, and I pray you don't burn yourself in the process."

"Well, I knew I could count on you to give it to me straight, and you did. But trust me, I know what I'm doing."

"Okay. If you say so."

As I checked on the cakes in the oven, the bell rang at the front counter. Allison and I headed up front and there stood Regina waiting to pick up her order.

"Morning ladies."

"Morning Regina." I assisted Allison in packing Regina's order. "The kids are going to love these. We hid caramel brownies in the middle of each cupcake."

"Ooh, that sounds so good. The kids have been begging me all week to tell them what type of treats you were making them. It was hard trying to keep them at bay."

"Well, all I can say is what you're doing for those kids is truly amazing. I know you don't have to do it, but I admire the devotion you give to your students."

"Thanks, Maya, that means a lot. I like rewarding them for their hard work. We always have a quiz one day before a big test, so I choose to make it into a game to keep it interesting. The kids love it and the cupcakes are the prizes."

"Well, tell your students to keep up the hard work; and since you're such an awesome teacher, this order is on the house."

"No, you don't have to…"

"No, I insist. Now go out and corrupt some young minds." I fanned Regina away from the counter.

"Thank you, Maya. This means a lot."

Regina walked out the door and I could feel Allison staring at me.

"What?"

"Nothing. That was sweet. Costly but sweet."

"I know, but I admire what she's doing. It can't be an easy job.

Besides, Mrs. Garcia left us a very generous tip for her cake yesterday which will cover Regina's order *and* our trip to the spa tomorrow."

"The spa. So, you're bringing me along this time?"

"I guess so. Anyway, you're my only true friend besides Matt who really doesn't count."

"So, what's up with you and Matt anyway? You two have a very strange relationship."

"I know it's crazy, but you know what's even crazier? The fact that he's dating and I'm not. He's a lawyer. When do lawyers have time to date? Besides, I've always pictured him with you anyway. The two of you would be perfect together."

"And why would you think that?"

"Well, for starters, both of you like to meddle in other people's business. To me, that's compatibility."

Allison and I started to laugh as we got back to work. For once I was going to let my hair down and have some fun. I knew the type of man Julian was, but I was tired of being alone. At some point, my truth would surface. Until then I intended to play along until I got caught. I wasn't the type of person who played games, but when it came to men like Julian, either you play the game or you get played.

Chapter 3

✦

Kisses Only

A week had passed and Julian finally decided on a location for our date. I was so excited to see where he was taking us, but I also had Allison's warning looming in the back of my head. Yes, Julian was a dog, but I felt as though I could control myself around him; or at least that's what I wanted to believe. Even though I was saving myself for Mr. Right, there was always the fear of never meeting him. I didn't want to abandon my morals because I was lonely. Yet, I didn't want to end up alone, simply because I was too picky about who I wanted to be with.

The Accounting Department at Julian's firm was being audited, and they asked if I would cater their meetings. I didn't mind taking on the firm because it gave me a reason to stop by and see Julian. Since the meeting was causal, I decided to wear a free flowing sundress, hoping it would catch Julian's attention. I was convinced that I would be able to get him to spill on the location of our date, if I played my cards right.

"Hi, are you busy?"

I could tell Julian was shocked to see me.

"Hey. What are you doing here?"

"We're catering for the accounting division downstairs. You seem surprised to see me. What's wrong?"

"Nothing's wrong. I'm just surprise to see you *here,* that's all."

"Well, don't worry. I'm not staying long. I only came by to give you this." I placed a bag on Julian's desk. "I couldn't allow accounting to have all the goodies, now could I?"

Julian opened the bag, and in it was his own personal pan of peach cobbler.

"You didn't!"

"Oh, but I did. Just a little something to brighten your day."

Julian walked from behind his desk, locked his office door, and then he made his way towards me.

"Thank you."

"It was nothing."

I smiled as Julian moved closer to me; and without warning, he kissed me. I couldn't believe what was happening. I pulled back and looked into his eyes, and at that moment, I knew I was in big trouble.

"What was that for?"

"That was me thanking you."

"But you had already thanked me, so what was the kiss for?"

"The kiss was just a proper thank you."

Julian knew how to turn on the charm.

"Okay, Mr. Foster. Your kiss was nice but it's time for me to go."

"What's the rush?"

"I'm not rushing. It's just time for me to leave. Besides, I'm probably needed back downstairs. I'm working, remember?"

Julian didn't say a word. He grabbed hold of me and continued to kiss me. It was like I hadn't said a word. His kisses were so hypnotic. I wanted to pull away but I couldn't. Julian picked me up with my legs straddled around his waist and sat me down on his desk. I had no idea where this was going but I needed to get control of the situation and fast. I forced myself to stop kissing Julian, but that didn't stop him from kissing me. He moved from my lips, to my neck, then my chest. This was not happening! I felt Julian's hands creep up my dress, and I pushed him away trying my best to control the situation.

"Stop. I told you from the beginning, kisses only."

"And that's all we're doing. Kissing."

Julian's hands moved back up my dress as he continued to kiss me. My emotions were all over the place, and then I felt him tug on my panties.

"Okay, that's enough! We have to stop now." I pushed Julian off of me as I tried to compose myself.

"Are you sure? We don't have to stop."

"Oh, yes we do! I don't know what just happened here, but I have to be very careful around you."

"You don't have to be cautious around me. I wouldn't force you to do anything you wouldn't want to do."

"Are you sure about that?"

"Oh, I'm sure, because what I got for you, you're not ready for it."

"Really? You're so full of yourself. You know what…this was nothing but a mistake and it won't happen again."

"Don't speak too soon. Date night is right around the corner."

"And that may be the case, but next time you'll have to keep your distance."

"We'll see."

I couldn't get over how I allowed Julian to get in my head. I knew I would need a prayer and full body amour for our upcoming date. It was clear I was weak around him. I really didn't need his kisses leading to other things.

"Good-bye, Julian."

I walked to the restroom to freshen up while still in shock over what had just happened. I needed to rediscover self-control, because apparently I didn't have any around Julian. I took the elevator downstairs and ran into Regina as I stepped off.

"Regina, it's good to see you."

Regina gave me a hug.

"It's good to see you too. So, what brings you here?"

"The Accounting Division, believe it or not. Its audit season and they asked us to cater the event. Since joining with Fosters, we are now catering breakfast, lunch, and dinner, which opens up an array of new clientele."

"Fosters? I didn't know you were in business with them."

"Yes. The owner thought it would be a good idea if we joined forces with his restaurant, and he was right. So, what brings you here?"

"Oh, one of my students has gotten himself into a bit of trouble, so I'm here to seek some legal counsel."

"I'm so sorry to hear that. I know how you feel about your students."

"They are my life. I would do anything for them and they would do the same for me."

I could see Allison signaling for me.

"Well, I hope everything works out. I have to go."

"Thanks."

I walked over towards Allison to see what the commotion was about.

"So what's up?"

"Where have you been? I was looking all over for you."

"Oh, I ran into Regina and she was telling me about one of her students who seemed to have gotten into some legal trouble." I didn't like lying to Allison, but I'm sure she didn't want to know what I was really up to. Hell, I was there and I still couldn't wrap my head around what happened. Besides, if I would have told her the truth, then for the rest of the day, I'd have to listen to her say, "I told you so." I was so not in the mood to hear her chastise me, so I lied. "So, what's up?"

"Well, the firm enjoyed the food so much that they want to sign us to a contract for their next couple of events."

Allison pulled the contract from behind her back. We looked at each other and smiled with excitement.

"Are you serious? This is great news! Wait until my father hears about this. I can finally tell my dad I'm working for a law firm. Ha! Even though I know it's not the same thing as being a lawyer, it's still cool to say."

"Okay, I get that your father wanted you to become a lawyer, but look at everything you've accomplished. He has to be proud of you."

"I know he is, but I would give anything just to hear him say it. Anyway, before I get too excited, I have to call Brandon to see what he thinks about the deal."

"Well, you go ahead and take care of the paperwork and I'll finish up here."

"Are you sure? I can stick around just in case something else comes up."

"No, you go ahead. If something comes up that I can't handle, then I'll give you a call."

"Okay. Well, I'll see you tomorrow."

I went by to see Brandon and I told him about the deal. We went over the contract line by line and decided to take on the firm as a new client. As Angela walked into the room, Brandon informed her of the good news and we celebrated the occasion with cake and wine. Business was booming and my so called love life was trying to take off. After the celebration, I left for my dad's to inform him of the good news; but before I could pull into his driveway, I passed Julian who was parked in front of the house. Popping up at my house was one thing, but showing up at my father's was crossing the line.

"Julian, what are you doing here?"

"It wasn't my intention to come here, but I wanted to make sure you were okay."

"I'm fine, but that doesn't explain why you're here. And if Allison gave you this address, then we might have to rethink our friendship. . ."

"Don't blame Allison. She had nothing to do with me coming here. Like I said before, I wanted to make sure you were okay."

"I'm fine, but why do you keep asking? Did something happen that I don't know about?" I began to feel uneasy. I hadn't spoken with Mary all day. Did something happen to my father? I started towards the house in a panic, but before I could make it to the door, Julian stopped me.

"Wait! Before you go in, let me explain."

"What is there to explain? There could be something wrong with my father. I have to check on him." I tried to push past Julian but he wouldn't let me pass. "What are you doing?"

"I didn't mean to scare you, but I think I may have overreacted just a little."

"What are you talking about?"

"Okay, I'm going to be honest with you, but promise me you won't get mad."

"I'm not making any promises, so what's going on?"

"Fine. Here's the truth. I stopped by your shop earlier today and there was this guy delivering you some black roses, and on the card it read, "Sorry for your loss. Matt." I didn't know what was going on, so I raced over here to make sure you were okay, and I'm sorry if I scared you in the process." As much as I wanted to be mad at Julian, I couldn't. All I could do was laugh. "What's so funny?"

"You are. You scared me half to death over nothing."

"Nothing! Black roses were delivered to your job. I didn't know what to think."

"Well, I'm sorry if Matt scared you, but everything is okay. So you can go home now."

"Go home? Are you serious? And what's up with this guy Matt and why is he sending you black roses?"

"Nosey much? But if you must know, Matt and I are in the same softball league. His team slaughtered my crew on Friday so he sent me black roses to mourn the death of my ego."

Julian had a look of disgust on his face.

"So, to be clear, no one has died in this scenario and the only thing harmed was your ego?"

"That's about right."

"I'm going home."

I felt bad that my ongoing joke with Matt upset Julian, but in my defense he had no right to be snooping around my shop.

"Are you mad? You read a card that was addressed to me and now you're upset because you weren't in on the joke?"

"I'm not mad, but I am disappointed that a grown woman would play such childish games."

"Childish games! Are you serious? You snoop around my shop, come across something that wasn't addressed to you, and you have the nerve to be disappointed in me. Please! You are free to leave at any time."

As I headed towards the door, Julian grabbed my waist and pulled me into a kiss. Why was he playing mind games with me? I didn't want to kiss him, but I couldn't force myself to break away. Allison was right. Julian was different than any other guy I had ever dated, and if I didn't form some kind of self-control, then I could kiss my virginity goodbye.

"I'm sorry. I didn't come over here to upset you. You're right. I shouldn't have been snooping around and it won't happen again."

Oh, was I in trouble. When a man is caught doing wrong, he tends to throw on the charm, and here I was eating it up. What was wrong with me and where was my common sense when I needed it?

"We'll see. Anyway, I have to go and check on my dad, but this…this was interesting." I opened the door to go inside and Julian followed me. "What are you doing?"

"I'm staying too. Besides, it's late. So when you finish up here, I'll escort you home.

"No, you don't have to wait. Plus, I don't know how long I'll be here."

"It's fine…"

"No! You don't get it. You shouldn't be here. My father doesn't react well to strangers. You should go."

"I'm not leaving you."

What was I going to do? My father's moods would change like the wind. He could barely recognize me on a good day, so there was no telling how he would react to seeing Julian. As I walked in the house, I heard yelling coming from the living room. Just my luck, my father was having one of his bad days. If he wasn't medicated quickly, he would scream, curse, and go on a raging rampage all night long. I went into the living room and I tried to talk him down while Mary fixed his syringe; but then my father caught sight of Julian and he went wild.

"Patricia! What is this? Are you screwing around on me? Are you bringing strange men into my house?"

"Dad, it's me, Maya, your daughter and this is my friend Julian."

"Patricia, what's wrong? You don't love me anymore?" My father looked at me, then started to charge towards Julian. "You wait until I get my hands on you! You son of a…"

"Dad, stop!" I tried to grab hold of my father and without warning he turned around and slapped me. I looked down and there was blood coming from my mouth.

"Maya, are you okay?" Julian asked as he tried to evade my father.

"I'm fine. Just help me hold him down."

My father was violent and belligerent but Julian was able to restrain him. I tried to help hold him down while Mary tranquilized him. After my father was sedated, I went into the bathroom to clean up. I closed the door and locked it. I was so embarrassed.

"Maya, are you sure you're okay?" Julian asked through the door.

"Yes. I'm fine." Tears ran down my cheeks and I quickly wiped them away. I tried to compose myself so I could face Julian. As I walked out, Mary was waiting for me in the hallway.

"Ms. Davenport, we need to talk. Your father is getting worse, and I don't know how much longer I can continue to do this."

"Mary, I understand, but I promised my father a long time ago that I wouldn't put him in a senior care facility. This is his home. So, if this is too much for you, then let me know so I can look for another caregiver."

"I understand what you're saying, Ms. Davenport, but I don't think you understand the severity of this situation. Your father is very sick and needs constant care. The type of care he's not receiving here. I know what you promised him, but you also have to think about what's best for him."

Mary was right, yet I had no intention in breaking my father's promise. I loved him and there was no way I would agree to send him away.

"You're right. This isn't the best place for him to live, but this is where he wants to be. So, can I count on you to assist me with his care, or do I need to get someone else?"

I could sense Mary was upset, nonetheless, I wasn't about to betray my father just to make her job easier.

"Someone else? Are you kidding me? I've been with your father for the past five years, and it doesn't take a genius to see that he's not getting any better. I can't keep fighting him off. He's too big, too strong, and his moods are becoming highly erratic."

"I'm not heartless, Mary. I get what you're saying and I don't want my father to accidently hurt you in any way; so if you need a male nurse to assist you, then let me know. I'll be more than happy to hire you some help; but as for my father, he's not leaving this house."

Mary seemed as though she was contemplating my offer.

"Okay, Ms. Davenport. If you're able to provide me with an assistant, then I'll stay."

I was glad Mary decided to stay. I would move mountains to protect my father, but I didn't want him to hurt anyone in the process. If Julian hadn't been around, there's no telling how long it would've taken to sedate him.

"Thank you, Mary. I know that I'm asking a lot of you, but this house is all he knows." I felt the tears coming as I tried to dry my eyes. "And I promise you'll have an assistant tomorrow morning."

"Thank you, Ms. Davenport. This may sound insensitive, but will hiring another nurse affect my pay?"

"No, Mary. If anything, I'll pay you more. My father really likes you and that means a lot to me."

Mary smiled as we headed back towards the living room. To my surprise, Julian was still there. He was bent over picking up pieces of broken glass off the floor. Mary looked at me, then Julian, and smiled.

"I'm sorry, Mary, I didn't get a chance to introduce you. Mary, this is Julian, and Julian, this is Mary."

"It's nice to meet you, Mr. Julian."

"It's a pleasure to meet you as well."

"He's very handsome." Mary whispered to me.

I smiled then looked around the room and my heart sank. I prayed I was making the right decision regarding my father's welfare. Julian and I helped Mary clean up before heading out. Afterwards, I stood on the porch feeling the fresh air as it gave my body life again. I looked up and noticed Julian was staring at me.

"Look it's late, and we're both tired; so you're off the hook. You don't have to follow me home."

Julian didn't say a word. He walked over and gave me a hug. I didn't know how to react. I didn't know him well enough to cry on his shoulder, so I just let him continue to hug me. Once Julian released me from his embrace, he gave me a soft kiss on the cheek.

"Let's go."

"No. You go home. I'll be alright." All I wanted to do was drown in my sorrows. I didn't want to be around Julian or anyone else.

"No. You're coming with me." Julian grabbed my hand and walked me to his car.

"I can't. It's late and I have to get up early in the morning."

"Stop making excuses. Now get in." Julian opened the passenger door of his car and I got in. I didn't know what Julian had planned, but I was tired. My lip was busted and all I wanted to do was be alone. As we were riding, I noticed Julian was heading in the direction of my house. Before long, he was pulling into my driveway. "I promised I would see you home."

Julian exited the vehicle and opened my car door.

"Thank you." As I walked to the front door, Julian's steps were in sync with mine. I entered the house and didn't know how to feel. I had so many emotions running through me and was afraid of feeling vulnerable. "You're welcomed to come in."

"Thanks. I won't stay long. I know you need your rest."

I walked into the kitchen and poured two glasses of wine. As I entered the living room, I handed Julian a glass and crashed on the couch. Julian placed his glass on the coffee table, grabbed hold of me, and removed the glass from my hand as well.

"What are you doing?"

"Just relax." Julian held me in his arms and I melted. I should never have felt as comfortable as I did lying in his arms, but I was physically and mentally drained. "I get it now."

"You get what?"

"Why you only want to do fun things on a date."

"And why's that?"

"Because, you're so busy taking care of everybody else that you leave no time for yourself. So, I get it. Sometimes you have to let go, relax, and try to have fun."

"Fun. Now that's an understatement."

"Well, we need to change that. So, I hope you own a pair of walking shoes because I'll be here bright and early on Saturday morning to pick you up for our date."

"Saturday morning?"

"Did I stutter? Saturday morning. So be ready."

"Okay. Saturday morning it is."

I motioned as if I was about to sit up, but Julian wrapped his arms around me and held me close.

"Maya, can I ask you a personal question?"

"Sure."

"How long have you been seeing about your father?"

"I don't know. Maybe a little over five years. Why?"

"Because it seems like a lot to be doing by yourself. I mean no disrespect, but your father appears very ill, and…"

"And I get it. I know my father is sick but he's all the family I have. I promised him when he was first diagnosed that I would always take care of him, and I intend to keep my promise."

"And I'm not saying that you shouldn't, but this has to be heartbreaking for you to experience day after day." I felt myself tearing up. "I know you love your father, but this can't be easy on you."

"It's not, but what most people don't understand is when my mother was sick, my father devoted all of his time to her. I saw the love and compassion he gave her; and even through the mist of all that hell he experienced, he still found time for me. He wanted me to know that no matter what happened, he would always be there for me…and I think I should be able to return the favor."

Tears began to fall. Julian gently wiped them away as he pulled me into a kiss. His kiss was comforting and the attraction between us quickly intensified. We went from a slow roll to full speed ahead. I needed to stop this train and fast, but my mind was thinking one thing while my body was doing the complete opposite.

"We have to stop."

"Why?" Julian asked as he kissed me along my neck.

"Because…" My mind was all over the place. "I can't do this. I'm sorry but you have to go. Now!" I tried to push Julian off of me but he wouldn't move.

"Are you sure?"

"Yes."

"Okay." Julian retracted as if he was about to get up, but then he leaned over and began kissing me again. He was making it harder for me to say no.

"We have to stop."

"Okay then stop." Julian was right. I was telling him to stop, yet I was continuously kissing him.

"You first." Both of us laughed. It was like a game that neither one of us wanted to stop playing. "Okay, I'm serious. You have to stop." Julian ran his hands up my dress, and the feeling of his hands stroking my thighs made my thoughts race and my emotions peak. "Please stop." I could hear love songs playing in my head. Julian ran his hand between my legs. Before I could comprehend the situation, I pushed him off of me and onto the floor.

"What the hell?"

"I'm sorry. I shouldn't have invited you in. I knew this was a mistake."

"A mistake? Are you serious? I'm a big boy but you threw me off of you like a paper weight. So what's up, Maya? What is it about me that scares you?"

"Trust me, it's not you. It's me. I'm just not ready to go there with you. Not yet."

I began to feel uncomfortable. I didn't want Julian to leave but he couldn't stay either.

"So, you acting weird has nothing to do with me?"

"No, and I'm sorry if I misled you in any way."

"See, I want to believe you, but I feel as though there's something you're not telling me."

"And why do you think that?"

"Because as long as I'm kissing you Maya, you're fine. But as soon as I touch you – you damn near jump out of your skin. So tell me the truth. What's really going on?"

I contemplated on whether or not I should tell Julian the truth, but it seemed as if the truth was inevitable. I thought I'd be able to drag out this charade, but I couldn't. I wasn't as strong as I thought I was. At least not around Julian.

"I don't know if I can tell you."

"And why not? Trust me, whatever you have to say can't be that bad. So, what is it?"

"Okay. So, here's the truth." I was so nervous that I started to laugh. "I'm really a man."

The expression on Julian's face was priceless. It was obvious he was not amused by my sense of humor.

"Okay, so we're still playing games? Fine, I'm going to leave and when you decide to be an adult about this, call me."

"No, don't go. It's just. . . "

"It's what? Come on Maya. Talk to me or I'm gone."

"This is hard for me." I didn't know what to say. How do you tell a man that you're a 31 year old virgin?

"Alright. Well, I guess I'll see you on Saturday." Julian began to head towards the door.

"Don't go."

"Then talk to me. What's going on with you?"

I was so afraid to speak the truth but I knew it had to be done. "I'm a virgin."

Julian looked shocked. He looked at me and then he sat down on the couch.

"Are you serious?"

"Yes."

"I don't believe you. You're still lying, because you don't want to have sex with me. Just admit it."

"No, I'm not lying to you. I promise. I've never had sex before. Ever. And that's why I'm so afraid of getting close to you."

"Wait a minute. So the emails and texts we were sending each other, what was that? A tease? Was all of this just a game to you? Because based off what you're telling me, you were never going to sleep with me, were you?"

"No, this wasn't a game to me. I like you, but how can I expect you to respect me as a woman if I don't respect myself. I'm not saying I'm waiting for marriage, but I would like for my first time to be with someone who..."

"Who what?"

"Who I can trust."

Julian looked at me, went to the door, put on his coat, and walked out. At that moment I felt crushed. Being rejected by men was the main reason why I've always kept my virginity a secret. I wiped away my tears and decided to take this hit like a woman by moving on. I started to clean and just as I proceeded to lock the door, Julian came walking back in.

"Hey, I thought you left?"

"No, I went outside to get my overnight bag."

"You keep an overnight bag in your car?"

"And you don't?"

"No, I don't. So, what's up with you and the bag?"

"Well, I'm staying the night. You won't allow me touch you because you don't trust me, so I think it's only fair I'm given the opportunity to prove myself."

"Prove yourself how?"

"First." Julian dropped his bag. "I'm going to kiss you over and over again and you're going to let me." Julian began kissing me along my neck. "And I may touch you, and that's okay. I'm going to do some things to you that you may question, but when it's all said and done, your virginity will still be intact. I promise."

I was afraid. I didn't know what to say. Julian wanted me to give him permission to do whatever he wanted with my body and I didn't know how to feel about that.

"I don't know if I can trust you just yet."

"Then try."

Julian started kissing me. Before I knew it, he was on top of me and my heart was racing. He tried to pull off my dress but I stopped him.

"Trust me."

"I'm trying."

Julian moved my hands away from my dress as he took it off. His lips were all over my body and at that moment, I felt like giving in.

"Julian…"

"Remember you told me kisses only."

"Yes."

"Then let me keep up my end of the bargain."

Julian continued to kiss me and then I felt his hands tug on my panties. In what seemed like an instant, I was lying naked in bed with Julian on top of me, and I was supposed to believe that nothing was going to happen. I needed for him to stop kissing me before I allowed something to happen that I couldn't take back.

"Julian…"

My breathing had intensified. Julian started kissing along my inner thighs and, unexpectedly, traded one set of lips for another. No man had ever parted those lips and here I was letting someone, whom I barely trust, put his lips on my most prize possession. The feeling that came over by body was uncontrollable. Surprisingly, I began to enjoy it; and before I knew it, my body began to shake all over. I tried to make myself stop, but I couldn't. The sensation I felt was unlike anything I had ever experience before.

"Oh my God!" Julian unlocked my legs from around his head, then he grabbed me and held me tightly in his arms.

"It's okay."

I was experiencing my first *real* orgasm. My legs were wrapped tightly around Julian's waist, and as much as I wanted to let go, I couldn't.

"I'm so sorry. Are you okay?"

"I'm fine. Are you okay?"

"Yeah. I'm good actually."

We looked at each other and started to laugh.

"You see. I told you that you could trust me. I kept my word and you're still a virgin."

"Am I?" We continued to laugh.

"Kisses only. You know I'm starting to like that rule."

"Yeah, me too."

Julian had found a way to use my words against me. He took kisses only to a whole new level. I didn't know what the future held for us, but I was now curious to see where this relationship was headed. In the back of my mind, I knew Julian couldn't be trusted, but part of me was starting to fall for him. And that scared the hell out of me. He was charming and knew exactly what to say. Most of all, he wanted to be with me. What would happen if we had another kisses only episode? Would I be able to control myself, or would I give in? I was heading down an unknown path, which frightened me, yet I continued to move full speed ahead.

Chapter 4

Be Careful

The next day while at work, I was trying my best to focus but found it extremely hard to concentrate. All I could think about was Julian and the night we spent together. For the most part it felt like a dream. Our encounter had taken control of my thoughts. My mind was so preoccupied that I could barely stir the batter in the mixing bowl.

"Maya!" I was zoned out. "Maya, do you hear me talking to you?" Allison caught my eye and I snapped out of my trance.

"Hey, what's up?"

"I don't know. You tell me. I've been trying to get your attention for the past ten minutes. What's going on with you?"

"Nothing. My mind is somewhere else today. So, what do you need?"

"Matt is here to see you."

"Matt? I wonder what he wants."

"I don't know, but he's out front asking for you."

I put the bowl down and headed towards the front counter. I

had no idea what Matt wanted…until I saw him in his softball gear. It was Friday and I had forgotten about our game.

"Matt. I forgot!"

"I see. And you forgot about last night's game as well."

"I'm sorry. Give me a few minutes and I'll get dressed."

"You sure? Because I don't want the league to become a burden to you. I know you have so many *other* things to do."

"Wait a minute. Do I detect hostility in your voice? Are you mad at me for missing the game?"

"No. I'm not mad."

"Then what am I sensing here? Because you seem a little upset to me."

"I'm not upset. I'm just frustrated. Samantha showed up at the game last night while Amy was there. Long story short, it wasn't pretty."

"Samantha? I thought it was over between the two of you."

"And so did I, but she surely didn't think so. I could've really used your help last night to run interference between the two of them."

"Oh, so you needed some muscle last night, is that it?" I motioned as if I was slapping Samantha in the face, then both of us started laughing.

"No. Who I needed you to slap last night were your teammates."

Nikki, one of my employees who worked the front register, was helping Allison clean up. Both of them played in last night's game and they were trying their best to eavesdrop on the conversation I was having with Matt.

"My teammates? Are you serious! So, what happened?"

"Well, for starters, the game was horrible. You really need to talk to your team. They are not the same when you're not around. They were flirting with the guys from the firm, and I caught one hitting on Mr. Murray. It was crazy!"

"Are you serious?" I looked over at Allison and she looked away. "Don't worry I'll talk to them."

"So what happened to you last night?"

"My dad had another episode and it was bad. Notice the swollen lip." I motioned my hand across my lips.

"He hit you?"

"Yeah, but he didn't mean to. He was just having another one of his fits." Matt began to examine my lip. I was taken off guard by his action, but it was nice to know he cared. "Oh, and before I forget. I received your flowers yesterday."

"Yeah, about those. I don't know if I should get you black roses again."

"And why not? I thought it was funny."

"And so did I. But to be honest, I think a shovel would be more appropriate next time, so you can dig your team out of the hole they put you in last night."

"Really? We lost that badly?" I turned to Nikki who was sweeping the floor and she looked away. "Well, don't worry. We'll be ready tonight." I went into my office and noticed my gear was not there. I went back up front and Allison was in the process of closing up shop. "Allison, I have to stop by my dad's to pick up my gear, so I'll meet you at the field."

"Okay, I'll see you there." Allison began locking the doors.

"Hey, Matt, can you give me a lift? I left my car at my dad's house last night."

"Sure."

As we were riding in the car, Matt looked over at me and smiled.

"So, what's up with you?"

"What do you mean?"

"You've been smiling since you got in the car. So, what are you thinking about?"

"Not what. More like who."

"Oh, so you found someone?"

"You can say that?"

"Well, I don't believe it. Jeremiah Davenport is finally dating. So who's the lucky guy?"

"I don't know if you know him or not, but he's a lawyer as well. Julian Foster."

"Julian? Yeah. I know him." The intensity in Matt's voice dropped.

"You do? So what can you tell me about him?"

"Well...he's..."

"He's what? Come on spill."

"I don't really know the guy that well, but..."

"But what? Come on Matt. Tell me. Is he married, gay, or crazy? I need to know."

"I don't know a lot about the guy but I will say this: be careful. I've heard talk about him at different firms and rumor is he's definitely a ladies' man."

"Yeah, I've heard that too. So have you heard anything else about him?"

"Wait a minute. I tell you this guy is a player and you don't flinch, which leads me to believe he's already in your head."

"No, it's not like that. He's nice to me, and..."

"And I'm sure he's nice to a lot of other women as well. Come on, Maya, you can't be that stupid."

"Stupid? Really!"

"I'm sorry. I didn't mean it like that."

"Oh, but I think you did. Look Matt, I need you to understand something. Just because I'm willing to give Julian a chance doesn't make me stupid. My eyes are open, but I'm not going to turn him away simply because of his reputation.

"And I'm not telling you to. All I'm saying is watch your back. I know you may like Julian, but are you sure about him? You're my friend and I don't want to see you get hurt."

"I appreciate that, but not everyone gets an Amy in their life. I can't keep waiting around hoping to find Mr. Right. Besides, I'm not looking for a husband. I'm not even looking for a commitment. I'm just tired of being alone."

I couldn't believe I admitted that out loud, but it was the truth. As much as I wanted Julian to be relationship material, I knew he wasn't.

"You say that now, but once you allow your emotions to come into play, then its game over. You've seen some of the clients I've represented in the past. Now think about how they got there. Betrayal is a beast."

Matt was right, however I didn't want to accept it. I just wanted to be happy even if it was based on a lie. As we pulled up to my father's house, I asked Matt to come in to help me carry out the extra softball gear to my car. Hopefully my father was in a better mood then he was yesterday and wouldn't try to attack Matt.

"Hi, Mary. How's he doing today?"

"He's doing better. By the way, the center sent Kevin over this morning, so thank you."

"Good. So how is Kevin working out? Can he handle the job?"

"Well, your father fought with him for a while, but then gave up when he realized Kevin wasn't going anywhere."

I hated my father's illness and what it was doing to him, but what upset me the most was the fact that he was always afraid.

"I know my father is probably confused about Kevin's role here, but I need you to feel safe so you're able to do your job." I kissed my father on his forehead. "I'll be at the softball field tonight. If anything comes up you know how to reach me."

"Okay, Ms. Davenport."

I noticed Mary observing Matt as he stood in the foyer.

"I'm sorry, where are my manners? Matt, this is Mary. She's practically family."

"Hi, it's nice to meet you." Matt said to Mary then Mary looked at me and smiled.

"It's nice to meet you too." Mary began walking with me towards the kitchen.

"Keeping your options open I see." Mary whispered to me.

"Oh no, don't get any ideas. He's just a friend."

"Sure." Mary winked at me. "I'm not judging you."

"Yes, you are." Both of us laughed. "Oh come on, Mary. It's hard enough to juggle work, but men? You know that's out of my element."

"I know. I'm just teasing you."

I noticed Kevin sitting at the kitchen table. I decided to introduce myself while my father was distracted by the television.

"Hi Kevin. It's nice to meet you."

"It's nice to meet you as well. I've heard nothing but nice things about you."

"You have! Well that's good to hear. I know my father can be a handful but I'm glad you're here and able to assist."

"It's my pleasure. My job is to make your life easier."

"Well, that's comforting to know." I looked at the clock and it was getting late. "Please excuse me. I'm running behind schedule. If you don't mind, we can finish our conversation at a later date."

"I'll be looking forward to it."

I noticed Matt was still standing in the foyer. "Come on in. I won't be long, and then we can leave."

As I was rambling in the closet, I could overhear my father talking to Matt.

"So, Second Chair, what are you doing in my house?"

"I'm here with your daughter, Sir. We play for the same softball league."

"Softball. Now that's the game to play, and I see it's helped you to slim down as well."

"That and working out. You know, trying my best to look good for the ladies."

I heard a noise coming from the living room. A noise I haven't heard in a long time. It was my father laughing.

"You better watch out for ADA Madison. I think she likes you."

"I don't see that happening, Sir. Madison married Chambers last year."

I stood in shock as I watched my father carry on a lucid conversation with Matt. I visited my father everyday, and even on a good day he could barely recognize me. But to see him carrying on a conversation with Matt like it was old times was heartbreaking.

"Dad, do you know Matt?"

"Yes, I know Mr. Cole. He's an excellent litigator and he's always on time. I have a good feeling that one day he's going to be first chair during a major trial. What you think, Patricia? You think he has the talent to be first chair?"

For a moment I thought my father was having a major break though until I heard him call me Patricia. I didn't understand how was he able to remember Matt from his days serving as a judge, but couldn't remember me, his own daughter.

"Yes. I think he has what it takes." My eyes teared up as I handed Matt the softball gear. I knew I had no right to be upset, but I would've given anything for my father to remember me, laugh with me, and reminisce with *me*. My heart had shattered into a million pieces. "Okay, well I'll see you guys later. Come on, Matt. Let's go."

Matt placed the gear in the trunk of my car as I tried to fight back the tears. My heart was aching and I couldn't make it stop. I felt betrayed by my father's actions and all I wanted to do was scream.

"Thanks. I'll see you at the field."

"Are you okay?"

"Yes, I'm fine."

"Are you sure? You seem a little upset."

I was beyond upset. I was livid. I had no right to be angry at Matt, but I was. Given the fact my father remembered him and not me was very upsetting. The entire incident felt like a cruel joke.

"I'm not upset. I'm pissed! It's not fair that my father recognizes you, but for some strange reason he thinks I'm his dead wife. I'm not my mother. I'm his daughter, yet he treats me like I never existed."

I began to cry. I was infuriated with the entire situation. Matt gave me a hug as I tried to wipe away my tears. I didn't want him to see this side of me. Even though we were friends, I always tried to keep our relationship on a platonic level.

"It's okay to be upset, Maya, but you have to keep in mind your dad is sick. Yes, he may have remembered me today, but he could easily forget who I am tomorrow. You know how this works."

"I know, but it still hurts. We shared so many memories together and now he can't remember any of them." I tried to compose myself but it was hard. I began to pace back and forth trying to calm myself down.

"I know this is upsetting for you, but you have to know that your father loves you. You do know that, right?"

"Yeah, I know." I tried to pull myself together as I got into my car. I sat there for a few minutes trying to psych myself up before heading to the game. All I could hear was my father's laughter echoing in my head. It wasn't fair, but there was nothing I could do about it. When I arrived at the field, I saw my team in the dugout waiting for me. I decided not to think about the incident with my father and to transfer all my energy towards beating Matt's team. As soon as I stepped into the dugout, Nikki approached me.

"Okay, boss. I know we messed up really bad last night and we're sorry." The entire team started nodding their heads in agreeance. "So, we've decided to make it up to you tonight by going hard against Mr. Coleman and his team. Deal?" I looked at my team, and they didn't know how bad I truly needed them at that moment.

"Deal."

Everyone was excited and began to dance with Nikki leading the crowd. "Now work it out. Now twerk it out. Now work it out. Now twerk it out." Nikki was singing out loud while everyone was dancing. The entire situation was okay until they started dancing as if they were in the club. Matt witness the incident and glared at me from the pitcher's mound with a baffled expression on his face.

"Okay, that's enough. Come on. Let's play some ball." We took the field and played as if we were in a tournament. I was so proud of my team. Matt looked at me in disbelief. By the time we took our final break, my team was up by six runs. During the break, I walked to my car to call Mary to find out how my father was doing. After hanging up the phone, I looked up. To my surprise, Julian was walking in my direction.

"Hey. What are you doing here?"

"I stopped by the shop earlier and Allison told me you guys were having a game tonight. So, I decided to swing by to see how you were doing."

"Well, I'm good. My team is up by six points, which is great, because if we get four more runs, that's game!"

Julian started to laugh.

"Why are you laughing?"

"You're really into this, aren't you?"

"Who wouldn't be? I get to hang out with my employees and have fun while dominating against some lawyers who think they should win at everything."

"Really? Is that what you think about us?"

"For the most part, yes. Anyway, are you sticking around for the rest of the game?"

"Well, I was going to stay but…"

"Oh, come on. Don't make excuses. You know you want to stay so you can see us beat up on your comrades."

"So it's like that, huh?"

"I guess so." Julian leaned over and kissed me, then headed to the bleachers. I felt myself blushing as he walked away. As I turned to make my way back towards the dugout, I spotted Matt heading in my direction.

"I see your boyfriend made it out. I'm surprised he showed up."

"Don't start, Matt."

"I'm not, but be on the lookout. You don't want to run into one of his groupies out here." Matt started to laugh.

"You know what's really funny?" I smiled as I looked over Matt's shoulder. "*Your* groupie just showed up." Matt turned around and noticed Samantha heading in our direction.

"Are you kidding me?"

"So who's laughing now? Sorry, Matt." I walked off smiling.

"Come on, Maya. I was just joking about Julian. Help me out here! Please!"

Even though Matt got on my nerves talking about Julian, I couldn't stand to see Samantha come between him and Amy.

"Fine." I signaled for Matt to walk ahead as I intercepted Samantha. "Samantha! Hey, girl. What are you doing here?"

"Hey, Maya. I'm here to watch Matt play ball." Samantha was trying to veer around me keeping her eyes focused on Matt.

"Okay, but why? You know he's moved on, right. His girlfriend, Amy is sitting over there in the bleachers cheering him on."

Samantha glared at Amy and rolled her eyes.

"She's not his girlfriend. Merely a distraction. Nothing more, nothing less."

"No, Samantha. The only distraction out here is you." Samantha looked at me in disgust. "I know you so I don't understand why you're allowing yourself to be 'that' girl. Look around. There are available men everywhere so why are you so dead set on chasing after the one who doesn't want you."

"Because I love him."

"I get that, but Matt's happy and you need to go out and find your own happiness." Samantha looked over at Matt and Amy with tears in her eyes. I could sense she was hurting, but it hurt me even more to watch her chase after a man who didn't want her.

"But I don't know how to let him go."

"I understand. It takes time. I mean, think about it. Most women during this stage are holding on the idea that their ex will have a change of heart and take them back; but you and I both know that's not going to happen."

"You don't know that. Matt could change his mind and take me back."

"You're right. He could. But would he?" I glanced at the dugout and saw my teammates signaling for me to return. "I have to go, but think about what I said. You deserve your own happiness too."

Samantha looked at me, then Matt, and left the field. As I walked back to the dugout, I signaled Matt to let him know the situation was handled. I was hot and tired, Julian was sitting in the bleachers, and I was ready for this game to be over with. Allison walked over to me smiling.

"So, I see Julian is here. I'm surprised he came."

"Now you sound like Matt. Why are you guys so dead set on Julian being the bad guy?"

"Because guys like Julian usually are."

"Anyway." I looked passed Allison and addressed the team. "It's time to shut this down. I need a drink and I know you guys want one too; so let's do Around the World, and end this." Everyone started screaming! Around the World was when we loaded the bases and then brought out Ms. Tina. Tina was a guy who transitioned into a woman. Whenever she went to bat, she always scored a homerun. The bases were loaded, and when the lawyers saw Tina step up to the plate, they all began to gripe and whine.

"Oh, come on, Maya. Really?" They all yelled out.

Tina did what she does best and hit the ball out of the park. That was the end of the game, and I was glad. We cheered as Matt and his team looked on in disbelief. Ecstatic by the fact that we won and the game was finally over, we gathered our gear so we could head out to celebrate. Julian met me at my car with a huge grin on his face.

"What? Why are you smiling like that?"

"You know why. You guys are so wrong."

"Wrong how?" I started to laugh because I knew what Julian was insinuating.

"The last hitter. What was that?"

"That was Ms. Tina hitting a home run. Why?"

"Ms. Tina….yeah, and I'll say it once again, you guys are so wrong."

"Well, say what you want but it doesn't change the fact that we won! Anyway, we're about to head out for drinks. You're welcomed to join us if you want."

"I don't know. It's late and…"

"Julian it's only nine o'clock. Really?"

"I know but I have to finish planning our date for tomorrow."

"Excuses, excuses. All I can say is this date better be awesome considering the amount of time you're spending on it."

"And it will be. So, enjoy your night but don't stay out too late. Remember, I'll be at your house bright and early tomorrow morning."

"Yeah. Yeah. See you in the morning." Julian kissed me and it became so intense that I almost forgot where I was. "What was that?"

"I don't know." Part of me didn't want him to go, but I knew he had to leave.

"Come and have one drink with me. Just one and then you can go."

"It's temping but…" Before I knew it, my body was pressed against his and he couldn't resist the softness of my lips. The chemistry between us was amazing. "Okay. Maybe just one drink."

Julian followed me to the bar where my team was awaiting my arrival. I opened a tab with the bartender for my teammates and we began to drink and let loose. Matt soon showed up with Amy, and we teased him about his team losing, about us winning, and Tina joked about our around the world strategy. I thought Julian was going to leave early, but he stayed around and joked with us the entire night. Soon it was time to leave. Matt went around the room taking everyone's keys. He made sure everyone caught a cab, and he took my keys as well.

"Wait. What are you doing?"

"I'm taking your keys. You know the routine. They will be waiting for you at the shop and your cab is on its way." Matt looked over at Julian. "Are you good being alone with him in your condition?"

"I'm fine, Matt. You and Amy have fun. I'll call you tomorrow."

"Okay." Matt gave me a kiss on the cheek, then he and Amy left. Julian walked over looking tipsy.

"Where are your keys?" I held out my hand to Julian.

"They're in my pocket. Why?"

"Good. They can stay there and you can share a cab with me because no one is driving home tonight."

"Okay. Whatever you say, Ms. Davenport."

On the ride home, I looked over at Julian and I wanted to pinch myself. I couldn't believe someone like him wanted to be in a relationship with someone like me. It almost seemed too good to be true. My house was the first stop. I was so dizzy I could barely walk. I tried to search for some cash in my purse to pay the driver, but my vision was also impaired.

"Are you sure you're okay?" Julian asked in a concerned voice.

"Yeah. I'm fine." Which was a lie. My vision was so blurry that I could barely stand. As I turned to head towards the house, I almost fell but Julian was there to catch me. "I'm so sorry." If I wasn't so drunk I would have felt embarrassed, though that was not the case.

"Sir, can you give me minute." Julian asked the cab driver as he walked me to the door and helped me inside. I tried to sober up but it was no use. I was wasted. Julian laid me down on the couch, kissed me on the forehead, then left.

Could this be real? Was one of the many thoughts running through my head. As I laid on the couch, I began to think about my father's conversation with Matt and Julian's true intentions. It was late and I needed my mind to shut down in order for me to fall asleep. I was too intoxicated to have so many thoughts running through my mind all at once. I thought about the kiss that Julian and I shared and I was finally able to fall asleep. I was determined to give us a try. I didn't want to end up alone, but I also didn't want to wind up someone's fool. Tomorrow was a big day - my first official date with Julian, and I prayed I didn't get in my own way and screw up a good thing.

Chapter 5

Check Please

I woke up on the couch in a frantic. What time was it? Did I over sleep? I may have moved too fast because my head was spinning. I was experiencing the worst hangover ever. I looked at the stove and it was only eight o'clock in the morning. It was still early, which gave me some time to work on sobering up. Why and how did I drink so much? I started to feel nauseous. I raced to the bathroom to throw up, which actually made me feel better. I needed to get it together before Julian arrived. I went into the bathroom, took a long hot shower, dried off, laid across the bed, and then repeated the process. By doing this regiment, it allowed my pores to breathe and it made me feel so much better. I sat on the bed trying to figure out what to wear but my brain was moving in slow motion. I had no clue what Julian had planned which made it harder for me to figure out what to wear. So, I decided to dress casual - a pair of skinny jeans, a nice top, and sneakers. I went into the kitchen and made some coffee while waiting on Julian to arrive.

It was now nine o'clock and still no Julian. He told me bright and early. Was I up too early? I waited and waited, occasionally glancing at the clock. By noon, I was pissed. The least he could've done was call. I wanted to call him but I didn't see the point. I couldn't leave the house because my keys were at the shop, so I decided to call a cab. While sitting on the couch flipping through the television channels, I heard a horn blow outside. I opened the door, and, of course, it was Julian. I glared at him then closed the door. As I headed back towards the couch my doorbell rang. Annoyed, I decided to answer.

"What do you want?"

"Okay, Maya, hear me out. I know that I'm late but let me explain."

"What is there to explain? You told me to be up bright and early. I had the worse hangover ever, but I forced myself to get up because of you, then you decide not to show up! Typical!"

"Look, Maya, it's not what you think."

"Then what is it? What lame excuse do you have for standing me up?"

"There is no excuse. To be honest, the only reason I'm late is because I over slept."

"Are you serious? It's noon!"

Another horn blew outside. I peeked out the window and saw Julian casting off the cab service. Infuriated, I headed towards the front door. At that moment, Julian opened the door and prevented me from walking out by blocking the doorway with his body.

"Look, Maya, I don't know how you were able to get up so early, but I could barely move. I freaked out when I saw the time and I immediately got dressed and sped over here. I promise you I didn't mean to be this late. But, if you're willing to give me another chance, we can still make our date…if you want to go."

I thought about Julian's offer. I did crucify him before knowing the truth, so I decided to lower my guard and give him another chance.

"Okay. Luckily, I want to see what you have planned, so I'm ready whenever you are."

Julian escorted me to his car and we headed out. As we were riding, I noticed we were heading in the direction of the airport.

"What do you have planned?"

"You'll just have to wait and see."

Julian escorted me to a private plane and there were flowers with a card waiting for me on my seat.

"Are you serious? Julian this is too much."

"No...it's not." Julian gave me a kiss and all of my resentment towards him went away. "Besides, I had a friend who owed me a favor so stop stressing about everything, sit back, relax, and enjoy yourself."

I couldn't resist smiling. Julian remained secretive about where we were going, which only kept me intrigued the entire flight. Once we landed, he blind folded me, then escorted me off the plane. From there, it felt like we were getting into a car. The whole situation made me like a little kid. I was so excited to see what Julian had planned. We stopped, exited the vehicle, and then he removed the blindfold. I looked up and realized we were standing in front of the Universal Studio entrance.

"Universal Studio? Okay..."

"Wait. Before you judge, let me explain why I chose Universal."

"Okay. Explain."

"I've listened to you talk about how you really didn't have a childhood, because of your father's dedication to your mother when she was sick, and now your devotion to him due to his illness. I can see in your eyes how much you truly care about him, but you never really devoted that much time to yourself. That's why I bought you here…so you can be a kid again."

My eyes started to tear up. Julian was right. I dedicated most of my time to my father and no one else. So, I decided for one day I would let my guard down and enjoy myself. Julian and I explored the theme parks and rode as many rides as possible. I never laughed so much in my life. We ate cotton candy, played games, and made out in line while waiting for the rides. There was no doubt about it; this was one of the best dates I had ever been on. I hated for the day to end, but I knew that it was time for us to get back to Atlanta.

"Thank you for today. I really had a nice time."

"So did I."

Julian leaned over and kissed me, and before I knew it, we were making out. I wanted so badly to take things to the next level, but I couldn't. It was tempting, but I didn't want my first time to be on an airplane. I was a romantic and wanted my first time to be special, and becoming a member of the miles high club was not what I had in mind. Once we landed, Julian escorted me to his car. As we were riding along, all I could think about was Julian being the one.

"I have one more stop to make."

"Okay." I sat patiently in the car. When we stopped, I noticed we were parked in front of Fosters.

"What are we doing here?"

"I know you said you didn't want a candle light dinner, but I have something special in mind."

"Come on, Julian, and today was going so well."

"You'll love it. I promise."

Julian and I walked inside the restaurant and we were immediately seated. Before us was a table with a beautiful bouquet of roses and a bottle of wine. As soon as we sat down, the waiter began to serve us, immediately pouring the wine.

"So, tonight you will be dining on a couple of my favorites dishes. I hope you enjoy them."

Julian preselected a three course meal. We started with a combination balsamic bruschetta plate, then thin cut grilled lamb chops, and ended the night with peach cobbler and vanilla ice cream. Everything was delicious. After we finished our meal, we sat at the table, drank wine, and laughed over a great conversation. I was so wrong to dismiss candle lit dinners. What I thought would be a complete disaster turned out to be a great night. During the middle of our conversation, I spotted Regina walking by. She glanced over, and I must have caught her attention because she began to head in our direction.

"Hi, Maya. It's good to see you."

"Regina. Hi. I haven't seen you in a while. How are you doing?"

"I'm doing good. I didn't know you and Julian knew each other."

I looked at Julian who was awfully quiet.

"Yeah, we met a while back and…" Julian cut me off before I could say anything else.

"Regina. What are you doing here?"

I was confused at how Julian and Regina knew each other.

"I could ask you the same thing."

"I'm working. So, why are you here?"

I looked at Julian in disbelief. Did he say he was working?

"Do I look stupid to you Julian? And, Maya, how could you? I thought you were my friend."

"We are friends, and why would you think anything differently?" I looked at Julian waiting for him to insert himself into the conversation, but he didn't say a word.

"I don't know, Maya. Seeing you out on a date with my fiancé leads me to believe there's something more going on between the two of you. Now, am I wrong?"

"Fiancé?" Countless thoughts flooded my mind all at once. I knew Julian was a player, but the game he played on me was beyond hurtful. It was cruel. I looked at Julian in disgust. There were no words for him.

"I haven't been your fiancé in a long time." Julian said to Regina.

"Maya." Julian pleaded with his eyes, but I couldn't stand the sight of him.

"Don't." I looked away from Julian, stood up, and faced Regina. I felt flushed and overrun with emotions. "Regina, I'm so sorry. I didn't know. You know I would never intentionally date a man who was already taken." I wasn't only hurt but I was ashamed. I wasn't a home wrecker, but no thanks to Julian, I was now portraying the role as the other woman.

"Okay Maya, I get what you're saying, but it's hard for me to believe that you didn't know about me and Julian. We've been living together for the past five years, so you claiming ignorance is kind of hard for me to believe."

I looked at Julian and my heart shattered. How could he hurt me like this? I was starting to picture a future with him. I began to trust him even though I knew he wasn't trustworthy. I wanted the night to end with him making love to me; instead I was going home alone, feeling heartbroken and betrayed.

"Is that so? Then explain to me Regina, how was I supposed to know that you and Julian were together? You never mentioned to me that you had a boyfriend, and none of us at the shop ever saw you with anyone, but somehow I'm supposed to know that the two of you were a couple? You know, as a matter of fact, Brandon never mentioned you, and neither did Angela. To be honest, I think the only ones who were knowledgeable of this relationship were you and Julian. So, if you'll excuse me."

I walked off feeling dejected and full of anger. Julian came after me, but I didn't want to hear anything he had to say. I didn't want him near me. I didn't want to hear his voice and I definitely didn't want to look at him. He played me for a fool, and I wanted to be as far away from him as possible.

"Maya. Look, I'm sorry. I didn't mean to hurt you, but…"

"But what, Julian? You have a fiancé. A got damn fiancé! People warned me about you, yet I defended you every step of the way." I went outside to hail a cab and Julian followed after me.

"Maya, wait." I stood on the curb trying my best to keep it together. "Look, this thing between me and Regina has been over for a while."

"Really. Well, I guess she didn't get the memo. Oh wait. Why would she think it's over between the two of you when you're still living together? Get away from me, Julian." My cab finally arrived.

"Maya, please. Just hear me out."

"You don't get it do you! All I've been doing is listening to you. That's why I'm in the predicament I'm in now. So, how about this? Why don't I start doing something new like listening to myself for once? Maybe that will work out better for me." I saw Regina walk out of Fosters. Julian looked back and saw her as well. "Your fiancé is waiting on you." I closed the cab door and left.

I knew Julian couldn't be trusted but this took the cake. Everything changed so drastically. I went from wanting him to be the one to not wanting to know him at all. When I arrived at home, I didn't know how to feel. I wanted to cry, but I was so angry that I couldn't. I knew things between Julian and I were too good to be true, but I didn't think his betrayal would cut me this deep. My phone ranged and it was Julian. I turned off my ringer and ran myself a hot bath. I had heard enough of his lies for one night. I sat in the tub trying to figure out how I missed the signs of him and Regina being together. I thought back to when I ran into her at his job, but she didn't say she was there to see Julian. She said she was there to see a lawyer for one of her students. I wanted to see the clues, but there weren't any. I laid in bed unable to sleep, so I got dressed and went to my father's house. I called Mary to give her and Kevin a heads up that I was coming over. Once I arrived, I went into my old bedroom. It took a while, but I was finally able to fall asleep.

The next day, I called in to work and told Allison I was taking a sick day. Time passed as one day turned into a week. I didn't feel like hearing I told you so from Allison and Matt. They warned me about Julian but I didn't listen. Eventually, I would have to explain to them how they were right about him all along.

I decided to wait another week before returning to work. When I got there, everyone was so concerned about my health and wanted to know if I was feeling any better. I felt bad for lying to them, but I wasn't ready to discuss my failed relationship. I went into my office and there were flowers everywhere. Allison followed closely behind me.

"So, are you going to tell me what really happened?"

"Nothing happened."

"Oh really. Then explain this." Allison picked up one of the cards from a bouquet of roses. "Maya, I'm so sorry for what happened. Call me. Julian." So what happened, Maya? What is Julian so sorry about?"

I looked at Allison, but was so embarrassed, I didn't know what to say. My eyes started to tear up, but I refused to shed one tear over him.

"All I can say is that you and Matt were right. Julian is nothing but a lair, and I was a fool to believe anything he had to say."

Allison locked the door then gave me a hug.

"So, what did he lie about?"

"Hell…everything! I can't believe I let him get inside my head."

I started to feel flush, so I sat down. "Oh, and I almost forgot. He has a fiancé."

"Are you serious? Do you know this for sure?"

"Yep. As a matter of fact, she crashed our date. But you'll never guess who it is." Allison gave me a blank stare. "Are you ready for this…it's Regina." Out of nowhere, Allison started laughing.

"What's so damn funny?"

"It's not funny. It's just hard to believe. Regina? The school teacher, Regina?"

"Yep, that Regina. Apparently they have been living together for the past five years. How could I have been so stupid?"

"Being lied to doesn't make you stupid. Julian hid his relationship with Regina from everyone, so how could you have known? You couldn't. So don't beat yourself up over this."

"I'm trying not to, but it's hard. I believed him, Allison. Every word that came out of his mouth, I ate it up like one of those cupcakes out there." Allison and I started to laugh.

"I know you wanted to believe him. Hell, as fine as he is, I would have believed him too, but he's a lair and liars don't change. So now it's time to move on and forget about him. Okay?"

"I hear you, but keep this between us for right now. I'm still trying to process what happened."

"Of course."

I looked at the flowers scattered around my office and they angered me knowing that they came from Julian.

"Hey. Get with Tina and pass these out to any couples who come in today. I don't want them anywhere in my shop."

"Sure thing."

I walked into the kitchen and I tried to think of something new to bake. Whenever I had a problem, I would focus all of my energy on creating a new dessert. Music was my muse along with my blue KitchenAid mixer given to me by my mother years ago. They were my coping mechanism and they allowed me to turn something negative into something beautiful. Depending upon the song's mood and tempo that would determine what type of dessert I would create. I pulled out my iPod and searched for a song. I put on my headphones and placed the song on repeat. Everyone in the shop knew that if my headphones were on, not to disturb me. I stayed in the kitchen all day and night trying to come up with something new. When I finally finished, my end product were cookies instead of cupcakes. They were soft and flaky on top like a cake but firm around the edges like a cookie; and the icing on top melted in your mouth. I decided to call them KOs. If anyone were to ask, the KO stood for knock out...but they truly meant kisses only. I always named my desserts after something significant in my life. KO cookies were now added to the menu. They soon became a big hit at the shop. It was disappointing to know that something so good was created out of so much hurt and pain.

Time passed and I was finally able to function without thinking about Julian. Allison was good at keeping me busy, which kept my mind off a lot of things. Then one day while we were in the kitchen laughing about one of her blind dates, we heard screams emanating from the front of the shop. I peeped through the door and saw someone waving a gun.

Nikki and Tina were working the front counter and I was afraid of them getting hurt. I told Allison to go out the back door and call the police. I checked again to reevaluate the situation and I could hear the gunman specifically asking for me. I looked over at Nikki who signaled for me to stay put, but I couldn't consciously stand by and do nothing while their lives were in danger. The gunman became hostile. I was afraid of the situation escalating into something worse.

As I began to emerge from the back, Nikki professed to the gunman that she was me. The gunman looked as though he wanted to pull the trigger, but didn't. The customers in the shop stated to scream. I looked at Nikki and Tina looked at me. The gunman raised his weapon then fired.

Tina jumped in front of Nikki and was hit, as both of them fell to the ground. I fled to their side in a panic. I didn't think about the gunman, who could have easily shot me as well. I could hear the sirens outside the shop. A police officer announced over a mega phone that the building was surrounded, the gunman should drop his weapon, and come out with his hands in the air.

"Tina, are you okay?" I applied pressure over Tina's wound.

"Yeah, I'm fine. Besides, that fool couldn't kill me if he tried. His aim was all off, but the real question is, are you okay?"

It was just like Tina to be hurt, but still be worried about others.

"Yeah, I'm okay. I just need you to be okay. Okay?"

"Okay."

I looked at Nikki who was crying, and so was I. The gunman must have lowered his weapon because I could hear the cops as they entered the building. One of the officers spotted us on the floor as he cleared our area carrying a large semiautomatic weapon.

"Please call an ambulance! She won't stop bleeding!"

The officer yelled for a medic. Before long, medical technicians were wheeling Tina out of the shop and to the hospital. I looked at Nikki in disbelief.

"And, what were you thinking by telling that idiot you were me? He could have killed you."

"I know, but I didn't want you to get hurt. Just in case you didn't notice, you were the only person who gave many of us a second chance when everyone else said no. So, yes, I put your life above mine because there are too many people here depending on you."

"But I depend of all of you. Understand? So, don't ever do that again. You hear me?"

"Yeah. I hear you, but you don't understand just how important you are to us."

"Listen to me. Your life is just as valuable as mine and I don't want to you ever underestimate your self-worth. You are important to me. Hell, everyone in this shop is important to me. It's killing me that something has happened to Tina and it would hurt me just as much if something would have happened to you as well. So, please don't ever do anything like that again." Nikki and I started crying. We both seemed traumatized by the shooting.

"I'm so sorry, Maya. I promise I won't ever do anything like that again."

I hugged Nikki, then tried to compose myself for the cops who were waiting to take my statement. After everyone left, I closed up the shop and headed to the hospital to check on Tina. I sat in the lobby and waited on the status of her condition. Before long, a nurse came and escorted me to Tina's room.

"Hey. So how do you feel?"

"I'm okay. The doctor gave me some happy pills, so I'm feeling pretty good right now." Tina started laughing and I started crying. "Maya, what's wrong?"

"Today… today could have gone wrong really fast. You were shot and…" I was too emotional to talk.

"Maya, I'm okay. Look at me. I'm okay. So, stop crying. You know we would do anything for you. We love you."

"And I love you too, but. . . ."

"No buts. Listen to me. Nikki would be dead right now if I hadn't jumped in the way of that bullet. You ladies are my family and I would do anything to protect you."

"And we would do anything for you too. I love you, Tina, and

I don't know what I would do without you. I mean, who would keep me laughing, and up on the latest trends. As you put it, I'm so fashionably challenged."

"That you are." Tina and I started laughing.

"I don't get why this happened. Why was this guy looking for me and why did he want to hurt me?"

"We don't know why, but thank God he's locked up. Now, he won't be able to hurt anyone one else for a long time."

"Yes. Thank God for that."

I sat and talked with Tina until she fell asleep, then I headed home. I sat in my driveway too afraid to get out of the car, but somehow I was able to force myself to move. I went inside the house and locked all the windows and doors, and then I sat on the couch and cried like a baby. I noticed the light blinking on the answering machine, so I pulled myself together long enough to check the messages. There were calls from Mary, Allison, Brandon, Nikki, and various vendors all wanting to know if I was okay. There was also a message from Julian begging me to give him a call, but I didn't feel like talking to anybody. All I wanted was some time alone. So, I grabbed a blanket and curled up on the couch trying to figure out why someone would have wanted to hurt me. Then out of nowhere, the doorbell began to ring, which startled me. I wasn't sure if I should answer it or not. My nerves were getting the best of me. The bell rang again, so I slowly proceeded to the door and peeked out the side window. I breathed a sigh of relief when I realized it was Matt. I opened the door and invited him in.

"Hey. I heard about the shooting. Are you okay? How do you feel?" Matt quickly gave me a hug and I tried my best to not fall apart in his arms.

"I'm a little shaken up but I'm okay." I answered too quickly. I was not okay. "I take that back! I'm pissed, afraid, angry...I'm just... Ugh! Why did this have to happen? Why?"

"I take it you haven't heard?"

"Heard what?"

"I just left the precinct and the kid they arrested finally admitted why he was after you."

"Wait a minute. Did you say kid?"

"Yes. Sixteen years old. He pulled this stunt today all because he didn't want his teacher to quit her job."

"You mean to tell me a kid came into my shop today trying to kill me because his teacher was threatening to quit her job. Are you serious? Who does these things? Who is his teacher?" And before Matt could respond, it dawned on me who it was. "Regina."

"Yeah. Regina Thompson. You know her?"

"You can say that. I can't believe it. I knew she was upset when she found out about me and Julian. But this? This is too much."

"Why would she care about you and Julian?"

"Because you and Allison were right about him. He's nothing but a low down lying bastard, and apparently Regina was his fiancé of five years who he failed to mention he was in a relationship with."

"I don't believe it. This dude is unbelievable. Five years?"

"Yes, and Regina had the nerve to come after me like I knew she was in a relationship with Julian. How was I supposed to know they were together? Hell, no one knew they were a couple, and then she pulls this kid into her psychotic scheme. This is crazy! What they should do is file charges against *her* instead of the poor kid she's manipulated."

"Well, actually they did."

"What are you talking about?"

"We found out that she intentionally discussed her issues regarding you and Julian around this kid. Apparently, she was able to get some charges he had pending against him dropped, and in return he felt obligated to help her. She knew he was coming after you, but the prosecutor can't prove it. So, he's filing criminal harassment charges against her on your behalf, unless you decide you want them to drop the charges."

I didn't know how to feel. Yes, I was angry with Regina for blaming me for Julian's betrayal, but being responsible for her freedom immediately began to weigh on my conscience.

"Why am I the one responsible for dropping the charges? I don't understand."

"Because the act was made against you. You don't have to decide right now. You have until her appointed court date to make your decision."

"And when is that?"

"Three months from now."

I thanked Matt for the information, then he left. I had three months to decide if I wanted to drop the charges against Regina, or not. What I felt should have been an easy decision, turned out to be a hard one. Someone could've died because of her recklessness, yet I felt sorry for her. I didn't know what to do. I was glad I had time to debate my decision because in the end, Regina's freedom was ultimately in my hands.

Chapter 6

✦

Moving On

Once I returned to work, I decided to brief the ladies at the
shop to ensure them everything was okay. Even though I
didn't believe the words coming out of my mouth, I wanted my
employees to feel safe while they were at work. Extra security was
incorporated throughout the shop. More cameras were installed
and patrolmen were asked to frequent the area. Even though extra
measures were taken to ensure our safety, I still felt nervous at work.
I loved my shop. It was like a second home to me but I didn't want
to feel afraid in my own home. So, I had a panic button installed at
the register to relay a distress alert to the police department as soon
as a threat was encountered. The extra security bought some piece
of mind not only to me, but to my employees as well.

After a while, things became normal again. Tina found it hard
to stay away, even though the doctor had restricted her to bed rest.
Although she was disobeying doctors' orders, it was nice to hear her
laughter in the shop again. I tried my best to not to think about
Regina, but it was hard. The prosecutor issued a restraining order

against her as well, stating that it was in my best interest to have one. Regina wasn't allowed within 100 yards of me or the shop. I felt the restraining order was a little extreme, but I understood the provisions regarding my safety. I honestly didn't know how to handle this situation. I was confused on whether or not I should drop the charges against her. The entire ordeal was still unbelievable to me. Julian called several times begging me to drop the charges against Regina and every time my answer was always no. He was the last person I wanted to talk to and I didn't want to hear anything he had to say. Whatever decision I made would be my decision and no one else's.

So, to lighten the mood in the shop, I decided to take the ladies up on their offer by going out on blind dates with whoever they chose for me, regardless if I liked them or not. I thought it would be fun and bring some much need laughter to the shop. In the beginning, the dates were everything we imagined them to be…hilarious. The first guy I went out on a date with was old enough to be my father. Enough said. The next guy expected me to pay for everything. Even though I paid for dinner, I figured the least he could've done was leave a tip; but I soon discovered that was asking too much. I went on one disastrous date after another, and Nikki being Nikki decided to set me up on a date with her cousin, Frank. The guy favored a pimp from the 70s with his velvet suit and outrageous hat and cane. I thought someone was playing a practical joke on me. I didn't want to be seen in public with him but I knew that it was all in good fun, so I sucked it up and tried to enjoy myself. The date turned out better than I expected. If you removed Frank's attire and his misguided words towards women, he would make some lucky woman very happy one day…but not me. Matt decided he wanted to get in on the fun by setting me up with his friend, Tommy. Tommy was a gentleman, but he seemed exceedingly nervous like he had never been out on a date before. My hand accidently brushed against his and he almost jumped out of his skin. I knew he was young and inexperienced, but I didn't have time to babysit a grown man. I expressed to Matt that Tommy was a nice guy, but he wasn't the guy for me. Although the dates were fun, I still felt an overwhelming sense of loneliness. I wanted to continue, but it was time for a break. So I informed the gang that I was putting a pause on dating for a while. I still had some emotional issues I needed to work through, and I needed some time alone in order to work them out.

Then, one night after leaving my father's house, I decided to stop by the local bar for a drink. I sat and thought about all the craziness I had experienced within the past couple of weeks, and all I could do was laugh. I finished my cocktail, stood up to leave, and a guy bumped into me spilling his drink all over my shirt.

"I'm so sorry."

I tried to dry myself off with napkins from the bar.

"Don't worry about it. It was an honest mistake."

"Please, let me take care of that for you. I'll pay for your dry cleaning. It's the least I can do."

"No. You're fine. Besides, I was already on my way out."

"Then, at least allow me to buy you a drink before you leave."

The guy was very handsome, but my shirt was wet, so I didn't feel comfortable staying.

"That's very nice of you, but as you can see, my clothing situation is less than ideal right now. So how about a rain check?"

"No problem, but I *will* hold you to it. I'm Nathan, by the way."

"Maya."

"Well, it was nice meeting you, Maya."

"And it was an experience meeting you, Nathan."

We laughed as I walked out the bar. Nathan seemed like a

very nice guy. Too bad he wasn't one of the mystery men from my pervious blind dates.

The next day I caught myself humming at work. I didn't know why I was so happy. Nothing was going right, yet I found a little happiness over a spilled drink. Nikki walked by me and smiled.

"You seem mighty happy today. So tell me, did you let my cousin, Frank, put it on you last night?"

"No. Your cousin did not touch me nor is he allowed to come anywhere near me. Frank needs to see a therapist, but that's a whole other conversation."

Everyone in the shop started laughing.

"Say what you want, but my cousin knows how to treat a woman."

"Yes. If I was a hooker and he was my pimp, then we would be a match made in heaven. I'm sorry Nikki, but your cousin doesn't have a cold chance in hell with me."

Everyone continued to giggle to themselves.

"You guys can laugh all you want, but some of you would be lucky to have someone like Frank. Considering who you're lying up with, let's just say that Frank would be a step up for some of you." Nikki fanned her hand up in the air and walked off. All of us looked at each other and started to laugh out loud.

As I went up front to put out some fresh pastries, a delivery guy came walking into the shop.

"Can I help you?"

"Yes, I have a package here for a Maya D."

"That's me."

"Sign here, please."

I signed for the package and began to wonder who it was from. I glanced at the box and noticed there was card attached.

"I'm sorry about last night. I had to ask around to find out who

you were. The gift is for you just in case you decide to leave me hanging on our rain check."

I smiled to myself as I opened the box. Inside was a designer shirt that looked as if it cost three times the amount of the shirt I was wearing last night. Allison walked by grinning.

"Oh, I see someone has a secret admirer."

"Not really."

"If that's the case, then spill. Who sent you this Derek Lam, blouse?" Allison asked as she held it up in the air.

"A guy I met last night at the bar. He spilled his drink on my shirt, and I guess this was his way of making it up to me."

"Are you kidding me? You met a guy last night and didn't tell me about him. A guy who has the money and taste to buy you a designer blouse? Come on, Maya! Do you know how much a blouse like this cost?"

I looked at the tag and then at Allison.

"I do now. I can't believe he spent that much money on a shirt."

"No. Not a shirt. A blouse. A Derek Lam, blouse."

"Okay. I can't believe he spent that much money on a blouse. Sound better?"

"Yes, it does." Tina walked into the shop and Allison stopped her. "And this is all your fault. You have not been doing your job."

"And what did I just walk into?" Tina seemed confused.

"Maya received a designer blouse as a gift and she called it a shirt."

Tina gasped and I laughed.

"That is not funny. Baby girl, I know you're a work in progress, but Maya, come on. Please learn the difference between a shirt and a blouse. Learn who the current designers are, and for the life of me, please learn how to coordinate." Tina turned to face Allison. "And this is all your fault, not mine."

"My fault? How is this my fault?"

"Because you're the so call fashion designer and you have yet to teach your pupil how to dress."

"Because Maya doesn't like it when I try and dress her up." Which was true in my case.

"Look, now you guys know how I feel about fashion. I don't have the time to stay up on the latest trends or designers. I'm grateful if I'm able to match my shirt to my shoes."

"And sometimes that's a hit or miss," Tina said in a snide voice.

"Tina! Come on. I try."

"I know, but you need to try harder." Tina started walking off towards the kitchen. "Your fault, Allison. All! Your! Fault!"

Allison and I laughed at Tina as she walked away. I looked at the blouse contemplating on what I should do with it.

"I can't keep this. I have to send it back."

"No. No. No. You don't give it back. You smile, say thank you, and move on. Think about it, Maya, this guy could be the one and even if he's not, it doesn't hurt to get to know him."

Allison was right. Nathan was very handsome and what did I have to lose. Considering the past couple of dates I had been on, I didn't see the harm.

"You're right. He seems like a nice guy. So, I'm going to give it a shot and see where it leads."

Allison was so excited that she hugged me.

"I'm so happy for you."

"No you're not. You're just happy this guy knows what a Derek Lam, blouse is."

"And that too." As I was about to place the card back in the box, I noticed there was something written on the back of it. To my surprise there was a phone number written on it that said call me.

"Are you serious? I really like this guy, Maya. Please call him."

I contemplated on whether or not I should call. I wanted to see Nathan again, but the butterflies had already made their way to my stomach. I was so nervous.

"I don't know, Allison. I want to call but..."

"But what? What is there to think about? Just do it."

I may have been over thinking the process. So, I pulled out my cell phone and dialed the number. Before I could speak, a voice came over the phone.

"Is this Maya Davenport?"

"Yes, it is."

"My name is Daniel and I'm your personal assistant for today. Mr. Roberts left clear instructions for me to follow in case you called. I will arrive at your shop at 6 p.m. sharp to pick you up. You should wear the blouse you received today along with a smile. See you soon."

I was taken by surprise. No guy had ever done anything like this before. All I could do was smile.

"So, what happened? What did he say?"

"That wasn't Nathan. It was some guy name Daniel."

"Who's Daniel?"

"Apparently he's the personal assistant Nathan assigned to me for the day, and he'll be here at six to pick me up." I was still in shock.

"Maya this is some "Pretty Woman" stuff going on here. This guy is amazing."

"He's something."

I was so amazed by what had happened that I couldn't concentrate for the rest of the day. All I could do was stare at the clock waiting for six o'clock to roll around. As the time neared, I went and changed into the blouse and a pair of slacks Allison ran out and bought me to match. The blouse fit perfectly. I walked out and the staff began to whistle.

"You look great," Allison said while grinning ear to ear.

"Thanks, ladies." As I turned around, a guy walked into the shop dressed like a chauffeur wearing a black suit and hat.

"Good evening, ladies. I'm looking for a Ms. Davenport."

"That would be me."

The guy pulled out a bouquet of flowers from behind his back and handed them to me.

"These are for you."

All the ladies in the shop looked on in admiration.

"Awe." They all echoed.

"Thank you."

"I'm Daniel. I spoke with you earlier. I'm here to assist you for the evening." Daniel held out his hand. "Please follow me?"

I waved goodbye to my staff as I walked away. I felt out of my element because I didn't know what to expect next. Daniel walked me to a stretch limousine, opened the door, and assisted me inside. We drove for a while, and when we stopped, the door opened and there stood Nathan. I smiled as he helped me out of the limo.

"You look beautiful."

"You don't look too bad yourself."

I looked around and the scenery was beautiful. Flowers surrounded the driveway. Lushes bushes, water fountains, and vineyards were far as the eye could see. The view was breathtaking.

"I hope you didn't mind the ride. I wanted to do something special for you."

"No, the ride was fine."

"Great. Well, welcome to Château Élan. You've probably been here before, but this place by far is one of my favorite places to come to. Also, the food here is incredible."

"Believe it or not, I've never been here before. Of all my years in Atlanta, this is a first."

"Well, I hope you enjoy but before we head to dinner, I would like for you to take a walk with me."

"Okay."

As we walked, Nathan didn't say a word. We strolled around the property and the sights felt like a romantic backdrop you would see in a movie. I had to give it to Nathan; he was as smooth as they come. On the way to dinner, he was such a gentleman, holding my hands and pulling out chairs. It felt nice to be wined and dined in a proper manner.

"So, while I was searching trying to figure out who you were, I discovered a lot about you."

"Oh really? And what did you uncover?"

"Well, you're an only child, your mother passed away when you were young, and your father is one of the most respected judges that ever served. By the way, what was that like?"

"I'm confused. What was what like?"

"Growing up with Judge Davenport as a father. I only ask because I grew up with demanding parents, so I can only image how crazy it was for you growing up with the infamous Judge Davenport as your father."

"Well, what can I say? My father is a perfectionist. To him, I was a Davenport and I had to be the best at everything, which made his vision for me a struggle. What I had envisioned for myself versus what he wanted for me were two different things."

I started to squirm in my chair. My nerves were getting the best of me. What if Nathan discovered something about me he didn't like? I began to worry about the level of digging he may have done into my past.

"And what was his vision for you?"

"To become a lawyer, but not just any lawyer, a great defense lawyer."

"So what stopped you from becoming a lawyer?"

"My mother." I smiled at the thought of my mother and the level of love I felt for her. "She was the total opposite of my father. She was a free spirit who believed in chasing dreams, not titles."

"Nice. Do you ever regret not becoming a lawyer?"

"No. Starting my own business gave me clarity. I felt I had a purpose to serve, but not on the judicial platform. My service was to the people who were denied a second chance by society."

"In what way?"

"Well, all my shops house men and women who were once convicted criminals."

"Wow! It doesn't scare you to work with those types of people?"

I felt insulted by Nathan's comment. Who did he think those type of people were?

"Those people, as you so politely put it, are no more dangerous than the men and women who work on Wall Street. So no, I'm not afraid of my employees. Some people don't get a second chance in life, however I believe that we all deserve second chances regardless of our past mistakes."

"Well, Ms. Davenport, all I can say is that you are one amazing woman."

"I try."

"So, tell me something."

"Sure. What else would you like to know?"

"Why did your parents name you Jeremiah?"

I smiled, considering Nathan was the first guy to ever ask me about my name.

"Well, when my mother was pregnant with me, the doctors told my parents they were having a boy. So, naturally, my father chose a name that was near and dear to him to name his first born son. Overtly when I came out a girl, my father refused to change the name."

"Why?"

"Because, Jeremiah was the name of his brother who drowned when they were kids. The fact that my father still wanted me to carry on his brother's name meant a lot to me, and for that reason alone, I never once thought about changing it."

"Well, I think your name suits you. Besides, how many Jeremiahs do you know who look as beautiful as you?"

I couldn't stop blushing. Nathan was definitely putting on the charm. My first date with him felt magical and I didn't want the night to end. On the ride home we laughed and talked about everything under the sun. Once the limo stopped, the butterflies returned as Nathan escorted me to the door.

"Well, Ms. Davenport, it has been an honor and I hope we can do this again very soon." I blushed as Nathan leaned in for a kiss. Considering the effort he put into our first date, I felt like he deserved a kiss and so much more. His lips felt nice. It had been a while since I was last kissed, but I pulled away because I didn't want to mislead Nathan in any way. After the fiasco I had experience with Julian, the last thing I wanted to do was to rush into anything new. "Good night, Ms. Davenport, and I hope to hear from you soon."

"Goodnight."

I walked inside and melted. I didn't know what to think. Nathan was such a gentleman, and I was so excited for our next date. I didn't think that someone like him existed; he was established, charming, and very handsome. I was so excited that I called Allison and told her all about my date.

The next day at work, I was floating on cloud nine. Everyone wanted to know how my date went, and I couldn't help but share. I didn't think I could feel this way again, but thanks to Nathan and his charm, Julian was becoming a distant memory. Later on that afternoon while I was sitting at my desk daydreaming about my magical date, Matt walked in.

"Hey, long time no see, stranger."

"I know. It's been a while. So, how are you doing?"

"I'm great. So what brings you by?"

"Well, it's that time again. You know I have to ask."

"I know and my answer is still no."

"Okay. So, how's the case going? Have you decided whether or not you're going to press charges against Regina?"

"No, not yet. Part of me wants to drop the charges and move on, and the other part of me can't forget that she tried to have me killed. So, I'm no closer to a decision than I was a month ago."

"I'm sorry. I know this is hard for you."

"No, what's hard is having Julian constantly begging me to drop the charges. He doesn't understand his presence only makes me want to press charges, not drop them."

"You know, I knew he was a jerk, but this is ridiculous. What is it going to take for him to get a clue?"

"I don't know. Maybe if he saw me with my new friend he would stop coming around."

"New friend? Did one of your blind dates work out?"

"Oh hell no!" Both of us started laughing. "I didn't meet him on a blind date. I accidently ran into him at the bar and from there, things took off."

"I'm glad to hear that. So tell me, would I approve of..."

"Nathan. And yes, you would like him. He is such a gentleman and he makes me feel like there are no other women around for miles. All eyes are on me."

"Well, I'm happy for you, and I hope things work out between you and Nathan."

"Thanks, Matt. That means a lot."

"So, are you and Nathan busy tomorrow night?"

"I don't know. Why?"

"Well, I have an extra pair of tickets to the Falcon's game, if the two of you wanted to join me and Amy."

"Awe that's so sweet of you unless you're doing this so you can size up Nathan."

"Really, Maya. You think I would stoop that low just to see who the guy is?"

"Yes, I do."

"And you're right. I would." We both started to laugh. "But all joking aside, if you guys would like to join us, the tickets are yours."

"Thanks! Once I talk with Nathan, I'll let you know."

Matt left and I contemplated on whether I should invite Nathan to the game. I had a valid excuse to call him and I was eager to hear his voice again. So, I dialed the number and once again Daniel picked up. I explained to him that I needed a direct line, and he had Nathan return my call. During our conversation, I explained to Nathan how I needed a direct number in order to contact him. I liked Daniel, but I didn't need a middle man screening my phone calls. I also informed Nathan of Matt's offer, but he politely declined stating he had already made plans. So, I called Matt and explained to him why we wouldn't be able to join him and Amy, and I thanked him for inviting us to the game.

I wasn't sure about a lot of things, but I prayed that the connection between me and Nathan manifested into something genuine. He provided a sense of hope when I felt I didn't have any, and I was thankful that we were somehow able to meet, even if it was through unconventional circumstances. Regardless of what happened next, Nathan was an escape that my mind needed and a distraction my heart warranted.

Chapter 7

Pinch Me

Things between me and Nathan were gradually heating up. We would go on one incredible date after another, and even though we had conversed over several different topics, I still felt as though I was in a one-sided relationship. Nathan knew a lot about me yet his life remained a mystery. The more I thought about it, the more intriguing he became, and I was determined to figure out what skeletons he had hidden in his closet.

Then, one evening while Nathan and I were sitting on the couch watching television, I decided to sort through the mail. While I was fumbling through some ads, I came across a letter from the court stating Regina's hearing was only two weeks away. I was so caught up in my relationship with Nathan that I almost forgot about the hearing. I sat in deep thought contemplating on what to do next. I was so confused. I thought about the many conversations I shared with Nathan regarding forgiveness, but in my heart I didn't know if Regina deserved my forgiveness.

"Hey, are you okay?"

"Yeah, I'm fine."

"So, what's wrong? You read that letter and then you went ghost."

"It's nothing. I'm okay"

"You sure?"

"Yeah, I'm sure." I placed the letter on the coffee table and Nathan picked it up. "Hey, what are you doing?"

"I'm trying to see what you're so secretive about."

"I told you it was nothing."

I tried to reach for the letter but Nathan had already read it.

"Nothing? Maya, this letter says you have two weeks to make a decision about Regina."

"I know what it says."

"Well, what are you going to do?"

"I don't know. I thought Regina was my friend until she decided to believe Julian over me. He lied to both of us and yet she tried to have me killed. I don't know if that's forgivable."

"I know it seems hard, but let's say you were to press charges. Would that make you feel any better?"

"I don't know but who's to say she wouldn't try this again? I'm trying to be compassionate by giving her the benefit of the doubt, but I have to be realistic as well. She tried to have me killed." I was starting to get a headache. "I don't know what to do."

"How about this. Just breathe." Nathan held my hands as he looked into my eyes. "Here are the facts. You're no longer with Julian, so he's not a factor. If anything was to happen to you, then Regina would be the number one suspect. So, whether you decide to press charges or not, it wouldn't change your current situation. You're with me now and that's the only thing that matters."

Nathan was right. Whatever I decided wouldn't change my relationship with him. So, I concluded at that moment I would go to the court by the end of the week to give them my decision.

"You're right. We're together and that's the only thing that matters."

Nathan and I started kissing and I wanted so badly to take things to the next level, but I couldn't. We had only been dating for a couple of weeks and I didn't feel mentally capable of making such a decision. I had planned on telling him about my virginity in advance, but with everything that was going on, the moment never felt right.

The next day I went to visit my father, and Mary and Kevin met me at the door. They both seemed pretty excited.

"Hey guys. So, what's going on? Is my father okay?"

"Are you ready for this?" Mary could barely contain herself.

"Ready for what?"

"Your father…he asked for you."

At that moment my heart stopped. I must have been dreaming. I pinched myself just to make sure it was real. I couldn't believe my father asked for me. Tears quickly formed in my eyes. I was so elated but I didn't want to get my hopes up. I walked over towards my father and he grabbed my hand.

"Maya."

I immediately broke down in tears. I didn't know how long his memory of me would last, but I wanted to make the most of it.

"Yeah, dad, it's me…Maya."

My father looked at me and smiled.

"You look just like your mother."

I couldn't stop crying. I looked over at Mary who was in tears as well. Kevin bought us tissues, and all we could do was laugh.

"So, dad, how are you feeling?"

"I feel good. I sat here all day waiting on you to bring me some pound cake."

I looked at Mary and couldn't stop smiling.

"You know I couldn't forget your cake." I grabbed Mary's hand as I walked to the kitchen. "So, how long has he been like this?"

"Since this morning. I tried calling you but you never answered."

"My phone." I looked for my phone in my purse. "I turned my ringer off yesterday and I forgot to turn it back on." I placed my phone back in my purse and stared at my father. "Oh my God, Mary this is so amazing."

"I'm so happy for you, Ms. Davenport."

"Thanks, Mary."

I pulled the cake out of my carrier and poured my father a glass of milk. We sat and talked the day away. I didn't want to leave.

"I know I'm a hand full and I see you've kept your word because I'm still here, but know that while I'm in my right mind, if I ever become too much for you guys to handle, then you have my permission to put me in a home."

"You know I couldn't do that. I love you."

"And I love you, but you're my baby girl, and you deserve better than this. Seeing about your old man isn't living. You deserve a family of your own…"

"And one day I'll have one, but for right now I'm going to enjoy *this* family. Me, you, Mary, and Kevin. I love you guys and I wouldn't have it any other way."

"I love you, Jeremiah."

"I love you too, dad."

I stayed until my father fell asleep. I was so afraid for him to close his eyes knowing that when he awakened, he may not remember anything that had just happened. I sat in the living room and cried. Mary walked over and gave me a hug.

"You see. He loves you. Regardless of what happens from here on out, you know in your heart that your father loves you, and no decision you make in the future can take that away."

"I know."

I was so excited that I wanted to call and tell someone the good news, but I didn't know who to call. Allison was always my go to person, but for some strange reason I called Matt.

"Hey, are you busy?"

"No, why?"

"Meet me at Murdock's."

"I'm on my way."

As I sat at the bar waiting for Matt, Brandon caught my attention as he walked through the door.

"Brandon. Hey, what are you doing here?"

"I could ask you the same thing."

"Well, I'm here meeting Matt for drinks. I had a pretty amazing day today."

"Really? Well, do you mind if I sit with you until Matt gets here."

"No, I don't mind."

"So, what happened? What has you so amped up?"

"My father. Long story short, he regained his memory today and we talked for hours." I couldn't stop smiling. "I'm sorry. I'm just really happy right now."

"I can tell. Well, I'm happy for you. Let's drink to memories. To the good and the bad ones."

I tossed back my shot then I looked over at Brandon. I was so happy that I overlooked the sadness in his eyes.

"So, what's going on with you?"

"Nothing much."

"Really, because you look depress and it's bringing down my high. So what's going on?"

"It's Angela. She's being considered for a job out in California,

and I don't want to hold her back, but I can't move to California
either. My life is here."

"Wow. That's a bummer."

"Really? That's all the advice you have for me? I don't know
what to do."

"And I can't tell you want to do, but I will say this. Listen to
your heart because the heart doesn't lie. If you love Angela, you'll
figure it out."

"I do love her, but not in the way I think I should love her."

"Excuse me?" I was confused and my drinks weren't helping the
situation any.

"In my heart I know I should have married Angela a long time
ago, but something was holding me back. I don't know what it is,
but I'm afraid if I don't figure it out soon, she may end up going to
California alone."

"Well, only you know how you truly feel about her. If you let
her go, it doesn't mean you don't love her. How does the saying go?
If you love something or someone, then set them free; and if they
come back, then it was meant to be. Or something like that."

"I love her, but I don't want to let her go."

"Then it sounds like you have a problem." I looked up and Matt
was walking through the door. "Well, Matt is here. You're welcomed
to join us if you like."

"No, you two go ahead. I think I know what I need to do."

"Okay, well it was great seeing you." I gave Brandon a hug and
he left.

"Hey, Maya. What was so important that I had to come out in
the middle of the night to meet you here?"

I couldn't stop grinning.

"Okay are you ready for this?"

"I don't know. You seem very..."

"Happy. I'm so happy."

"So what happened?"

"My father. He had one full day of clarity. He remembered who I was. We talked, and talked, and talked. The entire day was perfect!"

"Maya. I'm so happy for you!"

"I know its crazy right, but today felt so good. It was like the old days, and the icing on the cake...he reassured his love for me regardless of any decisions I may need to make in the future regarding his well-being."

I felt the tears fall but I was so elated I didn't care.

"Now, I hope you'll stop questioning whether or not he'll still love you if you decided to put him in a home."

"You're right. There's no reason for me to doubt his love for me anymore."

Matt looked around the bar.

"So, I have one question for you."

"Sure. What's on your mind?"

"Why did you call *me*?"

"Why wouldn't I call you?"

"Because you could have called anybody to tell them the good news. So why me?"

"Because my father remembered you, "Second Chair," and to me, that means something." Matt and I smiled at each other. "He hadn't recognized anyone in a long time, and yet he recognized you; so it was only fitting that I call you."

"Are you getting sentimental on me?"

"Shut up and drink."

Matt and I took another shot.

"So, I hate to be a bearer of bad news, but have you decided on what you're going to do about Regina."

"I have. I talked with Nathan yesterday and I think I'm ready to make my decision."

"You've been talking to Nathan about this?"

"Yes, and he's been a big help. After my breakup with Julian it was hard, then Nathan came along, and now everything doesn't seem as bad anymore."

"Well, I'm glad he's there for you."

"Me too."

Matt and I had a couple more drinks then I headed home. When I arrived, Julian was sitting in my driveway. It was late and I was not in the mood to hear any of his nonsense.

"No."

"Wait, hear me out."

"No, we have nothing to talk about."

"Yes, we do. Look, I get that you're mad at me, but I'm begging you to not take your anger out on Regina."

"Are you serious? I could give a rat's ass about you. You weren't the one who tried to have me killed. Regina was! Remember that! So, if you'll excuse me."

"Maya, please."

My entire mood changed. Julian killed my good vibe and now I was pissed.

"You know, before you came over, I had already made my decision, and now you've caused me to change my mind."

"Maya, don't. This is hard for me. None of this would have happened if it wasn't for me and for that, I'm sorry. I fell for you and didn't know what to do."

Listening to Julian talk only angered me more.

"You fell for me. Really? You know, if you would have been honest with me from the beginning, then none of this would've happened. You knew you had a fiancé, but you chose to play with my heart, and now I'm supposed to have all this compassion for you and Regina! Well, I don't! I hate what you did to me, and I hate myself even more for believing in you."

"Maya, how I felt about you wasn't a lie."

"Whether it was a lie or not, it doesn't matter anymore. I've moved on and I ask that you don't come around here anymore."

"Maya."

I closed the door and I tried to catch my breath. Julian was the only person who could take me from 0 to 100 in no time flat. Why was he doing this to me? I wanted nothing more than to move on with my life but he was constantly reminding me of how stupid and naive I was to have believed in him. All I wanted to do was forget. I went into the kitchen, found a bottle of wine, and drank the night away.

I woke up the next day with a serious headache. I needed to control my emotions, and stop drinking in order to forget my problems. In my mind, it was easier said than done. I looked over at the court notice sitting on the coffee table and I questioned if I was making the right decision. I was tired of stressing over the situation, so I decided to go to the courts early to give them my decision. While I was getting dressed, I heard the doorbell ring. I answered and it was Nathan.

"Hey, so what brings you by so early?"

"I decided to stop by to see if you wanted to spend the day with me."

"Well, aren't you sweet. Let me finish getting dressed then we can go." I walked into the bedroom looking for a pair of shoes to put on. "So, what do you have planned for today?" I yelled from the bedroom.

"I was thinking about getting away for the weekend. What do you think?"

I couldn't go away with Nathan for the weekend. I still hadn't told him about my virginity, and besides, I still needed to settle my issue with the courts.

"That sounds nice, but I can't."

Nathan walked into the bedroom while I was sitting on the bench putting on my shoes.

"And why not? You seemed pretty stressed yesterday. I figured you needed some time away in order to relax and clear your head."

"See, that's the thing. I've already made up my mind. I plan on going to the courts today to give them my decision."

"Today? I thought you were waiting until next week?"

"I was going to wait, but then Julian came by last night and let's just say that I'm ready for this to be over with."

"Julian. What did he want?"

"What he always want. His way. He tried to hassle me into not pressing charges, but all he did was make matters worse."

"Well, all I can say is don't allow Julian be your deciding factor. Listen to your heart when you go in there today and then make your decision."

"I will." I went into the kitchen to fix myself a cup of coffee, then the doorbell rang. "I wonder who that is."

I opened the door and it was Brandon.

"Brandon. It's nice to see you. So, what brings you by this morning?"

"Julian."

"I don't want to talk about him."

"Wait, hear me out. I spoke with him last night and he told me he came by to see you regarding Regina. I want to apologize on my brother's behalf. You're my business partner, and I don't want Julian's behavior to cause any friction between us."

"You don't have anything to worry about because I wouldn't

allow that to happen. Besides, I know how to keep my personal life and my business life separate."

"Thanks. So, we're good?"

"We're good."

As Brandon was about to walk off, he spotted Nathan in the living room. He could see Nathan, but Nathan couldn't see him.

"Really? He sent Nathan over here to hassle to you as well. I swear he doesn't know when to stop."

"What are you talking about?"

"I'm talking about Julian sending over Regina's brother to bother you. Is he pressuring you too?"

At that moment I felt sick. I didn't know what to think. I was starting to fall for Nathan, and now I realized that our relationship had been nothing but a lie. My hands began to shake. I was so upset, but I didn't want Brandon to know I was unaware Nathan was Regina's brother. It was hard to control the shock. I could feel my eyes watering, but I had to be strong.

"No, he's only here to plead Regina's case. I'm making my decision today, and I wanted to hear from somebody other than Julian as to why I shouldn't press charges against Regina, and who better to do that than her brother?"

"Okay. If he becomes a hand full, you let me know. I have no problem turning around and coming back."

"Thanks, but I'm good."

Brandon left, and I had to figure out how I was going to handle Nathan. He lied to me, while attempting to use me, when his only goal was to betray me. On the inside I felt as though I was about to explode. I was truly at a loss for words. I walked into the living room, and Nathan walked over and gave me a hug. I didn't want him touching me. I stared at him and I was so angry. He was the second guy to play me within a year. What was I doing wrong, but most importantly, why was this continuously happening to me?

"Who was that?"

"It was no one."

"So, what time to do you want to head to the courts?"

"Now is a good time. Since I'm pressing charges, do you think there will be a lot of paperwork involved? I don't want it to interfere with the rest of our day."

"So, you're pressing charges?"

"Yeah. You know, the more I thought about it, I figured the streets would be a whole lot safer with that lunatic locked behind bars."

"And you're sure this is what you want to do?"

"Yeah I'm sure. I don't feel safe knowing she's free to take another shot at me." I grabbed my coat and headed for the door. I could tell Nathan was bothered by my decision. "Let's go. I'm ready to get this over with."

"Wait."

"What's wrong?"

"I need to know if this is what you really want to do. I don't want you to beat yourself up over this later, because once you make your decision, there's no going back."

"You're right. There's no going back, but I prayed about it, and I think this is the best alternative." I stood at the door waiting for Nathan to move, but he didn't. I knew he was tormented over my decision, but my heart was broken over the lies he told. "Nathan what's wrong?"

"It's just…this doesn't feel right."

"I get it, but the woman who tried to have me killed would be locked behind bars. What's not right about that?"

"I understand, but…"

"But what? What's going on Nathan?"

"It's..."

"It's what? Oh, it's because Regina's your sister. Is that it? Is that why you don't want me to press charges?" I was so angry that I started to shove Nathan. "Tell me, Nathan. Come on. Be truthful with me. Or do you even know how to do that!"

"Maya."

"Don't Maya me. You've been lying to me since the day we met. So, what was this? Some kind of play to soften me up so I wouldn't press charges against Regina? Is that it? Was I just a pawn in your creepy little game?" I slapped Nathan as hard as I could. "Answer me!"

"No, Maya. That's not it."

"Then explain it to me. Why did you do this?"

"I did it because I wanted you to see that, yes, what my sister did was wrong, but that doesn't mean you have to stoop to her level by pressing charges."

"Oh, there's no way I could ever stoop to her level. She's below low. She tried to have me killed, then sends in her brother to clean up her mess. The two of you are truly one of a kind."

"Maya, please don't hate me. I started out doing this for my sister, but then I fell for you, and...."

"Don't!"

"No! Please understand. I was too far in to tell you the truth. I'm sorry, but please...please don't hold this against me. I don't want what we have to end."

"Are you kidding me! Whatever this was, it's over. There's no us and there will never be an us. You played me, Nathan, and I don't want to have anything else to do with you or your crazy ass family. Now get out of my house."

"Please, Maya, hear me out."

"Get out of my house! Now!"

I was crying and I wanted Nathan to leave. I was hurt by his betrayal, and certainly done listening to his lies. I didn't know who was worse. Him or Julian. The infatuation of love broke my heart while deceiving my mind in the process. I wanted to forget, but the ramifications of betrayal was haunting my every thought. How do you force yourself to get up, when the depth of your fall causes all of your emotions to collapse? I didn't want to be alone nor did I want my heart to be broken; but when you entrust your future to manipulative men, the outcome you seek will never be the one that you receive. I had hoped that I would be different. That my virtue would somehow lead me to the right guy, but I was wrong. In the end, I played the fool, not once, but twice.

My breathing intensified as I tried to calm myself down. I sat in silence trying to clear my head. I felt like the most naive person in the world. How could I have been so foolish? I applaud whomever came up with the statement, "love is blind," because they were right on the mark. I was so blinded by love that I had allowed myself to overlook suspicious behaviors, incomplete timelines, and a lot of too good to be true moments. I sat on the couch obsessing over what to do next. How do I utter out loud what I allowed myself to fall victim to once again.

Tears began to fall, but I quickly wiped them away. I didn't know what I was doing wrong. Maybe I was too trusting when it came to men, or maybe I was too eager to be in a relationship, but one thing was certain, I was done with dating for a while. I couldn't deal with my heart being broken over and over again by men whom I trusted. In time, I would eventually meet the right guy; or at least that's what I had hoped, but one thing was certain. I was in no hurry in becoming another man's fool.

Part
II

Try Again

Prologue

D amage control was an understatement. The divinities in my mind had manifested into a full blown nightmare. What was I thinking? How could I have allowed myself to play the fool? Yet, again? I couldn't fathom what I was doing wrong. I was a smart, independent, and a very wealthy woman. Yet, I allowed myself to do the one thing I promised I would never do. Fall for a man who I knew couldn't be trusted. I allowed myself to cross a line that was forbidden. My heart wanted what my mind knew I couldn't have.

I faced myself in the mirror but didn't recognize the reflection looking back at me. Who was this woman and how could she have been so stupid? I knew the game and how it was played, but somehow allowed manipulation to undermine my every decision. I allowed myself to be fooled by a man who I knew was a complete liar, and yet I fell subject to his every word. I paced around the room, praying I was about to make the right decision.

Tears began to fall. I looked around the house and could only see images of past and present mistakes. The whispers of broken promises and the dilapidation of shattered dreams bled through the walls like screams in the night. I went into the closet and began to pack. Running away was never my strongest suit but it seemed like my only option. I had no clue where to go, but getting out of Atlanta was at the top of my list.

My phone rang, but I ignored it. One stupid choice. One weak moment, and now my life was forever changed. Thinking back, if I could reverse the hands of time, I would. I would go back to the day when I first laid eyes on Julian Foster and run full speed in the opposite direction. Sometimes it's hard to see the truth when you're surrounded by depictions of false hope. I'd convinced myself my actions were because of love; but in reality, the fear of loneliness trumped love each and every time.

Chapter 8

❦

Low Key

I decided to wait until the last possible day to give my decision. I wanted Regina to sweat it out for a while. I went to court and informed the judge I was dropping all charges. I didn't want to have anything else to do with Regina or her family. After I left the courthouse, I headed to work. I was amazed at how somber I felt. I wanted to be mad but I wasn't. I was truly at peace with my decision and readiness to move on. When I arrived at work, everyone wanted to know what Nathan had planned for us, but I had to explain to them that Nathan and I were no longer together. They all wanted to know what happened, and the only thing I could stomach up, was the fact that we were on two different paths. I knew no one bought what I was saying, but it was the only excuse I could think of. I decided to retreat to my office for some peace and quiet. While I was reviewing some receipts, Allison walked in.

"Different paths. Now that's a good one. So tell me. What really happened?"

"It's the truth. He was going in one direction and I was heading in another."

"Really? Something tells me there's more to this story."

"I wish, but that's it. There's nothing more to tell."

"Okay, since you won't tell me the truth about Nathan, can you at least tell me how it went in court today?"

"Sure. I dropped all charges against Regina, and now she is free to wreak havoc once again."

"Are you serious! Why would you do that?"

"Because I was tired."

"Tired of what?"

"I was tired of being lied to. From the day I met Julian, I've dealt with nothing but lies. I was tired of him coming around and harassing me about Regina. I was tired of receiving notices reminding me that I needed to make a decision regarding her case. More importantly, I was tired of Nathan lying to me as well."

"I knew it. So, what did he lie about?"

"What did he lie about?" Once again I was ashamed to explain why. "Let's see. You know how, lately, I've been attracting men who come with baggage? Well, Nathan was no different except his baggage was Regina."

"Regina? How?"

"Brace yourself. Nathan is Regina's brother and he was only with me to persuade me into dropping the charges."

"Nathan is Regina's brother? I don't see it. How could that fine specimen be related to Regina?"

"I don't know but he is. They don't share the same last name, so Matt nor anyone else was able to catch it. I don't understand why this keeps happening to me?"

"Trust me. It's nothing you're doing. Nathan tried to use you and your only mistake was trusting him. There was no way you could've known he was Regina's brother. As a matter of fact, how did you figure out they were related?"

"Brandon told me. He thought I already knew. I'm just thankful he stopped by when he did or I would have never known the truth."

"Maya, I hate that this keeps happening, but I know the right guy is out there waiting for you."

"And he'll be waiting for a while because I'm done with dating for the moment. It's time I put the focus back on me and figure out what I want to do next with my life."

"Knock, knock."

We turned around and there was Matt standing in the doorway.

"Hey, you! So what brings you this way?"

Matt gave me a hug.

"I just left the courthouse. Can we talk?"

"I'll give you guys some privacy. We'll finish our conversation later."

"Okay."

Allison walked out and Matt closed the door behind her.

"So tell me…what were you thinking?"

"What are you talking about?"

"Regina tried to have you killed and you dropped the charges against her. Why?"

"Because I wanted this situation to be over. I forgave Regina a long time ago for what she did."

"Well, isn't that nice. You forgave her, but tell me this: do you know if she's even sorry for what she did to you? And what makes you think she wouldn't try this again?"

"You're right. I don't know if she's remorseful or not, but I can't live my life wondering what she would or wouldn't do. That's why I dropped the charges. I'm finally ready to put this behind me."

"Okay, but if crazy comes knocking at your door, just remember you're the one who allowed her to be there."

"Thank you Matt, for you unsolicited advice. Now is there anything else I can help you with?"

"Just be careful. That's it. I'm done."

"Awe, Matt, if I didn't know any better I would have thought you cared."

"I do. You're my friend, Maya, and I would hate for something to happen to you. Sometimes you're too nice for your own good." Matt's phone began to ring. "I'm due in court. You be safe, okay."

"I will. Thanks for stopping by."

Matt left and I thought about what he said. Who's to say Regina wouldn't come after me again, but I couldn't live my life around a lot of what-ifs. It was time I moved on. I needed to move on.

I decided to go on a delivery run with Allison. Interacting with my customers truly lifted my spirits. When we stopped at Fosters, I questioned getting out of the vehicle. Even though Brandon had nothing to do with the case, he was still Julian's brother. When I went inside, I spotted Brandon, but he seemed deep in thought. I didn't say anything as I continued to unload the desserts. When I returned with another rack from the van, he was gone. I let out a sigh of relief. I wasn't in the mood to converse with him about Regina or anything else. As I approached the van, Brandon startled me because I didn't see him standing beside the door.

"Oh my God! You almost gave me a heart attack!"

"I'm sorry. I really need to talk to someone. Are you busy tonight?"

"I can't."

"Come on. I know my brother hurt you, but I need a friend right now. Please."

"Brandon, I would like to help you, but I can't. I'm in a weird place right now and..."

"And I need a friend, Maya. You're the only person I can talk to who knows my situation. Please."

I thought about it. I didn't want to have anything else to do with the Foster men, but Brandon was my friend, and if it wasn't for him, I would have never known the truth about Nathan.

"Fine. Meet me at Murdock's at 8:00. If you're late, I'm leaving."

"Thanks, Maya."

Allison walked over looking confused.

"What did he want?"

"Nothing. So are we done?"

"Yes, that was the last of it. So how do you feel?"

"I'm okay. A lot of this still feels unreal, but I'm going to figure out a way to work through it."

"Well, if you need someone to talk to, you know you can always call me."

"I know."

When I got off work, I went home, changed clothes, then headed to Murdock's. I didn't know what drama Brandon had going on in his life, or if I was mentally capable of helping him resolve it. I looked up, it was eight o'clock, and Brandon came walking through the door.

"Hey, thanks for coming. I know I'm asking a lot, but I really do need someone to talk to."

"Okay, so what's going on?"

"Remember when I told you Angela was considering a job in California?"

"Yes."

"Well, she took the job and I broke her heart by not going with her. I don't know what I was thinking. Why didn't I go with her?"

"I can't answer that, but I do know it's never too late to go and be with her. If you truly love her, then go. Trust me, finding the right person these days is harder than you think."

"I do love her, but I don't know how to leave the life I have here."

"Look, Brandon, you're the owner of Fosters, which means you don't have to be here to run it. You can always leave someone you trust in charge while you're away in California. Besides, they have an invention called airplanes that allow you to travel back and forth, if for some reason you just can't stay away."

Brandon and I started to laugh.

"I hear you. I want to go and support her, but I don't know how to let go of this place, and this crazy fixation is about to cost me my relationship with Angela."

I looked into Brandon's eyes and I could tell he was torn. I wanted to give him some good advice or some great words of wisdom, but who was I to say anything considering my recent circumstances.

"I'm going to be honest with you. There is nothing I can tell you to make you go or stay, but as your friend I will say this: if I had someone who loved and truly cared about me, he wouldn't even have to ask. I would follow him anywhere."

"Thanks, Maya. And for what it's worth, I'm sorry for the way my brother treated you. You're a true friend and I hope one day you'll find the happiness that you deserve."

"Me too."

"So, how about a drink?"

"A drink sounds good." Brandon and I talked and drank for hours. It was late, and I had spent far too much time with another Foster man. "Okay, I'm going to call it a night. Thank you for the drinks and I hope things work out between you and Angela. You're a good guy and I want you to be happy."

"Thanks and I want the same for you as well." I looked around to ensure I had all my belongings as I prepared to leave. "Do you need a ride home?"

"No, I'm good."

"Hey, before I forget, I meant to tell you about this farmer's market I found just north of here. If you don't have anything to do tomorrow, would you like to go and check it out?"

"I don't know. You're supposed to be figuring out your situation with Angela, not hanging out with me."

"And who says I can't do both."

"I don't know."

"Awe, come on. You'll love it. You're a Farm Geek just like me."

"That may be true, but don't try to use my love for all things fresh to persuade me."

"Really? So you're going to pass up a chance to get first pick on some juicy berries, exotic fruits, and fresh milk? You know you want to go. So what do you say?"

Brandon was right. I did want to go but wasn't sure if I should be going with him.

"Ahh, what the hell. Swing by and pick me up when you're ready to go."

"Alright. I'll see you tomorrow."

"See you then. Goodnight."

On the cab ride home, I did my best to not think about Brandon. Even though he was my friend, he was still a Foster. Once I made it home, to put my mind at ease, I took a long hot shower then went to bed. I was in a deep sleep when suddenly my phone began to ring. Who in their right mind would call someone so early in the morning? I looked at the number and it was Brandon.

"Hello."

"Good morning. It's time to get up and go."

"Are you serious? It's five in the morning."

"I know, and if you want to get the best products, you have to get there early. So get dressed. I'm waiting for you outside."

"You're already here?"

"Yes, so hurry up. It's time to go."

It took everything in me to move. My eyes were unfocused and my body felt like a heavyweight. I walked outside dressed like a bum. I got into the car and tried my best not to fall back asleep.

"It's too early in the morning for this."

"Oh, come on. You'll thank me once you get there."

"We'll see."

I tried to stay awake but couldn't. I was fast asleep before I knew it. After a while I felt a nudge that woke me.

"We're here."

I looked around and wondered how I was able to miss such an amazing market. As we walked around I felt like a kid in the candy store. There were three times the vendors compared to the market I would frequent. Brandon laughed at my excitement for the myriad of berries and spices. The entire morning gave me a renewed spirit. We bought a cup of homemade yogurt and enjoyed the scenery.

"So, was I right?"

"You were right. This place is amazing. How did you find this treasure?"

"Well, as a chef, I've met several entrepreneurs who've been eager to attract new customers with product sampling."

"Well, I'm glad you bought me here. This was a much needed treat."

"Now don't go off telling everyone about this place. We don't want our secret to get out."

"Don't worry, you're secret is safe with me."

Brandon and I explored more shops then headed back to the city. After dropping me off, I was in such a good mood that I decided to stop by and see my father. Once again he didn't know who I was, but we shared some pound cake and watched television.

Weeks passed and Brandon and I found ourselves hanging out more than usual. He would invite me over to taste dishes he'd paired together, and I would invite him over to sample desserts I was creating for the shop. Our friendship was unusual, but I was glad to have him around. I lied to Allison and Matt about how I was occupying my time. If they knew I was hanging out with Brandon, the criticism would never stop. So, I started rotating my time between Allison and Matt so they wouldn't be suspicious about my whereabouts and time not spent at the shop. For a while, my plan was working, but soon I discovered just how bored Brandon really was. Sometimes when I went to the movies with Allison, I'd spot Brandon at the same showing. The same thing would happen when I went out with Matt as well. I felt like he was stalking me.

Then one day, while I was at home cooking in the kitchen, my doorbell rang. It was Brandon.

"Hey. So what's up? Your message sounded urgent."

I stopped Brandon at the front door. I was so use to being coy with him; however at that moment, I needed him to understand the seriousness in what I had to say.

"Are you stalking me? I'm asking because, every time I go out with my friends, I see you? So what's the deal?"

Brandon started laughing.

"No, I'm not stalking you. You know for a fact I have no one to hang out with. Julian is never available, so I'm usually out alone. Besides, you tell me everywhere you're going. So if you're out at the movies, then I'll go see the same movie so we can have something in common to talk about. I didn't mean to make this awkward for you. In that regard, I'm sorry."

"Okay, I get it. You're lonely. But you can't go around following people. That's creepy."

"I understand…"

"Do you really…because we can't be friends if you keep this up. I can't have crazy in my life right now, and lately your actions are on the verge of crossing the line."

"I'm sorry for making you feel uncomfortable. That was never my intention, and I promise you nothing like that will ever happen again."

"Well, I hope you're right." I unblocked the doorway and allowed Brandon inside the house.

"So what are you up to?"

"Baking as usual. I researched some of the spices we bought from the market and tried to incorporate them in my cakes. And guess what? Since you're here, you get to be my taste tester."

"I'm down for that."

Once the cakes were ready, Brandon and I began to sample the desserts. Some were okay and some were just down right awful. We laughed and joked around while discussing the taste and texture of each cake.

"Hey, you have some frosting…" I could feel the frosting on my lips and out of nowhere, Brandon removed it with a kiss. I was shocked. I didn't know what to say. "I'm sorry. I didn't mean to."

"Don't be."

What was I thinking? Was I really doing this? Brandon kissed me again and this time it was intense. I couldn't believe what I was allowing to happen.

"Are you sure about this?"

"No. Are you?"

"Not really." Brandon looked into my eyes and then he kissed me again. I felt conflicted with what I was doing but I didn't want him to stop.

As Brandon and I were making out, I was still in disbelief over what I was allowing to happen. He didn't know I was a virgin, and if I didn't stop him, he would soon discover the truth. Was I really going to let Brandon be my first? I was so tired of over thinking the issue. I've had my heartbroken by guys I've trusted in the past, nevertheless Brandon and I weren't in a relationship, so I didn't see the harm in moving forward.

"Wait. There's something you need to know."

"What is it?" Brandon asked as he continued to kiss me.

"I'm a virgin."

Brandon stopped kissing me and looked at me in disbelief.

"You're a virgin? So, you've never?"

"No. Never."

"And you and Julian? The two of you never?"

"No. So, if you want to stop I understand, but I felt it was only fair that you know the truth."

Brandon pulled me close and continued to kiss me. I tried to hide my nervousness, but it was too hard to conceal.

"It's okay. I promise to take it slow." My breathing intensified as Brandon undressed me. "Maya. Look at me." I looked into Brandon's eyes and prayed that my nerves wouldn't scare him off. "Don't think about what's going to happen. Just follow my lead and everything will be fine."

"Okay." I decided to loosen up a little and enjoy the moment. Brandon continued to kiss me as he ran his hands all over my body.

"You're so beautiful."

"And you're full of crap."

As we both began to laugh I felt the penetration. It hurt at first, but after we continued on, there was nothing but pleasure. I couldn't believe what I had allowed myself to miss out on. As I began to climax, Brandon's rhythm slowed. After I had my moment, we continued on. My mind was in shock. I was having sex with Brandon Foster. I had to look past the fact that he was Julian's brother to truly enjoy the moment.

When I woke up, Brandon was still in my bed. I didn't know if what we had done was a mistake, but it was too early in the morning to think about it. I tiptoed to the bathroom to take a shower. As the hot water washed over my body, all I could think about was the fact that I wasn't a virgin anymore. When I came out of the bathroom, Brandon was still asleep, so I decided to go out for coffee which gave me time to meditate over the situation. By the time I returned, I found Brandon in the kitchen cooking breakfast.

"Morning."

"Good morning to you too. I didn't know if you were hungry or not."

Brandon placed a plate in front of me as I sat down at the table.

"I bought us some coffee. I would usually make it here, but I needed the fresh air this morning."

"Are you okay?"

"Yeah I'm fine. I just have a lot on my mind."

"I get it, but if you felt like last night was a mistake, I understand. But know that for me it wasn't."

"That's sweet. But in all honesty, I don't know how to feel. One minute I'm a virgin and the next I'm not. You're my friend and I don't know what to make of this."

Brandon pulled a chair from the table, sat down next to me, and then turned my chair around to face him.

"I get this is a lot to take in, but know that last night happened because we wanted it to happen. Yes, we're friends, but there's no rule that says we can't be more than friends. I like you, Maya, and I would like to see where this goes."

"That sounds nice, but what about Julian and Angela. If Julian was to ever find out we were together, he'd flip. And believe it or not, I like Angela. Oh my God, what was I thinking? I knew better." I was rambling. Brandon pulled me out of my chair and straddled me over his lap.

"If someone finding out about us bothers you, then we can keep our relationship a secret. I don't want to end things before they begin. I'm not Julian. I want to be with you and only you. I have no secret relationship out there, except this one if you'll have me. So what do you say, Maya? Can you give us a chance?"

I didn't know what to say. I knew I was playing with fire if I started a relationship with Brandon, but I was tired of being alone and desperately needed companionship.

"Sure. Let's give it a shot."

Brandon began to kiss me and before long we were making out again. The fact that I was with Brandon said a lot about where I was mentally. I knew the fall out of us being together would be great, but the body wants what the heart can't comprehend. My father once told me, "what you do in the dark will come to light," and I know that one day I would be confronted with this secret, but for now I was all about enjoying the moment, and dealing with the repercussions later.

Chapter 9

⚘

Into The Light

Brandon and I became successful at keeping our relationship a secret. He treated me as if I was the only woman in the world, and I loved it. We were in hibernation for months. Lying in bed and doing absolutely nothing. Often, we switched up our sleeping arrangements so no one could pick up on a pattern. However, everyone at work noticed a difference in my mood and behavior, but I credited it all to my father's improvement and no one ever questioned my motive. Before long, a year had passed and Brandon and I were still going strong. I was so in love, and Brandon reassured his devotion for me every chance he could. In some ways, being in love scared the hell out of me because I didn't know it was possible to feel so deeply for someone else.

Then, one morning as Brandon and I were about to leave the farmer's market, a woman stopped and offered me flowers. Brandon bought me white lilies and beautiful sunflowers, then he kissed me. As we pulled away, I saw Nathan out of the corner of my eye, and my heart dropped. We had been so good about hiding our relationship, but Nathan was now aware that we were together.

"Maya, what's wrong? You look as though you've seen a ghost."

"I did and his name is Nathan. He saw us kissing."

"So what. He saw us kissing. You knew eventually someone would find out."

"Yes. Someone other than Nathen. You know he's going to tell Regina, and then she's going to tell Julian. I can only imagine how Julian is going to react. I thought you kept this place a secret."

"I did, but Nathan gets around. There's no telling how he knows about this place."

I looked at Brandon and the thought of losing him made me tense.

"Just promise me you won't allow anything to come between us."

"You know I wouldn't. Come on, Maya, I love you."

"I love you too."

"Besides, you and Julian were never in a real relationship, and Angela and I have been over for a while; so what is there to stop us from going public?" Brandon started yelling, "I love this woman! I'm in love with Jeremiah Davenport."

I couldn't refrain from smile. I may have found my Mr. Right. As we headed back to my place, Brandon's phone began to ring. First Julian called then Angela. I knew things felt too good to be true.

"Julian and Angela. I guess they know now. I told you this would happen."

"And I told you I loved you. This means nothing. We're together, and that's the only thing that matters."

I wanted to believe Brandon, but I knew better. We had a fight ahead of us and I for one didn't know the outcome. Brandon tried to reassure me everything would be okay, but my mind was all over the place. As I was lying on the couch watching television, I didn't notice Brandon waving his hand back and forth in front of me.

"Hey, are you okay? I told you not to worry about us. We're going to be okay."

"I know, but its' hard. When morning comes, who knows what we're going to be faced with. I love our relationship and I don't want it to end."

"And it won't. Come here."

Brandon started kissing me all over. Before long we were making love...but this time it felt different. It was emotional and it scared me. Even though Brandon wouldn't admit it, I felt as though he was afraid of our relationship coming to an end as well. The passion I felt was so intense that I began to cry. Brandon was the first guy I truly loved and I was afraid of losing him. He wiped away my tears and I melted in his arms. I didn't want the night to end.

Morning came and I knew I would have to face the truth. I made coffee and within minutes Brandon's phone started buzzing. It was Julian.

"You know you're going to have to answer that, right?"

"I know, but not now. Right now it's about me and you."

I didn't want Brandon to leave the house because I knew, once he stepped outside, things would change. I wanted to live in the moment for as long as I could. We sat on the couch and watched T.V. in silence, and within an hour, the doorbell ranged. We looked at each other as I answered the door, it was Julian. The light my father once spoke of was now here, and it was shining brightly in my face.

"Julian. How can I help you?"

"All I want is the truth. Are you and Brandon together?"

"Who I choose to see is none of your business. Bye, Julian."

I tried to close the door but Julian blocked it.

"It is if that person is Brandon. He's my brother, Maya."

"Goodbye, Julian."

Brandon came to the door and I could see the fire in Julian's eyes.

"How could you?"

"How could I what? Maya is free to see whoever she wants and she wants to be with me."

At that moment, Julian punched Brandon in the face and he fell to the floor.

"You knew how I felt about Maya! Then you hooked up with her behind my back!"

I tried to help Brandon stand as he wiped the blood from his lip.

"You have some nerve. You lie about having a girlfriend, who later tries to have me killed, and you're mad because your brother and I are dating." I was getting upset. "You got back with Regina after everything she did to me! And you have the audacity to claim you felt some type of way about me. Get out!"

"Regina and I never got back together."

"What are you talking about? She's living with you."

"No, she's not. After Regina lost her job, I allowed her to stay in my guest room until her brother was able to get a bigger place for the both of them. I haven't dated anyone since you. Ask Brandon. He knows."

"I don't care if you did or didn't. I'm with Brandon now, so the relevance of your relationship with Regina is none of my concern."

"You say that now, but how long do you think your relationship with Brandon is going to last once Angela comes back to town. That girl has some sick and twisted hold over Brandon and he won't choose you over her."

I looked at Brandon and didn't know how to feel.

"So, is that true? You told me we were good and nothing would break us up, but if Angela came back to town, would you leave me for her?"

"Maya, you know I love you…"

"That's not what I asked you. Would you leave me for her?"

"He can't answer you because you know what his answer will be. You were just a filler, Maya, and deep down you know it."

I slapped Julian and then I faced Brandon.

"You made love to me and told me that nothing would come between us. All I want to know is…was all of this a lie? Do you really love me?"

"You slept with Maya!" Julian started moving towards Brandon. "You slept with Maya!" Before I knew it Brandon and Julian were fighting in the living room.

"Stop! Stop it!" I tried to pull the guys apart. Finally, Julian stopped hitting Brandon.

"How could you, Maya?" Julian eyes were watery. "He's my brother! My got damn baby brother. How could you do this to me?"

I felt like I was in the Twilight Zone. Why was I feeling sorry for Julian when he was the one who betrayed me?

"Leave, please." Julian composed himself and left. I looked at Brandon and I didn't know what to feel. "You too. I need to be alone right now."

"Maya, please. Don't listen to him. You know I love you."

"I hear what you're saying but that doesn't excuse the fact that your brother knows you very well. So, is it true? If Angela came back, would you leave me for her?"

"Maya…"

Tears fell from my eyes.

"Just answer the question." Brandon didn't say anything. "You know what…just leave. You can let yourself out." I was so heartbroken. I knew dating Brandon wouldn't be easy, but I wasn't prepared for this. My heart was broken once again.

I tried to move past everything that had happened but it was hard, because I loved Brandon. I couldn't work. I found myself crying in the cookie batter, and no matter how hard I tried to pull myself together, I couldn't. Days went by and I thought I was doing okay until I had a breakdown in my office. I was wreck. I locked my door and didn't leave until everyone had gone home. I decided to take some time off. I wasn't fit to work and needed time to heal. At home, all I did was cry. I was a mess. Allison came over and sat with me. She didn't ask any questions, she just let me cry. The next day, I got dressed, and went to see Brandon. I rang the doorbell and he answered.

"Can I come in?"

"Sure."

I walked in and it hurt to be near him.

"I don't know what to say. I miss you."

"I miss you, too."

"Look, I just want us to be together. I love you and that's the only thing that matters."

I felt so ashamed. I felt like I was begging for Brandon to be with me, when all I wanted was for my heart to stop aching.

"I love you too, Maya, but you know we can't be together. Not anymore. I didn't know how much I had hurt Julian until we had a chance to really talk. He's my brother Maya, my blood, and I hurt him deeply by being with you."

I started crying. I tried to control myself but couldn't. I'm sure I was experiencing the pain Samantha probably felt when I advised her to let go of Matt. It's easy to give someone advice when you're on the outside looking in; but it's a different story once you've experienced that pain for yourself.

"I understand."

I turned to leave and my hands were shaking. I was consumed with emotions. Brandon grabbed my hands and pulled me in for a hug. All I wanted was for the pain to stop.

"I'm sorry about all of this. You know I never meant to hurt you."

"Yeah, I know." I tried to compose myself as I wiped the tears from my eyes. "Can I use your bathroom to freshen up?"

"Sure."

While I was in the bathroom, I looked at myself in the mirror wondering what I was doing wrong. I needed to pull myself together and let go. I knew Brandon wouldn't pick me over Julian, but I prayed he loved me enough to not let go. I cleaned myself up and walked out. When I looked up, I stood in disbelief at the sight of Angela standing in the living room.

"Well, well. Look who it is. You didn't waste any time, did you? As soon as I left town, you decided to make your move."

I was upset and heartbroken. There was no way in hell I was about to listen to Angela accuse me in the same manner as Regina.

"Are you serious? You know you're about as worse as Regina. FYI, I didn't pursue Brandon just like I didn't pursue Julian."

"And I'm supposed to believe that?"

"You can believe whatever you want, but know that Brandon pursued me, and my only crime was falling in love with him. So, before you go pointing fingers, why don't you ask yourself one simple question? Why were Brandon and I practically living together for over a year and he never mentioned you. Not once."

"You think you had Brandon. Please! You never had him because I never let him go. All you were doing was keeping his bed warm while I was away."

"And if you're proud of that, then you'll always be his side chick, but never his wife." I headed for the door looking at Brandon in disappointment. "You know, it kills me to say this, but Julian was right about you." I turned around and proceeded towards the door.

"Since you're feeling all sure about yourself, know this: as of today, you and Brandon are no longer business partners." Angela turned around to face Brandon. "Tell her, Brandon. Tell her your partnership is over."

I looked at Brandon in disbelief and he couldn't even look me in the eye.

"But, you can't do that and you know it. We have several events booked for the next couple of months."

"I know and we're dropping your service. I'm sorry."

"You're sorry! Have you informed our clients that my service will no longer be available? Or are you so stuck on trying to stick it to me that you didn't consider the customers or the business?"

"I'll call them this week."

"No, you won't, I will. You will not tarnish my name because your girlfriend can't get over the fact that we were together. I'll call the clients and straighten this out. Oh, and one more thing before I forget, ensure you make the check out to Jeremiah Davenport since you're breaking our contact. You have to pay me. Remember?"

"Oh, no he doesn't. There's a clause in the contract that breaks it if a workplace romance occurred between the promisor and promisee."

"You should've read the contract in its entirety. If you had, you would've known that I don't work for Brandon, nor do I work with Brandon. I'm a corporation that supplies Fosters with a product. And for future reference, whoever makes the first move is guilty of infringement; so either way the fault would've been on Brandon. He crossed the line the day he kissed me in my house. So, I'll be waiting on my check."

"You'll never see that check."

"My lawyer says otherwise."

As I was leaving, I could hear Angela cussing and fussing; screaming how they would never pay me a dime. I had mixed emotions about the entire situation. I was furious with Brandon but was angrier with myself. I knew better. I abandoned common sense all because I didn't want to be alone. I knew upfront that Brandon was a Foster, but I allowed my emotions to rule the situation; and once again I was the one suffering from a broken heart. I was determined next time around I was leaving emotions out of the relationship. I was tired of giving my heart away while receiving nothing in return. Men only knew how to take and it was time I returned the favor. I was going to do what I wanted, with whom I wanted, and the hell with everyone else. It was a new day for Jeremiah Davenport. I dried my eyes and promised myself that I would never allow another man to take advantage of me ever again.

Chapter 10

Double Trouble

Time passed and I felt my heart grow cold. It took a while but Brandon finally paid the fee for breaking our contract. I honestly didn't know how to feel about him or anyone else. He had done a true number on me and I was afraid of the person I was becoming. I found myself snapping at my employees over issues I knew wasn't their fault. I isolated myself, and would blow off Allison, Matt, and anyone else who tried to get too close. I would sit at home and drink the night away. I was in a downward spiral and wasn't doing anything to make the situation any better.

Then one day at work, Allison walked into the kitchen looking nervous. I could tell that something was up.

"Maya. Can I speak with you for a minute?" I walked over to Allison, trying to figure out what was going on.

"What's up?"

"Well, I don't want you to cause a scene or anything, but…"

"But what? What's going on?"

Allison walked me to the kitchen door.

"Take a look."

I looked out, and to my disbelief there sat Julian, Regina, Brandon, and Angela at one of my tables awaiting service. I couldn't believe them. They didn't know how to leave well enough alone. It was like they were trying to rub it in my face that they were together. I decided I wouldn't give them the satisfaction. I went back to work and told Allison to serve them so they could leave. I felt my blood pressure rise. I knew they were doing this out of spite. They left and I thought the situation was resolved, but it wasn't. They returned day after day sitting at the same table like clockwork. I felt like they were trying to goad me into saying something, but I kept my cool. If they wanted to spend their money in my shop, then who was I to refuse their business? This went on for weeks, but somehow I was able to make peace with the situation. Then one day unexpectantly, Matt dropped in to see me while I was reviewing some invoices.

"Hey, stranger."

"Hey."

"So, you don't know how to return a phone call? I've been worried about you."

"There's nothing to worry about. I'm okay."

"That's what your mouth says but I know better. You don't go out anymore, we haven't seen you on the softball field in months, and you look downright depressed. So, what's going on? And don't tell me it's nothing, because I know you."

I looked at Matt and I wanted to break down and cry, but I couldn't. I had bottled up my emotions for so long that I became numb to everything around me.

"You're right. A lot has happened since we last spoke. So, get ready to say I told you so. Long story short I was in a relationship with Brandon Foster for over a year, then he ended it. He broke my heart and I did what most women would do…I blamed myself."

"Maya…"

"Oh, but wait. It gets better. Him and Julian come by the shop every morning with their girlfriends to rub their relationships in my face. I didn't play the fool once, but twice, and with brothers. How irresponsible could I have been? I mean, I couldn't have been thinking straight to do such a stupid thing."

I felt a tear roll down my cheek and I quickly wiped it away.

"I don't get it. How did you end up dating Brandon?"

"I don't know. It just happened. He needed a shoulder to lean on, and in time, I became that shoulder and much more. In my head I knew that we shouldn't have been together, but I allowed it to happen anyway."

"So, now the four of them come into your shop every day and do what?"

"I don't know. I'm always in the back when they come in. It hurts when I see them together, so I chose to ignore the situation."

"Well, maybe it's time you stop ignoring the situation and confront it."

"Confront it how?"

"By fighting fire with fire."

"And how would I do that?"

"By moving on."

"And with who genius? You know I'm not dating anyone."

"Well, you can always pretend you're dating me."

"Oh no. I can't do that. I may have liked Angela, but I really do like Amy and wouldn't do that to her."

"You wouldn't be hurting Amy because we're no longer together…you would know that if you would've picked up your phone when I called you."

"You guys broke up? When did this happen?"

"About two months ago."

"You mean to tell me I've been out the loop that long?"

"Yes, you have. So, what do you say? Are you down for having a French Vanilla boyfriend?"

Both of us started to laugh.

"French Vanilla? You're more like a white chocolate."

"Awe, come on, Maya. I do have a little game."

"I'm sorry, Matt, but you fall into the category Tina calls, "White Boy". You're as white as they come, but I still love you."

Matt and I continued to laugh. It felt good to laugh again. I let out a sigh of contentment. Matt was right. It was time I fought fire with fire. I didn't know if Julian or Brandon would believe Matt and I were in a relationship, but we were about to find out.

"So, what time do they usually come in?"

I looked at the clock then at Matt.

"They're usually here by now. Why?"

"I say let's give them a show."

"What do you have in mind?"

"Just follow my lead." I followed Matt outside to his car which was parked in front of the shop. He stood by the driver side door with me standing in front of him. "Can they see you?"

"Yes."

"I'm going to wrap my arms around you, okay."

"Okay."

I rested my head on Matt's chest. He felt nice which was weird. Matt quickly glanced over to see if they were watching then he squeezed me tightly in his arms.

"Okay, we have their attention. Let's give them something to talk about."

"How? What are we going to do?"

"This." Matt leaned over and kissed me. It was shocking! Even though I've viewed Matt as a friend, his kiss felt nice...too nice!

He got into his car and let down his side window. "Same time tomorrow?"

"Yeah. Same time tomorrow."

I went inside and everyone including my staff gawked at me in disbelief. I looked at the expressions on Julian and Brandon's faces. Matt was right. Their expressions were priceless. I walked into the kitchen and my staff was astounded.

"Okay, boss lady. What's up with you and the lawyer?" Nikki asked awaiting my reply.

"Yeah, Maya, what's going on with you and white boy?" I laughed because Tina was right on cue with her comment.

"Okay, everyone calm down. What you saw wasn't real; it was just for show."

"What are you talking about?" Nikki was searching for answers.

"A guy I use to date has been harassing me by coming by the shop every day with his girlfriend. You've seen them. They're in here every morning. So, to make it seem as though I've moved on, Matt and I decided to pretend that we're a couple."

"So, the two of you aren't together?" Allison asked in an inquisitive voice.

"No. Matt and I are only friends, but I need you guys to pretend like we're dating."

"Anything for you, boss lady," Nikki said while glaring through the doorway at Julian and Brandon.

"Thank you guys for understanding."

Later on that day, as I was driving home, I thought about the great support system I had at work. I felt bad for the way I treated my staff while I was going through my rough patch. I had forgotten how much they truly cared about me. I needed to get my act together and fast. When I arrived at home, there were several messages on my answering machine. One in particular that surprised me. It was from Brandon. The fact that he thought it was okay to bring his girlfriend to my shop every day for weeks, irked me. Then as soon as I'm seen kissing someone else, he gets into an uproar. I deleted the message and began to cook dinner. After I ate, I sat on the couch and watched some television, but before I could get comfortable, the doorbell ranged. I opened the door and it was Julian.

"What do you want?"

"Can I come in?"

"No. Now what do you want?"

"Please, Maya, can we talk?"

"We have nothing to talk about."

"Oh really? So, what's up with you and Matt? I thought you guys were just friends."

"You want to know what's up with me and Matt, says the guy who brings his deranged girlfriend into my shop every day." I was so pissed that I slammed the door in Julian's face. He continued to ring the doorbell over and over again. "Go home, Julian."

"Not until you hear what I have to say."

"I don't want to hear anything you have to say. Now leave." Julian continued to ring the doorbell. "If you don't leave my property, I'll be forced to call the police to arrest you for trespassing; and then I'll have them arrest your nutty girlfriend too, considering she still has an active restraining order against her."

"Maya, please."

"Leave, Julian! There's nothing for you here."

Before long, the ringing stopped. I was amazed at how a simple kiss between Matt and I caused so much animosity. The next day, I waited for Julian and Brandon to show up, but they didn't. Maybe our plan actually worked. Matt came to the shop looking for them as well.

"So, where are they?"

"I don't know. They didn't come in this morning."

"I told you it would work."

"We'll see. The day isn't over." Matt and I went into my office to discuss tactics just in case we had to keep our charades going. "Okay, first thing first. There will be no more kissing."

"And why not? It seemed pretty effective to me."

"Yes, it was very effective, but I'm in a vulnerable state right now, and even though you wouldn't take advantage of me, I would probably take advantage of you. You're my friend and I don't want to lose your friendship because we allowed ourselves to cross that line."

"I get it, Maya, but I wouldn't do that to you. You're right. We're friends and I only want what's best for you. So, if you don't want to kiss, then we won't kiss. Anything else?"

"Yes. In order for them to believe that we're actually dating, we have to be seen together outside the shop."

"I'm already ahead of you. I have a special date planned for us tonight at 8:00."

"And what's so special about this date?"

"You'll just have to wait and see."

"Alright, since you won't tell me what it is, I'm going to drop the subject, but make sure it's nothing crazy. I know you and you're good for doing something crazy."

"It's not crazy. Trust me. You'll like it."

"Okay, if you say so. Now back to our plan. Is there anything else you can think of?"

"Yes, I want you back on the softball field as soon as possible."

I smiled at Matt because he was right. I needed to get back into my normal routine.

"Will do."

There was a knock at the door and Allison walked in.

"Hey guys. I wanted to let you know they just walked in."

"Thanks." Matt and I looked at each other and walked out. We strolled to the front counter and Matt grabbed my fingers.

"Okay, so I'll see you tonight."

"Yes, I'll be ready."

Matt let go of my fingers and kissed me on the lips. I was stunned. We just had a conversation regarding no kissing. Matt smiled at me as he walked out the door. I went into the kitchen and started baking.

"You know, if I didn't know any better, I would say Matt is getting more out of this pretend relationship then you are." Allison smirked as she checked on her cakes.

"Really? And why would you say that?"

"I don't know. It could be because of the way he looks at you."

"We're only friends. Nothing more."

"Okay, but watch him. You don't want another Brandon incident."

Allison was right. It started out as fun and games and before I knew it Brandon and I were in compromising positions. I had to make sure there were boundaries, not only for Matt, but for myself as well. Allison peeped out the kitchen door then looked at me smiling.

"What are you smiling about?"

"I think the guys are buying it. Both of them keep looking back at the kitchen door. And Angela looks pissed."

"Good. Maybe now they'll stop coming in."

"Look, Maya, I get why you're doing this, but I don't want you to get hurt in the process. So be careful, okay."

"I will and thank you, Allison."

"For what?"

"For caring."

I could tell Allison was truly worried about me and for good reason. For a couple of months, I shut everyone out including her. After work, I went home and decided to get dressed for my pretend date. I didn't know what to wear considering Matt and I were just friends. So to make it easy, I decided to dress up since we were pretending to be on a real date. Before long, the doorbell ranged and it was Matt.

"Hey, you look great."

"And you look over-dressed." Matt was dressed very formal. "So, where are we going again?"

"We're going to the orchestra. The London Symphony is in town and it's an experience you shouldn't miss."

"Are you serious? The orchestra?"

"Hey, don't knock it until you try it."

"Didn't we just have a conversation about you picking out something crazy?" Matt and I started to laugh. "Okay, since I trust you, I'll give it a chance."

When we arrived, I had my doubts; but when I heard the music, my doubts went out the window. It was beautiful. I was captivated from the beginning until the end. As we were walking out of the theater, Matt smiled at me.

"Okay, I'll give it to you. It was good."

"I knew you would like it." Matt and I turned to leave the theater and my smile quickly dissipated. There, standing in the lobby, was Julian. "Okay, pretend you don't see him and keep walking."

As we headed towards the exit, Julian followed closely behind us. Matt gave the valet our ticket, and I prayed they would find our car quickly, but to my luck they weren't quick enough.

"Maya!"

"Julian."

"I didn't know you guys were going to be here tonight."

"Same here."

I looked at Julian and had no further words for him.

"Well, our car is here. You ready?" Matt asked, as I glared at Julian.

"Yeah, I'm ready." In the car, my anxiety rose. "Did you mention to anyone where we were going tonight?"

"No, I didn't tell anyone."

"Then, how did Julian know we would be there?"

"I don't know. Then again, it is the London Symphony."

"Come on. You think Julian is really into the symphony?"

"I don't get it. Why are you so upset? Your plan is working."

"No, my plan was to get them out of my shop, not have them follow me everywhere I go."

"You know what I think you need?"

"What, Matt? What do I need?"

"You need a vacation."

"A vacation?"

"Yes. You need to get away, clear your head, and relax."

"As nice as that sounds, you know I can't leave my dad for a long period of time."

"Maya…you're rich. Take him with you. I'm sure Mary and Kevin wouldn't mind going on a vacation with you."

We stated laughing.

"You're right. I do need a break."

"And I have the perfect plan."

"What do you have in mind?"

"I have a business trip coming up and…"

"Matt…"

"No, it's not what you think. While I'm away on my business trip, you take your vacation at the same time. That way we're both gone at the exact same time giving the appearance that we left together."

"That could work. You're pretty good at this."

"I told you I got your back. They're going to be so worried about where you are and what you're doing, that they'll railroad their own relationships in the process."

"Remind me to never cross you." I smiled at Matt as he drove me home. When we arrived, he walked me to the front door. "Thank you again for a great night."

"Anytime. And before I forget, let me email you the information regarding my trip so our time frames will match up."

"You're the best! You know that?"

"Yeah I know."

Matt gave me a goodnight kiss on the cheek and left. I walked inside trying to think of a vacation spot. I was floored. I had no idea where I wanted to go, so I called Allison for help.

"Hey, are you busy?"

"No. What's up?"

"I'm planning a vacation but I don't know where to go."

"You're going on a vacation."

"Why do you say it like that?"

"Because you haven't been on a real vacation since your dad got sick."

"And that's why I'm in need of one. So where do you think I should go?"

"I don't know. There are so many places out there."

"I know and that's the problem I'm running into."

"So, what bought about this trip?"

"Matt suggested I needed a vacation and he's right. I need to get away."

"So, he's going with you?"

"Oh no. He's going on a business trip and we're planning to leave and return at the same time so it'll appear we're on a trip together."

"You two are crazy."

"I know, but help me figure out a location. Somewhere nice. I'm bringing my dad, Mary, and Kevin with me."

"Maya, that's not a vacation.

"It's the only way I can take a vacation. You know I can't leave my dad for a long period of time."

"I know, I know." Allison and I started brainstorming over the phone. "Okay how about Jamaica?"

"No, I've been there too many times. I want to go somewhere new."

"Okay, how about Paris."

"No. Too romantic."

"Okay. I got it. Greece."

"What's in Greece?"

"Charlie."

"Are you serious? Charlie is *your* friend, not mine."

"Oh come on Maya, she's your friend too. That girl did everything possible to be friends with you, and all you ever did was give her the cold shoulder."

"I did not. Besides, every time she came over, it was to hang out with you, not me."

"You know that's not true. So stop making excuses and go see Charlie. She hasn't seen you in over 10 years."

"I don't know. I'll think about it.

"Well, don't think too long. Besides, Charlie would love to see you."

"Yeah…yeah, if you say so, but now you have to reconsider opening up a new boutique."

"And why would I do that?"

"Because you brought up Charlie. You know the deal."

"Come on, Maya. That's not fair."

"Okay then. No Charlie."

"Fine. I'll think about it."

"Great! Who knows it may work out this time."

"We'll see. Anyway, back to you. How did your date go with Matt and where did he take you?"

"Are you ready for this? He took me to see The London Symphony."

"The Symphony? What was that like?"

"Believe it or not I liked it. We were having a good time until we ran into Julian."

"Julian? What was he doing there?"

"I don't know and I don't care."

"Well, at least you know your plan is working."

"It's working too well if you ask me."

"But this is what you wanted, right?"

"I don't know. All I wanted was Julian out of my life. Not popping up unexpectedly all the time. It's draining."

"Well, hopefully he'll get the clue and back off."

"We'll see."

"Well, if you need anything before you go, let me know."

"I will and thanks, Allison."

"Anytime. Goodnight."

"Goodnight."

I hung up contemplating whether or not I should go to Greece. I hadn't seen Charlie in years and considering how I left things, I wouldn't know what to say to her which is probably why I needed to go. So, I decided on Greece as my destination. I told Mary and Kevin about the upcoming trip and they were ecstatic. I aligned my flights with Matt's business trip, and everything was set. It was time I took a step back to reevaluate my life. After being in a relationship with two brothers, I was overdue for a break. I needed to put my thoughts together and figure out what I wanted to do next with my life. I had accomplished a lot, but I knew I was capable of doing so much more. I didn't know what the future held for me, but I was ready for the next chapter in my life to begin.

Chapter 11

Pièce De Résistance

It was time for our vacation and everyone was packed and ready to go. Mary tranquilized my father so he'd sleep the entire flight. When we arrived the sights were as beautiful as I imagined. The water was the bluest I had ever seen and the aromas in the air instantly made your mouth water. As soon as we walked into the villa, I felt the stress slowly melt away. It was breathtaking. Mary and Kevin readied themselves for my father's reaction once he realized he wasn't at home anymore. We were ready for him to fight everyone, but instead he was afraid. It broke my heart to see him in such a helpless state but once he saw the views, he calmed down, looked at me, and smiled. I didn't know what to make of it, but I was happy he wasn't freaking out. After settling in, we were jet-lagged from the long flight so we took a nap. After we woke up, we went out for food and my father was captivated by the scenery. Bringing my father with me was probably the best thing I could've done. I think he may have needed a vacation just as much as I did.

The next day, I informed Mary and Kevin that I was going out alone and would return soon. Allison emailed me Charlie's address and I rode a bike to her house. I was so fascinated with the scenery that I almost passed it. I stood outside contemplating whether I should leave or stay. After several minutes of rehearsing what I wanted to say, I decided to ring the doorbell. Charlie answered.

"Maya, is that you?"

"Yeah, it's me Charlie."

"Oh my goodness, it's so great to see you. Come in." Charlie invited me into her home, which was stunning. There were authentic plastered walls and an adobe fireplace. The entire concept took my breath away. "So, what are you doing here?"

"Believe it or not I'm on vacation. I heard you lived nearby so I decided to stop by for a visit."

"Well, I'm glad you did. I haven't seen you in ages." As soon as we sat on the couch, two little boys and a little girl ran in from the back and jumped on the couch with us. Hey guys, I want you to meet my friend, Maya, who's visiting all the way from…" Charlie glanced over at me.

"Atlanta, Georgia."

"Atlanta. So, what do we say?"

"It's nice to meet you." They yelled in unison.

"Maya, this is Andrew, Chloe, and Cristo." They waved at me and their smiles were too precious. Chloe and Cristo looked as though they were twins, and all of them had thick curly hair.

"Charlie, they are so beautiful. I can't believe you're a mom!"

"Yes, I'm a mom." Charlie then turned to face the kids. "Okay you little crumb snatchers, go to the back and play. I'll be in to give you a snack later."

"Okay." They sighed then they left the room.

"Wow, a lot has changed."

"Yes it has. So, are you married? Kids? What's going on in the life of Ms. Maya Davenport?"

"No, I'm not married and I don't have any kids. They will come in time, but right now I'm more focused on my business. Speaking of which, are you still in Foreign Relations? Is that why you're here in Greece?"

"Oh no, I don't work anymore. I met Thaddaios in Egypt, fell in love, and decided to have his babies. He's originally from Santorini, so we moved here and I never looked back."

"So, you gave up your career to be a stay at home mom?"

"You make it sound like I did something horrible, but yes. I wanted to stay at home and raise my kids. I help out at the restaurant when Thaddaios needs me, but for the most part, I'm usually here with my babies."

"You guys own a restaurant?"

"Yes, it's been in Thad's family for years and now he's the owner. It's just north of here. You should come by and have dinner with us tonight."

"That sounds nice, but my father is here with me and he can be a handful. He's suffering from Dementia and I don't want him to cause a scene in your restaurant."

"No, bring him. We have a room in the back and he can scream and shout and no one would care. It'll be fun and Thad can finally meet you."

"Fine, we'll come." As I scanned the house, there was an awkward silence in the room. I looked up and noticed Charlie was fidgeting with her hands, which led me to believe there was something bothering her. "Okay, Charlie, so what's on your mind?"

"It's nothing."

"No, it's something so spit it out. What's up?"

"It's…"

"It's what?"

"Fine. I want to know why you were so hard on me in college. I was always nice to you, and all you ever did was shut me out. So what was it? What did I do to make you hate me so much?"

I could tell my actions in college really did leave a mark on Charlie. Maybe Allison knew and that's why she wanted me to come to Greece.

"Charlie, the way I treated you had nothing to do with you, but more to do with me. My father was steadfast about me becoming a lawyer, but I was too busy trying to figure out a way to follow my own dreams. And besides, every time you came around, you were always looking for Allison, not me."

"I would only ask for Allison because you were short with me all of the time. It was like you didn't want me being friends with her."

"No, it wasn't like that. I felt like you always had something planned when you knew I was knee deep in exams. You always pulled Allison away during our study section when you knew I needed her help the most."

"Did Allison ever tell you why I would pull her away?"

"No, she never said anything? So, why did you do it?"

"I know she's going to kill me for telling you this, but Allison was pregnant. She was having her own little mini drama but didn't say anything because you were constantly making it about yourself."

My heart broke. How could Allison keep such a big secret from me?

"That's a lie and you know it. I was never a drama queen so don't make me out to be one. And as far as Allison is concerned, she was never pregnant."

"But, she was. She never said anything to you because you were steps away from having a nervous breakdown. So she allowed you to lean on her, and I allowed her to lean on me."

"I don't get it. She knew she could tell me anything. So, I'm assuming she had an abortion?"

"Yes."

Tears fell from my eyes. The person whom I claimed to be my best friend deceived me in the worst way possible. We were supposed to be each other's keeper yet she chose to treat me like the enemy.

"This doesn't make any sense. We told each other everything."

"Sometimes a true friend knows exactly how much you can handle. You were at your max, so Allison chose to confide in me instead."

I felt betrayed because I told Allison everything and she picked and chose what she wanted to share with me.

"Well, that's nice to know. So, tell me something. Are the two of you still Chatty Cathy's?"

"Maya, it wasn't like that?"

"No, I want to know if she still confides in you."

"Yes, she does."

I was upset but I was trying my best to not overreact.

"Okay. Since Allison tells you everything, explain to me why she closed her shop in Manhattan? I'm not angry, I just want to know what happened. Allison was at the top of her game and out the blue she up and quits. So what went wrong?"

"I don't know if she would want me to tell you."

"Charlie, she's the reason I'm here visiting with you today. So, I think it's okay to tell me what happened."

"Fine. As you know, her shop was thriving in Manhattan when she met Peter. They were so in love and Allison found out she was pregnant again. This time she wanted to keep the baby, but Peter had other plans and he beat her until she lost it."

"Charlie, why didn't someone tell me?"

"She was ashamed. Here you were at the top of your game but

she was crumbling behind the scenes of hers. Allison felt like she needed a fresh start. So, she left Peter, sold her business, and went to work for you."

"So, Allison's business didn't fail. She just chose to walk away from it."

"Basically, yeah. Peter took something from her and whatever it was it broke her spirit."

"Well, that explains a lot. Now I understand why she never took the money I gave her to open up a new boutique."

"Wait, have you heard of the clothing line called Mayhem?"

"Yeah, Allison is always trying to dress me up in their clothes. Why?"

"That's her line. So you see, she didn't give up on her dream; she just chose to pursue it a different way."

I was happy Allison was still following her dreams, but I was upset she chose to keep it a secret from me.

"I hate she wasn't able to confide in me, but with everything I had going on in my life, I don't blame her for not talking to me."

"Maya…you know how Allison feels about you. She loves you."

"And yet she has a stranger way of showing it."

"Maya, that's not fair."

"I know it's not, but I'm going to work through this like I do everything else. Allison wanted us to kiss and make up and that's what I'm going to do. There's nothing I can do about the past, but I am truly sorry for the way I treated you in college."

"Maya."

"I said I was sorry."

"I'm sorry too."

I looked at my watch and it was getting late. "Well, I need to be heading back. So what time do you want us for dinner?"

"How does eight o'clock sound?"

"Eight o'clock sounds good. I'll see you soon."

I left thinking about everything Charlie told me about Allison and I felt like she led a double life. I understood why she was so worried about me, but I hated the fact she wasn't able to confide in me. However, as much as I wanted to dwell on the issue, I couldn't. There was too much excitement going on around me. I was intrigued by tourists' accents and drawn to the subtle conversation between shop owners. Before I knew it, I was out shopping for ingredients to make a cake. Since I had my father in a strange place, surrounded by new people, the least I could do was make him his favorite dessert…pound cake. When I returned to the villa, to my surprise, it was empty. I went out back and there sat my father, Mary, and Kevin relaxing on the beach. It seemed like they were truly enjoying themselves, so I decided not to disturb them as I made my way back inside. I went into the kitchen to prep the cake. After I placed it in the oven, I decided to give Allison a call.

"Hey, I hope I didn't wake you."

"No, I'm up. So how's Greece? Are you enjoying yourself?"

"I am. Believe it or not, my father seems to be having a good time as well. He hasn't thrown a fit since we've been here. I think he needed a vacation just as much as I did."

"He probably did. Well, I'm glad you're enjoying yourself."

"I am."

"So, have you seen Charlie yet?"

"I have. She has a beautiful family."

"Yes, she does. So, how was it seeing her again?"

"It was good. We were able to resolve some issues *and* some other things were finally brought to light."

"Like what?"

"Like you keeping secrets from me. I thought we were friends."

"We are friends."

"Are we? You were my roommate in college and you never mentioned to me you were pregnant. Nor did you tell me Peter was abusing you in New York."

"I didn't want to burden you with my problems."

"We're friends, Allison, so your problems are my problems."

"It was never that simple with you and you know it. In college, you were always in a constant battle with your father, so it never seemed like the right time to say anything."

"Allison, you were pregnant! Not once, but twice, and I never knew about it. So, tell me, if I'm your friend, how am I supposed to feel about that?"

"I get it. You're upset and you have every right to be, but. . ."

"Upset? No, I'm not upset. I'm hurt. You confided in Charlie, Allison. Charlie! She wasn't your best friend. I thought I was but you've proven me wrong, yet again."

"Maya, you are my best friend and that's why I suggested you go to Greece. I wanted you to see Charlie because I knew she would tell you the truth about everything. I wasn't strong enough to do it myself, so Charlie said she would do it for me."

"Wait. You talk as if you have had this planned out for a while."

"Well, in a way I did. Matt felt as though you needed a vacation and I needed a way to get you to talk to Charlie. So, my plan above all else was to convince you to go to Greece."

"I don't know what to say."

"I know this seems crazy, but I couldn't continue to ask you to be open with me regarding your issues and keep you in the dark about mine. You deserved to know the truth."

"Well, I'm glad the truth finally came out, but I hate that you didn't trust me enough to handle it. I know my life may seem like a rollercoaster sometimes, but I'm never too busy to be your friend."

I could hear Allison sniffling on the other end of the phone.

"I know and I'm sorry, Maya. You know I love you, right?"

"Yeah, and I love you too."

"Okay, so listen. I want you to enjoy the rest of your time there and we'll finish taking about this when you get back. Okay."

"Sure. I'll talk to you later."

"Okay. Bye."

Upon hanging up the phone, my father, Mary, and Kevin came walking through the door.

"Oh something smells good," my father said while Mary escorted him to the bathroom."

"Go ahead and freshen up then you can have some."

We sat back, ate cake, and drank milk while enjoying the view. Everyone relaxed and lounged around the villa before heading out to dinner. I wasn't sure how my father would react, but I wanted him to get out and enjoy himself. When we arrived at the restaurant, we could hear music blaring out into the streets. As we walked inside there were people dancing and laughing throughout the restaurant. The atmosphere was so inviting, and as promised, Charlie had prepared a table for us in one of the reserved rooms. At first, my father was hesitant about going in, but Kevin was able to convince him that it was okay to enter. Charlie introduced me to Thaddaios and we sat, ate, and laughed for hours. During the course of dinner, Charlie and Thad relentlessly urged me to open a restaurant back home. The thought of owning a restaurant never crossed my mind, but it was time I branched out and did something different. And how crazy would it be if I opened my own restaurant?

I wasn't sure about the idea, but Charlie and Thad decided to walk me step by step through a restaurant start up. I didn't understand why they wanted to help me so badly, then Charlie explained how well my desserts were selling in Santorini. Surprisingly, Davenport Sweet Cakes were well known everywhere, including Greece. Allison had signed Charlie and Thad to a contract and they had been selling my desserts at their restaurant for years. Thad showed me how he paired some of my desserts with his famous entrees. He was also able to turn some of them into side dishes. It was amazing how the pairings actually worked together. I was so grateful for their help, and the remainder of our vacation was spent with Charlie and her family.

I wasn't sure if I was going to follow through once I returned home, but I was energized by the thought of doing something new. Once again life had thrown me a curve ball; but this time I was prepared for the outcome. My love life may have been in rubbles, but my career was in full speed and I didn't plan on slowing down for anyone.

Chapter 12

Ground Breaking

When I returned home, I couldn't stop thinking about opening a restaurant. I filled Allison in on the discussion I had with Charlie and she was on board. I didn't want to notify my staff until my dream of owning a restaurant had become a reality. So, I contacted my lawyer and we discussed different options and plausible locations. After several rejections, we finally received a yes, which would have been great if the location wasn't within close proximity to Fosters. I knew once Brandon discovered I was his newest competitor, he would explode. I thought about the animosity it could cause, but I was in this for the long haul, and I wasn't about to back down for anyone; especially him.

The final approvals came through and a date was set for the ground breaking ceremony. I notified my staff of my newest endeavor and they were thrilled. I offered them preference over the positions, before advertising them, just in case someone wanted a change of scenery. There was hesitation at first, but then a couple of them applied and the rest decided to stay on at the bakery. I was so excited. Everything was coming into perspective.

Finally, after a long day at work, I decided to head home. To my surprise, Brandon was there waiting at my door. I knew this day would come and I was prepared for anything he had to say.

"Maya, can we talk."

"We have nothing to talk about."

As I was about to close the door, Brandon blocked it with his foot and forced his way through.

"Get out!"

"Not until we talk."

"Like I've told you over and over again, we have nothing to talk about."

"Are you serious? You're going to pretend like what you're doing isn't wrong?"

"I'm not doing anything. What you're talking about?"

"Okay, then explain to me why you're opening a restaurant only steps away from mine. I know our relationship didn't end well, but what you're doing is callous."

"Really? What I'm doing is callous, says the guy who only strung me along until his ex-came back."

"Come on, Maya. You know it wasn't like that."

"Oh really?" I refused to get excited over anything Brandon had to say. "You know, I would love to stand here and go back and forth with you about this, but I'm not. I have a lot of decisions to make and a restaurant to build! So, if you'll excuse me."

"Fine, I don't know why I'm worried. It's not like you've ever ran a restaurant before. I'll give you six months to a year tops, and you'll be closed."

I laughed because I knew Brandon was afraid I'd be successful... more successful than Fosters.

"Wow. Well know this: I own a chain of bakeries that carry my <u>name</u>, I have friends all over the world, and I know celebrities who are only a phone call away. So, while you're sitting around waiting for my business to fail, you might want to keep an eye out on yours. Now get out of my house."

I watched Brandon's facial expression quickly change. I had no intention of opening a restaurant to get back at him, but now I was more determined than ever to make my business a success.

"Come on, Maya. Don't do this."

"It's already done. Goodnight."

I opened the door and signaled for Brandon to leave.

"You really hate me that much?"

"You know I don't hate you. I dislike a lot of things you've done to me in the past, but I could never hate you."

"And, I'm sorry about all of it."

"I know you are. Goodnight." Brandon walked out and I quickly closed and bolted the door. I was flushed. I poured myself a glass of wine and went to bed.

Finally, the day I had been anticipating arrived, and Kyle bought me the keys to the restaurant. I invited the press and all of my employees to the renovation celebration. We put on our construction hats, posed for pictures, had a couple of drinks, then headed home.

Now it was time for the real work to begin. I was so excited to start working on the interior design of the restaurant. Things were moving quickly and everything was falling into place. We gutted the inside and I received approval to add on another level which enhanced the view of the restaurant. I envisioned a grand staircase that led to rooms big enough to accommodate large parties and events. I chose warm paint colors and stylish furniture, which transitioned the mood from lavish to chill. I wanted evey customer to feel welcomed from the moment they cross the threshold.

While the contractors were busy revitalizing the property, I was on a mission to find the best chefs from around the world. I persuaded Allison to join me on my scouting mission and we traveled to several different countries in search of the best. We flew to India and the Philippians. We also visited Greece, France, and New York City. We went to culinary schools and spoke with only graduating students. I didn't want to hire anyone who was already established. I was only interested in new and up and coming chefs. I was captivated with the graduates who were ready to make a name for themselves, and who could offer everyone something new and exciting to savor.

Once all the chefs were selected, I held a tasting at the restaurant. Each chef would prepare six dishes for a panel review. The panel consisted of myself, other chefs, some of my employees, and the contractors. I wanted to have a diverse assessment of each dish, and what should have felt like work, turned into a lot of fun moments and incredible dishes.

The restaurant was nearing completion, and the contractors needed a name in order to generate a sign. I thought long and hard and none of this would have been possible if it wasn't for Charlie, so I decided to name the restaurant after her. I called her and told her the exciting news, and offered to fly out her and her family for the unveiling of the restaurant.

At last, the time had come and I was only hours away from the unveiling. I had butterflies in my stomach and found it hard to calm my nerves. Allison tried to help me relax but nothing was working.

"I can't believe it's done."

"I know and it's beautiful. I'm so proud of you, Maya. You had a dream and you followed it through. Charlie's is going to be a hit."

"Thanks, Allison, and don't forget you helped to make this possible as well."

Allison hugged me then my phone rang. It was Mary.

"Hello, Mary. Is everything okay?"

"Everything is fine. We're dressed and ready to go."

"Okay, I'm on my way."

Allison and I went to my father's to pick them up. I rented a limo for the night so we were able to arrive in style and drink as much as we wanted! Once we arrived at my father's house, I opened the door and Mary met me at the entrance.

"Okay, so are you guys ready to go?" I was excited to get the night started.

"Yes, we are, but first there's someone who would like to wish you luck." Mary was beaming from ear to ear.

Kevin wheeled my father to the door and he smiled at the sight of me. My father reached for my right hand, embraced it ever so slightly, then kissed it.

"Maya, you look beautiful," my father said as he caressed my hand.

I gashed in shock.

"Yes, out of all days your father just happens to be lucid today. This is nothing but a miracle," Mary said as she gave me a hug.

I was trying not to cry because I didn't want to ruin my makeup, but I was so overjoyed with emotions that the tears came anyway.

"Daddy..."

"Come here, Sweetie." My father gave me a kiss on the cheek, and all I could do was cry. "Mary told me what was going on and I want you to know that I'm so proud of you. You've achieved everything you set out for and more. Tonight is your night and I want you to enjoy it."

"Thanks, daddy. I love you so much."

"I love you too, baby girl. Now let's go. I don't want you to be late for your grand opening. Go. Go."

All of us laughed as we walked to the limo. Allison struggled to reapply my makeup because I couldn't stop smiling. My father grabbed my hand and held it for the duration of the ride. When we arrived at Charlie's, I took a deep breath and I thanked God for the blessings He bestowed upon me. I collected myself then stepped out of the limo. Cameras were flashing from every angle. I answered reporters' questions, then stood in silence as I marveled over the sight of Charlie's. I walked inside where there were more reporters waiting for me at the entrance. I smiled and answered more questions while Tina escorted my guest to their assigned table. I then headed towards the kitchen to check on the chefs. I wanted to ensure everything was running smoothly. As I made my way back through the crowd, someone stopped me from behind. I turned around and it was Julian.

"Maya, you look beautiful."

"Thank you."

As I turned to go back into the kitchen, Julian grabbed me by the arm.

"So, that's it. You have nothing else to say to me?"

I glared at Julian and he released my arm.

"You gave me a complement and I accepted it. What else do we have to talk about?"

"You're right. We don't have anything else to talk about. I just wanted to congratulate you on your big night. I know you may hate me, but believe it or not, I'm truly happy for you and I wish you the best."

"Thank you."

Julian's compliment ignited emotions, but I had to suppress them. I had a party to host, people to greet, and more interviews to address. Tonight was my night and I wanted everything to be perfect. I proceeded to the kitchen, gave my staff a motivational pep talk, and downed a couple of shots to calm my nerves. Once I felt composed, I headed back towards the party. As I made my way through the crowd, I quickly spotted Brandon heading in my direction. I tried to run back towards the kitchen but was blocked by a group of people who were being seated at their table. When the path was finally clear, it was too late. Brandon was standing in front of me.

"So, you're dodging me now?"

"That's the plan."

Before I could walk away, a reporter cornered Brandon and I into an interview. Brandon was very generous with his complements about Charlie's. I smiled as I tried to fake my way through it. My comments were brief but professional and was led by the most insincere smile as I occasionally peered at Brandon. Once the interview was over they wanted us to take a picture together.

"Now, was that so bad?"

"Why are you here? You want my restaurant to fail, remember?"

"I'm here to say I'm sorry. I was wrong for what I said and I hope you'll accept my apology."

"Apology accepted. Now, if you'll excuse me, I have other guest to attend to."

As I proceeded to walk away, Brandon grabbed me by the waist and whispered in my ear.

"Maya, I'm serious. I'm so sorry. For everything." He then leaned over, kissed me on the cheek, then walked away. Something as simple as a kiss on the cheek left me feeling confused and perplexed. I was convinced Brandon and Julian were trying to sabotage my night with their so-call apologies. They stated they were happy for me, but I knew better. As I headed towards my table and I saw Matt and Allison chatting. She casually walked over towards me with a concerned look on her face.

"Hey, are you okay?"

"Yeah, I'm fine. I had a little run in with Julian and Brandon, but I'm okay."

"Julian and Brandon? What are they doing here?"

"I don't know, but they both wanted to congratulate me on tonight's opening. Although it seemed like a nice gesture, I'm not buying it. They're up to something."

"Even if they are, we're not going to worry about it. Remember, tonight is your night. Charlie and Thad are on their way and we're going to have a good time. Okay?"

"Okay. I just hate they're in my head."

Matt walked over towards me and Allison.

"Who's in your head?" Matt asked in a concerned voice.

"No one…it's nothing. So, are you enjoying the party?"

"I was until I saw your face. What's going on?"

"It's nothing. Tell him, Allison, it's nothing."

"She's right. It's nothing. So let's party," Allison said while holding up a glass of champagne.

Matt looked at me and I felt like he knew I was lying.

"Allison can you excuse us for a moment."

"Sure."

Matt placed my arm inside of his and escorted me away from the table.

"What are you doing?"

"I'm taking you someplace where we can talk." Matt led me to my office and closed the door. "So, are you going to tell me what's going on?"

"It's nothing."

"You're lying. I saw you earlier and you were all smiles. Now you look like you're somewhere off in the distance. So, what's going on?"

"Like I said, it's nothing for you to worry about."

"Come on, Maya. You know you can talk to me. Tell me… what's going on?"

"Okay fine. It's the Foster brothers. They're the issue. They both showed up tonight wanting to congratulate me. I want to believe they're sincere, but I can't. I don't trust them."

"And you have good reason not to. But you shouldn't allow them to ruin your night. Remember, tonight is all about you and the opening of Charlie's. You need to figure out a way to get them out of your head so you can enjoy yourself."

"Trust me, I'm trying, but my head isn't where it should be. I hate I'm allowing them to get to me…tonight, of all nights."

"Okay, try thinking about something else. Your father is here. Put all of your focus on him and the fact he's here celebrating with you tonight."

"You're right. My father is here. He's lucid, and…"

"Wait, your father is coherent?"

"Yes. Of all days, his memory came back today."

"That's even more of a reason to be happy. So, let's go back out there and not think about whatever those guys' names are, and have a good time."

Both of us started to laugh.

"Thanks, Matt. I needed this distraction."

"Anytime."

I gave Matt a hug and may have lingered longer than expected, because when we pulled away, Matt looked into my eyes and kissed me. Something told me to draw back, but I didn't. I allowed the kiss to go on longer than I should have. Before I knew it, our kissing intensified. That's when I knew I had to stop.

"We can't."

"We can't what?"

"We can't do this. You're my friend, and I don't want to jeopardize what we have. Look at what happened between me and Brandon. We were friends then we allowed ourselves to cross the line. Now look at us. I don't want that to happen to you and me."

"And it won't."

"But you can't promise that." I held out my hand. "So, friends."

"Maya."

"Friends."

"Okay. Friends."

Matt kissed me on the cheek and escorted me back to the party. Even though I didn't want things to transpire between Matt and myself, I was still intrigued by the kiss we shared. I blushed whenever the thought came to mind. It appeared, Matt may have been the distraction I needed.

Once we made it back to our table, Charlie and Thad came walking through the door, and we partied the night away. After a while, I heard the music soften, and noticed the lights were shining on my father. He looked over at me and smiled as he signaled for me to come to him.

"Dad, what are you doing?"

My father didn't say a word. He pushed down the locks on his wheelchair and stood up.

"Dad." I wanted to help him, but he was determined to stand up on his own. Once he was up, my father escorted me to the dance floor. The DJ made a dedication to us as he played the song, "Dance with My Father Again." All I could do was cry. My father wiped away my tears and gave me a big hug.

"I love you baby girl."

"I love you too, dad."

The night was now perfect again. It was getting late and Mary and Kevin took my father home. As the party started winding down, I sat back in awe of what I had accomplished. After everyone left, Allison volunteered to stay behind to help close the restaurant. Finally, I plopped into the limo, poured myself a drink, and tried my best not to pass out. Once I arrived home, I took a long hot shower, changed into my pajamas, and readied myself for bed. Before I could lie down my phone rang. I was so tired that I ignored it, but, of course, it continued to ring. I looked at the caller-id and saw it was Mary.

"Hello."

"Maya, you need to get over here now!"

"Mary, what's wrong? What's going on?"

"It's your father, Maya. Please hurry."

My heart was racing. I didn't know what to do.

"I'm on my way."

I threw on some clothes and raced out the door. When I arrived at my father's house, I saw a police car and an ambulance parked in front. I felt like I couldn't breathe. I sprinted towards the house, but Mary stopped me before I could go inside.

"Oh, Maya, I'm so sorry."

"Mary, what's going on? Where's my father?"

"He's in the ambulance, but Maya. . . ."

I rushed towards the ambulance but one of the paramedics grabbed me.

"I'm sorry, Miss, but you're not allowed in there."

"He's my father! I need to see him! I need to know what happened!" I was scared, anxious, and probably a little erratic. I couldn't stop crying.

"We'll tell you as soon as you calm down. Okay? We need you to calm down."

"I'm clam. Now tell me what happened to my father."

In a somber voice, the paramedic holding me stated, "I regret to inform you that your father passed at two-thirty this morning from a heart attack. We tried to resuscitate him but he was nonresponsive. I promise you we did everything we could. I'm so sorry for your loss."

At that moment, I almost fainted. Mary came to my aid and tried to escort me into the house, but I didn't want to go inside. I wanted to be with my father. So, I hopped in the ambulance. All I could do was stare at his lifeless body. My heart was so full of grief that I couldn't stop crying. Mary hopped in the ambulance, and rode with me to the hospital.

"I don't get it, Mary. What happened? He was fine when you guys left, so what went wrong?"

"I don't know. He was in his chair watching television. I went over to escort him to his room, but he didn't move. I shook him and there was no response. So, I called 911 and then called you. After that, I performed CPR on him until the paramedics arrived."

"Thank you, Mary. I know you tried your best."

After we arrived at the hospital and my father's body was taken to the morgue. The hospital staff then engaged me for information in order to prepare the death certificate. Before I knew it, it was daylight. It all felt unreal. I called Allison and informed her of my father passing. She wanted to come to the hospital and help out, but I needed her at the shop. I advised her to leave Tina in charge of the restaurant in my absence. When I finally made it home, there were several messages on my answering machine. Everyone wanted to know if I was okay, but truthfully, I was still in shock. Everything I looked at reminded me of the family that once was. I went into my bedroom and cried. The phone rang continuously, so I turned off the ringer. I didn't want to talk to anyone. I just wanted to be alone.

Even though it was hard, somehow, I conjured up the strength to plan my father's funeral. I didn't want anything big so I decided on a graveside service. Everyone I knew was in attendance, and I could feel the love and support from all of my friends. My father was gone and I didn't know how to let him go. I laid a rose on his casket, said my final goodbye, and walked away.

For a while, it was hard to deal with the loss of my father but after a couple of days, I found the strength to go over to his place to handle his affairs. I packed up everything I wanted to keep, and the rest, I had the movers take away. I stood in the empty house that use to be my home trying to figure out what to do next. So, I called Mary over and gave her the keys to the house. I told her she could keep it or sell it. The house was now hers to do with as she pleased. Mary tried to convince me to keep the house in my family. I explained to her she was family. Mary gave me a hug, accepted my gift, and blessed me for my generosity. On the way home I stopped by the doctor's office because I was having a hard time falling asleep. The doctor prescribed me some sleeping pills to try and help with the insomnia. When I returned home, I isolated myself for a couple of days. I had no motivation to do anything to included taking a bath. I had allowed my depression to take over and nothing else seemed to matter. The doorbell would ring in the background, but I wouldn't move. I just wanted to be alone. Then one day, the doorbell started to ring and wouldn't stop. I tried to pretend like I didn't hear it, but the constant ringing was hard to ignore.

"Go away." I yelled, but the ringing continued.

I rolled over trying to block out the sound, but it didn't work. Suddenly the ringing stopped. Maybe the person ringing the bell, finally got a clue, and left.

"Maya! I know you're in there!" It was Julian. What did he want?

"Maya! Open the door!"

"Go away, Julian."

"Open the door, Maya."

I closed my eyes as I tried to fade Julian out. The next thing I knew, there was a loud noise that sounded like someone was trying to break down the door. As I rose from the couch my front door came crashing down.

"Are you crazy? Look at my door!"

"I needed to make sure you were okay. You're not answering your phone and no one has heard from you in weeks."

"I lost my father! You get that? The only family I had is gone, so I think I have the right to be alone. Now get out and don't come back!"

"I'm not going anywhere. Look at you. Look at your house. You're both a mess, and I'm not leaving until I know you're okay."

"Get out! I don't want you here, so please leave."

I was so embarrassed that I started to cry.

"Maya, I know you're hurting. Please let me help you."

"I don't want your help." I looked at Julian, and then I glanced at my door. "So please leave, and try to close the door on your way out." I laid on the couch, hoping Julian would get a clue and leave; but he did just the opposite. He pulled out his cell phone, and I heard him talking to a repairman about the door. After he hung up, I could feel him hovering over me.

"I know you may not want my help, but you're getting it."

Julian picked me up and headed towards the bedroom.

"Put me down."

"No."

Julian carried me into the bathroom and turned on the shower. I was getting drenched with water as I fought to get loose, but he held me tightly in his arms.

"Please, just leave."

"It's not that easy. I care about you, Maya, and that is why I can't leave you."

All I could do was cry while Julian held me in his arms. I cried for a while, and then I tried to pull myself together.

"I'm okay now."

"Are you sure?"

"Yes. I just need a few minutes alone."

Once Julian left out of the bathroom, I broke down in tears. My clothes were soaked. So, I took them off, showered, and got dressed. When I walked into the living room, Julian was still there. His overnight bag was on the floor and he had changed out of his wet clothes as well.

"You're still here."

"I told you I wasn't leaving until I knew you were okay."

"Well, as you can see I'm fine. So you're free to leave."

"No, you're not."

"And you know this because…"

"Because I know you."

"Why are you here, Julian? We didn't work, remember? And I was with your brother for over a year. So, there's no reason for you to be here."

"I'm here because I love you, Maya." The room became quiet. "The only reason we didn't work is because I lied to you."

"No, you did more than lie. You made me believe in something that wasn't real. I honestly thought you were the one, but I was wrong."

"Maya, I am so sorry for hurting you, but I don't regret what happened between us."

"Well, I do. So are we done here?" There was a knock at the door and it was the repairman. "You can leave. I can take care of this."

"No. I broke your door. The least I can do is fix it." Julian waited until the door was fix, paid the repairman, and grabbed his overnight bag. He hesitated for a moment, and then he dropped his bag. "I can't go. Not until I fix what's wrong between us."

"Are you serious? There is nothing to fix! And if there was, this conversation would've taken place over a year ago, not now. Now is too late."

"It's never too late. I hurt you and…"

"You're right. You hurt me, and then you and your girlfriend tried to manipulate me with her brother but…"

"No! I didn't know about that."

"The hell you didn't. You were constantly begging me to drop the charges against Regina, and then all of a sudden you stopped coming around, and Nathan miraculously showed up."

"I stopped coming around because I was in New York. I was out there working on a case for almost seven months. I swear, I didn't know what Nathan was up to, and I was definitely in the dark about you and Brandon."

I stood in silence. I didn't know what else to say.

"Fine. You didn't know, but that still doesn't excuse the fact that you and your brother came into my shop week after week harassing me with your girlfriends. So, what do you have to say about that?"

"We were only there because I wanted you to see me and to experience the pain I was feeling. Looking back, I know I was wrong for what I did to you. But at that moment in time, I felt like you deserved it."

"I deserved it? Are you kidding me? Get out! Now!"

"No! You don't get to be the victim this time. You were with my brother, Maya. For over a year. Regardless of what happened between us, he was still my brother. So, I made him come with me every day to your shop. I wanted you to hurt the same way that you hurt me."

"Well, you succeeded. I was hurt, but then I learned how to move the hell on. Something you need to learn how to do."

"You moved on? With who? Matt? You swore me up and down that the two of you were just friends, but once again I was wrong."

"Matt and I *are* friends but sometimes we're more than that."

"So, who's the liar now? I asked you if there was something going on between you and Matt, and on several occasions, you told me it was nothing."

"And I asked you if you had a girlfriend, and you told me no." I was getting angry.

"Because the only person I wanted to be with was you."

"Then why did you lie to me?"

"Because I fell in love with you. That's why. Once Regina found out the truth, she flipped. I never expected any of this to happen, but it did. So, when I came back from New York, all I wanted to do was to get you back; but then I found out about you and Brandon, and I lost it." Tears were running down Julian's face. "Trust me I don't want to feel like this. I wish I could turn this off, but I can't. I don't know how to stop loving you."

"Julian, we could never work. Even if I gave you another chance, it still wouldn't excuse the fact that I was with Brandon. I loved him. You get that? And it broke my heart when he chose you over me. So, regardless of how you may feel about me, I don't see anything happening between us."

"I don't get it! Why him? Why would you choose Brandon over me?"

"I don't know why…" Julian gazed into my eyes and then he kissed me. "No, we're not doing this."

"I need this to happen. Please, Maya. Let this happen."

"Why, Julian? Why?" I was in tears. "Because I was with Brandon? Is that it? So you have to be with me too?"

"No, it's not like that. I just want you to give me another chance."

"So, you can hurt me again? And what about Brandon? You didn't want him to be with me, but it's okay for us to be together?"

"Because it was never supposed to be him. It was supposed to be me." Julian kissed me again."

"No, I loved him."

"And I love you." Julian kissed me and then he picked me up.

"No."

"Yes." Julian laid me down on the bed as he continued to kiss me. I was so torn over what was happening. I looked at Julian and all I could do was cry. "Don't cry. I know that I hurt you, but I promise to never hurt you again."

"Lies." Julian kissed me, and as much as I didn't want to enjoy it, I did. He started out with kisses only, and before I knew it, we were having sex. How could I allow him back in? Why was I being so stupid? I knew better and I knew I'd regret it, but that didn't stop me from allowing it to happen.

Sometimes, in life, we create our own hell. I knew I was making a mistake by allowing Julian back into my life, and as much as I wanted to hate him, I couldn't. It was hard to live with the decision I had made, and as for my friends they could never know that Julian and I were back together. Sometimes in life, we try to do what is right, but our hearts and emotions tend to lead the way. Deep down, I knew I couldn't justify what I was allowing to happen, but sometimes the heart wants what the mind can't comprehend.

Chapter 13

Tell The Truth

I laid in bed trying to rationalize my behavior. My father's death allowed me to make some less than questionable decisions regarding my love life. I had been secretly seeing Julian for the past six months and I felt as though I was repeating the same mistake I made with Brandon. Both of us were single and yet we were sneaking around as if we were a married couple having an affair. I hated the secrecy, but I couldn't blame anyone but myself for what I was allowing to happen. Our deception was staring to weigh on my conscience. I wondered if I made the right decision by choosing to be with Julian. I rolled over, looked at him, and I wasn't sure about anything, anymore. I got up, put on some shoes, and went out for a walk. I needed to clear my head, so I headed towards the corner store and bought a drink. On my way out the store, I ran into Brandon.

"Maya. How are you doing?"

"I'm good."

"Look, I know we didn't get a chance to talk after your father passed, but I want you to know how truly sorry I am for your loss."

"Thanks. That means a lot." It felt weird talking to Brandon considering I was sleeping with his brother. "Well it was good seeing you."

I turned around to walk away but Brandon stopped me.

"Maya, wait. I want you to know I'm sorry for everything. I never meant to hurt you and I hope, one day, you can truly forgive me."

At that moment, my feelings were conflicted. In my heart, I didn't know how to feel about anything.

"I forgave you a long time ago. Bye Brandon."

I walked back to the house. When I opened the door, Julian was up watching television in the living room.

"Hey, where have you been? I woke up and you were gone."

"I went out for a walk. I needed to clear my head."

"What's wrong?"

"I don't know. I was out thinking about us, and…"

"You're questioning if we should be together? Aren't you?"

"And you're not?" I began to pace around the room. "Do you know I ran into Brandon while I was out? It felt unreal? Here it is I'm sneaking around with you after being in a long-term relationship with him. I honestly don't know what I'm doing anymore."

"You're following your heart, that's what you're doing."

"Am I? Or am I just tired of being alone? I care for you, but I'm afraid to love you, and that scares the hell out of me. So tell me, what type of relationship can we have if I don't know how to trust you?"

"It's my fault you feel that way, and it's up to me to change how you perceive us. I meant what I said when I told you I loved you. I understand it's going to take some time, but I'm willing to work at it as long as you're willing to give me an honest shot. Our relationship won't survive if only one person is putting in the work. Okay."

"Okay."

Julian kissed me. It was soft and passionate.

"Let me love you."

"I'm trying."

Over the next couple of months, I tried to let go of the past and give Julian an honest chance. I allowed myself to laugh and enjoy it. There were times when our conversations were heated, but nothing compared to the makeup sex afterwards. The attraction between us was intense and I knew from that moment on I was in trouble. Then one day, while sitting on the couch with Julian, I felt my heart flutter. The startling feeling sent a chill up my spine.

"Hey, are you okay?"

"Yeah, I'm fine. Why?"

"I could feel you shivering. Are you cold?"

"No, I'm okay."

Julian retrieved a blanket from the hall closet and covered us.

"Is that better?"

"Yeah. You know, this is nice."

"I know. It's moments like this where I never want to let you go."

"Same here."

"I love you."

"I love you too."

Julian sat up and looked at me in shock.

"What did you say?"

"I said, I love you too." Julian started smiling and so did I. "Why are you acting so silly?"

"I don't know. I just never thought I would hear you say it back to me anytime soon."

"Well, I said it, so don't make me regret it."

"Oh, you won't."

Julian picked me up from the couch and took me to the bedroom. He grabbed a chair from the kitchen table and sat me on the edge of it. I wasn't sure what he was up to, but I was more than curious to see what he had in mind. I stared in enjoyment as he took his shirt off.

"Okay, so what's going on?"

"Nothing. I just need to do a little workout before we start."

"Are you serious?"

"Yes. So sit back and relax."

Julian started stretching and I began to laugh.

"Are you serious right now?"

"Very." Julian walked towards me, stood me up, took off my pants along with my panties, and then he sat me back down in the chair. I was clueless about what he had planned, but, at this point, I was definitely intrigued. I sat in the chair wearing nothing but a t-shirt and a smile. Julian then placed his hands behind my knees and vigorously pulled me to the edge of the chair while slightly spreading my legs apart. "Okay, I need you to stay right there. You're going to be my motivation." His enthusiasm made me laugh.

Julian got on the floor and started during pushups. Up and down, up and down. I watched him as he stared at his motivation. During a quick glance across the room, I felt his lips taste me. I didn't know what to make of it, and then he did it again. My laughter quickly turned into moans. Every time he went down and came back up, my body anticipated his every move. He continued doing this until I couldn't take anymore. Then he pulled me out of the chair and he made love to me by *kisses only*. He then picked me up and put me on the bed. I didn't know if it was because I had finally allowed myself to be honest with him, but when we made love, I found myself having one orgasm after another. Both of us could sense the difference in the way we gravitated towards each other. I finally understood why Regina went crazy over him. The way Julian made me feel when I was with him was inconceivable.

The next day at work, I found myself daydreaming about Julian and his unique version of a workout. I began to smile and then I quickly stopped. After everything I had been through, I had to learn how to hide my facial expressions while at work. I didn't want anyone to ask questions that I wasn't prepared to answer.

Once I finished prepping the desserts, I headed towards the front counter to put out some fresh pastries; but before I could begin, a guy came walking into the shop with a bouquet of peach-colored roses.

"I'm looking for a Maya Davenport."

"That's me."

"These are for you."

I took the flowers and read the card. *You were such a peach last night and you taste like one too. J.*

"So, who are the flowers from?"

"I don't know. It didn't come with a card." I hid the card in my back pocket. I didn't want Allison to figure out the truth.

"Someone has a secret admirer."

"And whoever it is can remain a secret. I have a lot going on in my life right now, and what I don't need is more drama."

"But you could use a man. I'm just saying. Everyone needs their back blown out every now and then." I smiled to myself because that task had already been accomplished.

When I returned home, I fixed myself a snack and stretched out on the couch. I couldn't believe the things I was allowing to happen between Julian and myself. Not only did I give him another chance, but I also fell in love with him all over again. I was so afraid of getting my heart broken, but I feared loneliness more than heartbreak. While relaxing on the couch, I heard the alarm beep and Julian came walking through the door.

"Hey."

Julian gave me a kiss on the check.

"Did you get my flowers?"

"Yes, and what were you thinking? Are you trying to get us caught?"

"What are you talking about?"

"You sent the flowers to my job, Julian. No one is supposed to know about us. Remember?"

"We're together, Maya, and eventually it's going to come out. You can't be with me and expect us to remain a secret."

"Yes I can."

"In what world? You're going to have to face the fact that we're together, and sooner or later, you're going to have to tell your friends that we're back together as well."

"So, you're telling me you wouldn't have a problem letting your brother know we're back together?"

"No. Not at all."

I was shocked.

"And how do you think he's going to react once he knows the truth?"

"I don't know how he's going to react and I don't care. I thought I had lost the chance to be with you, and I'm not about to throw that away because I may hurt Brandon's feelings. He's a big boy. He'll be alright."

"Really! He'll be alright? You forced Brandon to break up with me, and he did because he valued his relationship with you, more than his relationship with me. But given the same opportunity, you're willing to spit in your brother's face all because you were with me first. Unreal."

I walked off feeling irritated.

"I love my brother and you know that! But Brandon knew how I felt about you long before the two of you ever hooked up. Besides, this has nothing to do with who was first. I laid everything on the line because I wanted to be with you, and he knew that but that didn't stop him from being with you. Now did it?"

"Look, Julian, I know Brandon and I shouldn't have been together, but it's not like we planned for it to happen. It just did. And even though you have no problem telling your brother we're back together, I have a big problem trying to explain this to everyone I know. Your ex tried to have me killed, and I don't know if that is something they can easily forget."

"And I get that, but answer this. Do you love me?"

"You know I do."

"Then nothing else matters."

Julian gave me a kiss, and then he went into the kitchen and poured himself a drink.

"So, for you it's just that simple. Nothing else matters?"

"Yep. Besides, we can't live our lives based on what other people may think. If we did, then we would never be happy."

"You're right, but for me it's going to take some time. I'm just not ready to tell everyone about us. Not yet."

"And I'm not rushing you. In your own time. Okay?"

"Okay."

My cell phone started to ring and I looked down and it was Matt.

"Hello."

"Hey, Maya. Are you busy?"

"Kind of. Why? What's up?"

"I need a date for the Gala tonight. You think you'll be able to help me out?"

"You need a date tonight…" Julian shook his head while whispering no. "I'm sorry, Matt, but I can't. I'm really busy tonight."

"Okay. I understand. I did wait until the last minute to ask."

"I'm sorry."

"It's okay. I'll talk to you later. Bye."

"Bye." I felt bad for lying to Matt. I turned to face Julian.

"Really? What was that about?"

"I don't trust the guy."

"You don't trust Matt? Why?"

"I just don't."

"Well, he's my friend Julian, and there are going to be times when I'm going to need a favor from him and vice versa."

"You know if there wasn't any history between you and Matt, I wouldn't feel this way; but after seeing how he is around you, it tends to make me a little leery towards the guy."

"Okay. So, what you're saying is that you don't trust me around Matt?"

"No, that's not what I'm saying."

"In so many words you are. If you don't trust Matt around me, then what you're really saying is that you don't trust me. I've told you over and over again that Matt and I are just friends. Nothing more, and if you can't believe that, then there's no reason for you to be here."

I could tell Julian was getting upset.

"What I see and what I believe are two different things. You told me you and Matt were just friends, but then I saw him kissing you at the bakery. Then to make matters worse, I saw the two of you kissing in your office on the night of your opening. It seemed pretty intense. So tell me, Maya, how am I not to be skeptical of this guy?"

I didn't know how Julian saw the kiss that transpired between Matt and me at the opening, but the fact remains he saw it. And considering the level of passion we felt for each other during the kiss, I knew Julian has cause to be alarmed.

"That wasn't Matt's fault; it was mine. Matt can only do as much as I allow. I was in a vulnerable state and needed an escape.

He provided it. So, I'm sorry if our kiss bothered you so much, but Matt and I are truly just friends."

"Okay, I hear what you're saying. But let's say you saw me kissing someone the way you and Matt kissed that night. Would you be okay with it if I told you we were just friends?"

"If I saw you kissing someone like that while we were together, then our relationship would be over. I wasn't with you or anyone else when Matt kissed me. So, stop trying to make this into something that it's not."

"That's not what I'm doing."

"Then what are you doing because right now I feel like you're harassing me about something that happened over a year ago. So, what's the deal, Julian? Why are you harping on old news?"

"You know what! Fine. I'll drop it." Julian went into the kitchen and poured himself another drink. "If you'll admit that you and Matt are more than just friends."

"O, M, G, are you serious? Where is this coming from? Are you seeing someone else? Is that what you're trying to tell me?"

"No, the only person I'm seeing is you, but I don't know if you can say the same."

"Okay! That's it. You can leave or you can stay, but I'm done with this conversation."

I sat on the couch and started watching television. Julian looked at me, and I could tell he was infuriated.

"You're right. I should go."

I couldn't believe how Julian was acting. Something was defiantly off. I wanted to stop him from leaving, but I couldn't. I was tired of him accusing me of things I weren't doing. When he walked out the door, I felt dishearten and confused. How could he accuse me of cheating with Matt when I was always with him? I didn't know where our relationship was heading, but I was too confounded to think about it. So, I took a shower and went to bed.

In my sleep, I heard a noise and woke up. I didn't know what it was, so I reached for the first weapon I could find, which were a pair of scissors on the nightstand. I began to tip toe towards the bedroom door. As I got closer, I saw the knob turn, so I hid behind the door. As the figure made its way into the room, I lunged to stab it then quickly realized it was Julian.

"Maya, wait it's me."

"Damn it, Julian! I almost stabbed you. What are you doing here?"

"I came back to apologize. I was wrong for how I acted and I'm sorry."

I didn't know how to react to Julian's apology. His vague behavior left me feeling perplexed about a lot of things.

"Julian, what's going on with you? You're all over the place and it's starting to scare me."

"I don't know." Julian took the scissors from my hands and walked me to the bed. "I won't lie. When I think about you and Matt being together, it bothers me. Anyone can see he has feelings for you which makes it hard for me to trust him." Julian began to caress my hands. "You know that I trust you, and I understand Matt is your friend, but I don't know how to be comfortable with you guys being so close."

I leaned over and kissed Julian on the cheek.

"Trust me you don't have anything to worry about. It doesn't matter if Matt wants to be with me or not. The only thing that matters is what I want, and I want you. I don't want anyone else, but you. Okay?" Julian gazed into my eyes and then he kissed me. The kisses weren't long and passionate kisses. They were short and sweet as if he was teasing me. "So, are we good?"

"Yeah, we're good."

I turned off the lights and got back in bed. Julian laid down beside me and held me close. He didn't say anything else for the rest of the night. When I work up, to my surprise, Julian was gone and there were two suitcases sitting by the door. I walked out of the room and Julian was in the kitchen cooking breakfast.

"Good morning."

"Morning. You're up early. And what's up with the suitcases?"

"I'm up early because I'm taking you away for the weekend, so you need to pack."

"You know I can't go anywhere. I have to work."

"Says who? You're the boss. I'm sure you can come up with something."

"Because I'm the boss doesn't mean I should abuse my power."

"But you can take advantage of it. So, what do you say? Are you going away with me or not?"

"Well, that depends. What's in it for me if I go away with you?"

"If you come with me, the only thing I can promise you is a good time. I can't disclose anything else."

"Well, I guess that'll have to do."

I packed my bags and we left. We headed towards the airport and before long we were standing in front of a private jet.

"What's this?"

"I promised you a good time, remember."

"But, Julian, once again this is too much."

"No, it's not so stop lecturing me and let's go."

We boarded the plane, and Julian refused to tell me where we were going. Once the plane landed, he blindfolded me and escorted me to a car. We drove around for a while, and then we stopped. Julian helped me out of the car then took off the blindfold. Once my vision cleared, I noticed we were at Universal in Orlando again.

"Universal. Why would you bring me back here?"

"Because this is where I fell in love with you. Our first date didn't go so well, so I decided to do it over."

"A do over. Well, I hope you can get it right this time!"

"Oh really." We started laughing. "Let's just see how it goes."

Julian and I had as much fun the second time around, as we did our first time at the amusement park. My heart fluttered again. It scared me to feel the amount of love I felt for him. While we were walking around the park, Julian's phone rang so many times that I figured we would have to return to Georgia earlier than expected. Once we left the park, instead of heading towards the airport, we checked into a hotel.

"So, what's going on? We're not going back tonight, are we?"

"No, and the night isn't over."

I walked into the room and there were flowers, chocolate covered strawberries, and champagne, sitting on the table. On the bed was a box with my name on it.

"What's this?"

"I don't know. Open it and see."

I opened the box and there was a beautiful cream dress in it.

"Julian. It's beautiful."

"And it'll look even better on you. So, let's change. We can't be late."

I wanted to ask where we were going, but I was too busy enjoying the moment. We changed and a limo picked us up from the hotel. We drove around for a while, then we stopped at a chic little restaurant on the outskirts of town. As we walked inside, I could hear the music emanating from the live band and people were up dancing. We were then escorted to our table and I couldn't stop blushing.

"This is nice."

"Only the best for you." After we ate dinner, the waiter came out with a dessert menu. As I was gazing over the menu, Julian took it from my hand, and laid it down on the table. "Dance with me."

"Are you serious?"

"Yes. Dance with me."

"Okay."

As we made our way towards the dance floor the song "Golden," by Chrisette Michelle began to play. Julian held me close as we slow danced to the song. He kissed me, and then he got down on one knee as Chrisette sang, *"Be the man of my dreams and get down on one knee, love Say you'll be all I need and then ask me to marry you, my love Let's take two golden bands and let's walk down the isle, love I'll say I do and you'll say I do, make a golden commitment…"*

"Julian, what are you doing?"

"Maya, I didn't plan on falling in love with you, but I did. Now I can't picture my life without you. So, Jeremiah Davenport, will you marry me?"

I was in tears. I couldn't believe Julian was proposing.

"Yes! Yes, I will marry you." I was shocked by my answer and I think Julian was too. He placed the ring on my finger then gave me the most passionate kiss. Everyone clapped as I struggled to regain my composure.

Once we made it back to the hotel room, Julian and I were all over each other. We made love and I felt like all my dreams were coming true. My business was thriving, and so was my love life. As we lay in bed, I looked over at Julian, and all I could do was smile. I was still in disbelief over everything that had happened.

"Tell me something. Is this why you've been acting so strange?"

"In a way. When you're putting your heart on the line the worst thing you fear is rejection. I had been planning this day for months, but I was afraid you were still in love with someone else…but I couldn't hold off any longer. I love you, Maya, and I want to spend the rest of my life with you."

"I love you, too." I gave Julian a kiss as I held up my hand and marveled over my engagement ring. "Mrs. Jeremiah Foster. You know, my new name doesn't have a ring to it at all, but we can work on that." I started laughing.

"Oh really! Ring or not, you're taking my last name." Julian began to tickle me. I was so happy and I didn't want the moment to end. "Mrs. Foster."

"Mrs. Foster. I love it."

I was engaged to Julian. I wanted to share that news with my friends, but I couldn't. I knew they wouldn't understand and the judgment would never stop. My relationship with Julian has had its ups and downs, but somehow we were able to survive the hardships, and make it to this point. It wasn't the most logical route, but somehow we found our way back to each other. I was in love, which excited and scared me at the same time. What if something went wrong or he decided he didn't want to marry me? I didn't know if my heart could take another breakup. Being with Julian was a catch 22 situation. He would either make me the happiest woman in the world, or he'd break my heart all over again. Either way, I was now committed to the ride; and whichever way it went, I couldn't blame anyone but myself for the outcome.

Chapter 14

Crazy Came A Knocking

Weeks passed, and I asked Julian not to tell Brandon about us, or our engagement. I needed to speak with my friends before they heard the truth about me and Julian from someone else. I especially didn't want Allison to find out; not before I was able to speak with her first. With each day that passed, I tried to stomach up the courage to tell her the truth, but I couldn't. As strong as I was, I was afraid of being chastised for getting back with Julian.

Then one day at work, while I was mixing up a bowl of cake batter I started to feel sick. My first thought was that I may have been stressing too much over the engagement. I tried to clear my head, but the nausea wouldn't go away. As I continued to stir the batter, unexpectedly, I began to throw up. I was shocked and embarrassed over what was happening. I had never been sick like that before. Once I was able to stop, I noticed there was vomit all over the counter and in the cake batter. Everyone in the kitchen was staring, as Allison rushed to my aid.

"Maya, are you okay?"

"Yeah, I'm fine. My stomach feels a little queasy, but I'll be alright."

"Are you sure?"

"Yeah, I'm good."

I threw away the cake batter and sterilized the bowl. I headed to my office to lie down, but before I could take another step, I fainted. When I woke up, I was in the hospital and Allison was sitting in a chair next to my bed.

"Allison, what happened?"

"You fainted. The doctors are running some tests so we can figure out what's going on with you."

"I don't know what's wrong. I was feeling okay this morning, then I wasn't. I've never felt like this before." There was an odd silence in the room. "Is there something else going on that I should know about?"

"You can say that. So, when were you going to tell me about Julian?"

"What are you talking about?"

"I don't know. You tell me. Your phone has been ringing since we left the shop. I pulled it out of your pocket and noticed all your calls were from Julian. He's been calling you for the past two hours. So finally, I decided to answer, and he became extremely concerned about your sickness and demanded I tell him where you were."

"Allison."

"No, you're not that stupid. I know you're not."

Tears ran down my face.

"Allison, please. . . just listen."

"Listen to what? Listen to you feed me more lies about Julian! This guy broke your heart, and then his crazy ex-girlfriend tried to have you killed. So, I'll say this again. I know you're not that stupid."

Before I could answer, the doctor walked in. I wiped away my tears and Allison walked out of the room. As the doctor was about to speak, Allison walked back into the room.

"And Doc, you might want to examine her head next because I think something is a little off up there as well."

"Allison!" Allison glared at me as she walked out the door. I looked at the doctor feeling embarrassed. "I'm so sorry for my friend's behavior."

"That's quite all right. I'm doctor Bridges by the way. So, how are you feeling?"

"Okay I guess. So what's wrong with me? Why am I so sick?"

"Well, we ran some tests and your friend stated you were throwing up before you fainted. Is that correct?"

"Yes. It happened very quickly. I don't remember much."

"Well, one of the tests we conducted was a pregnancy test and it came back positive. That could explain the nausea, but. . ."

"Pregnancy test? Wait, so you're telling me that I'm pregnant?"

"Yes. Were you unaware of the pregnancy?"

"You could say that, but I still don't understand how I could be pregnant. I always use protection, so this doesn't make any sense."

I was excited about the pregnancy, but also afraid. Was I ready to be a mother? And how was Julian going to feel about the pregnancy? My mind was racing.

"But, Ms. Davenport, there's another issue we need to discuss."

"Yes, I'm sorry. It's just a lot to take it in."

"I understand, but tell me something. Are you currently sexually active?"

"Yes, with my fiancée. Why? Is there something wrong?"

"Well, when we tested your blood levels, we noticed a discrepancy."

"What type of discrepancy?"

"Your white blood cells were really low and..."

"And what? What are you trying to say?"

"I'm sorry, Ms. Davenport, but you also tested positive for the HIV virus."

I sat in shock for a couple of seconds trying to wrap my head around the doctor's prognosis.

"Wait, what did you say?" I muttered in a low voice.

"I understand this may be a lot for you to take in all at once, but we have a proficient medical staff on hand who can assist you with your diagnosis."

"No. Your diagnosis is wrong! I can't be HIV positive! I've only had two sexual partners in my lifetime, so this has to be some kind of mistake."

"I'm sorry, Ms. Davenport, but I ran the test twice just to be sure." I was so shaken up over the news that it took a few minutes for me to digest the doctor's results. "We have several different options pertaining to your pregnancy, so there's no need to make any rash decisions. Nurse Summers will prescribe you some prenatal vitamins and I'll have Dr. Robinson come in and talk with you about the virus."

"I don't need a doctor to talk to me about the virus because I don't have it. Your tests are wrong! They're all wrong!" I was upset and very emotional. How could I be pregnant with HIV? I always used protection, so none of this made any sense. Dr. Bridges sat in a chair beside my bed and held my hands.

"I know this information is hard to hear, but I'll do everything within my power to help you."

I couldn't stop crying.

"Thank you."

While I was trying to come to terms with the doctor's diagnosis, there was a knock at the door. Dr. Bridges cracked it open and Julian walked in. I was so angry at the sight of him. I glared at him in frustration as tears ran down my face.

"Maya, baby, what's wrong?"

"I take it this is the fiancée." The doctor asked.

"If you want to call him that. So, Dr. Bridges, can you please inform this gentleman of my diagnosis."

"Are you sure?" Dr. Bridges asked in a concerned voice.

"Yes, I'm sure."

"Maya, why are you talking like that? What's going on?"

"The doctor will explain everything to you."

"Well, like I told Ms. Davenport, her pregnancy test came back positive, and…"

"You're pregnant! Maya, that's great news!" Julian tried to kiss me, but I pulled away.

"Continue on Doctor."

Julian couldn't understand why I was so upset.

"As I was saying, yes Ms. Davenport is pregnant, but she also tested positive for the HIV virus."

Julian looked at me as if I was the cause of the disease.

"Maya, what is he talking about?"

"I don't know. You tell me since you're the only guy I've been sleeping with."

"Wait a minute! Don't put this on me. We always used protection!"

"Exactly. So, how did this happen?"

"I don't know."

I looked away from Julian and then faced the doctor.

"Since he's my only sexual partner, shouldn't he be tested as well?"

The doctor turned to face Julian.

"Yes, it would be in your best interest if we tested you as well."

I glared at Julian with anger in my eyes.

"Don't say anything else to me until your test results come back."

"Maya."

"Not a word."

We sat in silence as I awaited Julian's test results. I continued to think about the baby I was carrying, and the fact that I was HIV positive. What was I going to do? It would be selfish to keep the baby, but I couldn't imagine terminating the pregnancy either. The doctor soon returned with Julian's test results.

"I'm sorry, Mr. Foster, but you also tested positive for the HIV virus."

I broke out in a loud cry. Why was this happening to me? I gave love a second chance and these were the consequences for my actions? Being pregnant with the HIV virus.

"Maya."

"Don't say anything else to me. My friends warned me about you, and somehow I allowed you back into my life. I knew better, but that didn't stop me from giving you second chance. And this is the thanks I get. HIV. How could I have been so stupid?"

"Really, and who's to say you didn't give this to me?"

Julian's comment made me so furious that I hauled off and slapped him as hard as I could. "How dare you! I was perfectly fine until I met you!"

"Then how do we explain this because we've always used protection."

"I don't know and I don't care. I just want you out of my room and out of my life."

"Maya…"

"Get out! Now!" Apparently I must have been too loud because a nurse came rushing into the room.

"What's going on in here?"

"I'm sorry, but this gentleman needs his own room. Can you please escort him out of mine? Thank you."

"Maya, we need to talk about this."

"We have nothing else to talk about."

The nurse escorted Julian out of my room and all I could do was cry. I felt like my life was over. What was I going to do? Minutes later, Nurse Summers entered my room and briefed me on information regarding my pregnancy. She also gave me a prescription for prenatal vitamins and a referral for their recommended obstetricians who would be better suited for my case. After Nurse Summers left the room, Dr. Robinson came in to discuss the virus along with the best treatments suited for my condition. He discussed antiretroviral therapy (ART) with me and informed me of various types of medications I could take. Thinking about the treatment devastated me. It all seemed unreal. I couldn't believe I had been diagnosed with an incurable disease. After I checked out of the hospital, I saw Julian pacing back and forth in the waiting room. As I turned to head in the opposite direction, he spotted me heading for the exit.

"Maya, please we need to talk."

"I have nothing else to say to you. Now go away." I made my way towards the parking lot, got in a taxi, and left.

I went home and cried for hours. I couldn't make sense out of what was happening. I also thought about my company. I was now HIV positive. What would the consumers say if they found out about my illness? It could ruin my brand and most importantly, my franchise. I had to save my business. I thought of several different options, but none of them would shield my franchise from scrutiny if the truth ever came out. I was at a lost. If there was ever a time I needed my father's guidance, it was now.

The next day, I decided to visit my parent's graves. I told them about my situation with Julian and admitted to being foolish for giving him a second chance. I asked them to forgive me for my lack of judgment and my vile choice in men. I was mad at the world; but, overall, I was disappointed in myself.

Time went on and I continued to receive phone calls from Allison apologizing for her behavior at the hospital. She wanted us to kiss and make up, but I was still hurt because she abandoned me when I needed her the most. Even though I was alone and heartbroken, it was time I devised a plan regarding my so-called future.

Then one day, while I was sitting in the living room staring off into space, the doorbell rang. I ignored it as usual, but to my surprise I heard the front door open. I jumped up from the couch and there stood Julian and Regina in my foyer.

"What in the hell are you doing in my house?"

"You wanted answers and I found them." Julian yanked on Regina's arm.

"What are you talking about?"

"You wanted to know how we got sick so Regina is going to tell you how that happened." Julian gave Regina a vicious look. "Tell her!"

"I have nothing to say to her."

"You either tell her the truth or you're going to jail. Your choice."

"You wouldn't."

"Try me."

"Fine." Regina glared at Julian. "But be careful what you ask for." She then turned to face me. "You want the truth and here it is. When I found out you and Julian were back together, I broke into his house and poked holes in all of his condoms."

"But, why would you do that?"

"Because I wanted both of you to pay for all the hurt you caused me."

"For the hurt we caused you! Are you serious!" I lunged at Regina but Julian kept us apart. "You're crazy, you know that…"

"Maya, wait. There's more." Julian squeezed Regina's arm. "Finish telling her."

"You sure you want me to do that?"

"Tell her!"

"Okay. Since Julian was out doing his own thing, I decided it was time I did the same. Long story short, I got with this guy who didn't want to use protection and he infected me. I was angry at the world. I was also annoyed by the fact that if Julian and I hadn't broken up, then none of this would have happened. So, when I discovered the two of you were *back* together, I wanted him to pay for all the pain he caused me."

"No, the only person you wanted to hurt was me. You could have done something less drastic to get back at Julian, but you poked holes in his condoms knowing it would affect me. So, now I'm curious. How did you know Julian and I were back together because we never mentioned our relationship to anyone?"

"Julian told me."

I looked at Julian in disbelief.

"That's a lie. I never said anything to you about me and Maya being back together."

"Oh, but you did. Remember the night I came over and got into bed with you? I started kissing on you and you called me Maya. You broke my heart. And when you opened your eyes and realized it was me, you had the audacity to put me out." I stood in shock as I listened to Regina explain herself. My emotions were in overload. "You've never put me out before and at that moment, I realized just how deep your feelings were for Maya."

"Really." Julian tried to reach for me but I pulled away. "But that still doesn't explain how Julian got infected."

"It doesn't?" Regina said in a sarcastic tone. "Oh wait, I almost forgot. You see a couple of days later, I went back to see Julian, you know, to apologize for everything I had done to him in the past. And I could tell he wasn't interested in anything I had to say, so I played on his emotions until he began to soften up. That's when I made my move. I started kissing on him, and…"

"Okay, we get it." Julian seemed uncomfortable. I looked at him and curiosity took over.

"No, continue on, and what?"

"And I asked him if we could have sex one last time. He refused in the beginning, which I expected; but then I stripped down to nothing and asked him again. He continued to say no so I started crying. I knew Julian had a soft spot for me and I used it to my advantage. I kissed him and before I knew we were having sex." Regina had a wicked smile plastered across her face.

"So, you intentionally infected Julian because he wanted to be with me?" I could feel the rage mounting inside of me. I was trying to stay calm but all I could see was red. "Unbelievable. So answer me this. When did this encounter take place?"

"Maya…" Julian pleaded with his eyes.

"I don't know. Probably over a month ago."

I looked at Julian and I became nauseous.

"Was it in July?" I stared at Julian. My body temperature was rising.

"Yeah. Which was crazy because he's usually not home around that timeframe, but that night he was. Why do you ask?"

"Shut up!" I looked at Julian and tears fell from my eyes. "That was around the time you accused me of being in a relationship with Matt. I kept asking you what was wrong and kept deflecting. Now I know why. You slept with Regina and you were feeling guilty."

"No, Maya it wasn't like that."

"Liar! The trip. The engagement. It was all a lie."

"No, it wasn't. I love you."

"Sure you loved her. That's why you slept with me." Regina's snide comment was my breaking point. I looked at her and my hands were shaking. I was afraid of what I would do next.

"Leave. Before I do something, I'll regret."

"Like what? Take Julian back? Again? I mean he must have been putting it on you real good for you to be this gullible. Which begs me to wonder…who was better? Him or Brandon?"

"Regina, that's enough. It's time for you to go." Julian tried to grab Regina but she pulled away.

"I don't know. Lick your lips and you tell me."

Regina started to laugh. "Now that was a good one, but not good enough. You see, I'm the one who's going to have the last laugh this time. So, enjoy, Julian. While you still…have…time."

"You selfish bitch! I hope this disease ravage you from the inside out."

"Selfish! I never would've been infected if Julian had taken me back. This is your fault! You took him away from me and you deserve everything you got."

I went after Regina and there was nothing Julian could do to hold me back. I tried to beat the life out of her.

"Maya, stop! Come on. Think about the baby."

"Baby?" Regina seemed surprised.

"Are you serious? Why would you mention the baby around her?" I was so upset with Julian that I started hitting him.

"I'm sorry, but you need to stop." Julian wrapped his arms around me trying to calm me down.

"You're pregnant?" Regina asked while trying to compose herself.

"I have nothing else to say to you. Now get out of my house!" I fought against Julian to release myself from his grasp.

"No. I need to know! Are you pregnant?"

"Get out! Now!" I threw a figurine at Regina's head as she rushed out the door. Then I turned to face Julian. "And that goes for you too. Leave."

"Not until we talk about the baby."

"There's nothing else for us to talk about. Whatever I decide to do with this baby is my decision and my decision alone."

"No, it's our decision." Julian seemed disappointed.

"No, it's not. You no longer have a say in anything I do and that includes what I decide to do with this baby."

"But that's my child too."

"Not any more. You lost rights when you slept with Regina after promising yourself to me. Now leave."

"Maya, it was a mistake."

"No, my only mistake was trusting you. Now get out. Now!"

"I'm not going anywhere."

"Please, just leave, before I call the cops on you for trespassing." Julian was upset. "Oh, and Julian, please leave my keys on the counter on your way out."

"Maya, please just talk to me."

"I'm done talking, now get out." Out of nowhere I thought about the engagement ring Julian gave me. "Oh, wait." I went into my bedroom and got the ring. "Don't forget to take this with you." I gave Julian back his ring. "Hopefully you can find someone else who would like to marry you."

"Maya, please don't do this."

"Do what? I loved you, Julian, with all my heart; but it's apparent you didn't know how to love me back. So, please leave and don't come back."

"Maya…"

"Just leave." Julian placed the key on the table and left.

Damage control was an understatement. The divinities in my mind had manifested into a full blown nightmare. What was I thinking? How could I have allowed myself to play the fool? Yet, again? I couldn't fathom what I was doing wrong. I was a smart, independent, and a very wealthy woman. Yet, I allowed myself to do the one thing I promised I would never do. Fall for a man who I knew couldn't be trusted. I allowed myself to cross a line that was forbidden. My heart wanted what my mind knew I couldn't have.

I faced myself in the mirror but didn't recognize the reflection looking back at me. Who was this woman and how could she have been so stupid? I knew the game and how it was played, but somehow allowed manipulation to undermine my every decision. I allowed myself to be fooled by a man who I knew was a complete liar, and yet I fell subject to his every word. I paced around the room, praying I was about to make the right decision.

Tears began to fall. I looked around the house and could only see images of past and present mistakes. The whispers of broken promises and the dilapidation of shattered dreams bled through the walls like screams in the night. I went into the closet and began to pack. Running away was never my strongest suit but it seemed like my only option. I had no clue where to go, but getting out of Atlanta was at the top of my list.

My phone rang, but I ignored it. One stupid choice. One weak moment, and now my life was forever changed. Thinking back, if I could reverse the hands of time, I would. I would go back to the day when I first laid eyes on Julian Foster and run full speed in the opposite direction. Sometimes it's hard to see the truth when you're surrounded by depictions of false hope. I'd convinced myself my actions were because of love; but in reality, the fear of loneliness trumped love each and every time.

Matt warned me if I dropped the charges against Regina, to not be surprised if crazy came knocking at my door, and he was right. Crazy came a knocking and broke the door down. But as hurt as I was, I knew I had to get my affairs in order. There was nothing else left for me in Atlanta, so I began to think of the different places where I would like to live. I thought about the great time I had with my father in Colorado. We were so happy and had nothing but great memories there. Even though I disliked cold weather, Colorado always felt like home. I wrestled with the thought of moving but knew it had to be done. So, it was settled. I was moving to Colorado.

I contacted a local realtor and flew out to Denver two days later to view some properties. The scenery was so beautiful and the air was breathtaking. I signed a contract for a house then flew back to Atlanta. The next day, I went to work and everyone was surprised to see me. I could tell they didn't know what to say. I went into my office and began analyzing expenditures. There was a knock at the door and Allison walked in.

"Hey. How are you feeling?"

"Why do you care?"

"Because I'm your friend. Come on, Maya."

"Come on what? You made me feel worst at a time when I was already feeling low. And instead of hearing me out, you walked away and had the nerve to call me crazy."

"Because being with Julian is crazy. I'm sorry, Maya, for walking out, but I'm not sorry for what I said. Julian is a mistake and you know it."

"You're right. He is. But as my friend, you should've stayed. I really needed you that day, but you were nowhere to be found."

"I'm sorry, Maya. I truly am and I hate it when we're like this. You're my best friend and I miss you."

"Are you sure about that? I thought Charlie was your best friend."

"Come on, Maya. Don't do me like this."

"I have work to do."

"Maya!"

I ignored Allison by pretending to read one of the documents on my desk. I wanted to make up with her; but if I did, then I would feel obligated to tell her the truth about my illness. Allison got upset and stormed out of the office. As I got up to go after her, Matt walked in.

"Matt. Hey, what are you doing here?"

"Well, it's good to see you too. Anyway, you know it's that time again. I have to ask."

"Right. I almost forgot. Well you're in luck because my answer is yes."

Matt seemed shocked.

"What did you say?"

"I said yes. So, what are your figures looking like?"

"Maya, what's going on? You said you would never sell your franchise. So what happened? What made you change your mind?"

"Life. Besides, it's time. My father is gone and there's nothing else holding me here. I'm finally ready to travel and see the world; and I can't do that if I'm tied down to this company."

"Are you sure about this? Davenport Sweet Cakes is a stable and once you sign over your brand, there's no going back."

"Yeah, I'm sure. And don't say anything to the staff, especially Allison. I'm trying to figure out a way to explain this to them."

"To them? How about explaining it to me."

"In time. But for now, I need this to stay between you and me."

"Sure. I'll draw up the paperwork." Matt headed towards the door then stopped. "I hope this is what you really want."

"It is."

"Okay. I'll get those numbers for you.

"Thanks, Matt."

Matt walked out and I thought about what I wanted to say to

everyone. Telling them that I was selling the business wasn't going to be easy. I was dying for a drink, so I poured myself a glass of wine. Since I wasn't planning on keeping the baby, I didn't see the harm in having a drink.

A couple of days passed and Matt came to the shop with a contract. Kyle and I reviewed it and made some modifications. There were special circumstances I inserted, along with specific details regarding my employees. I glanced at the tentative offer and it was laughable. I told Matt not to come back until he had a better proposal considering I was giving up my livelihood. Matt left and I decided it was time to let everyone know what was going on. I called together a meeting and everyone gathered in the kitchen.

"Okay, guys, as you know I've dwelt with a lot of personal issues lately. After consulting with my doctor, I was advised to reduce the stress in my life and to get plenty of rest. Because of his recommendation, I decided to sell my franchise to Jackson & Murray."

Everyone in the shop gasped and Allison looked at me in disbelief.

"You what?" Allison asked in shock.

"So, what about us? What's going to happen to our jobs?" Nikki asked.

"Your jobs are safe. That was one of the contingencies I negotiated in the contract to include a much-deserved promotion for everyone. You can call it my farewell gift."

"When does the firm take over?" Allison asked in a harsh tone.

"Probably in two months."

"Two months. Great. So, what are your plans? Are you leaving town?" I could detect the resentment in Allison's tone.

"Yes. I'll be moving away. It's not conducive for me to stay here anymore. I've had some great times here, and I love and appreciate all the hard work that you guys bring to the table every day." I began to cry. "I'm sorry. I'm truly going to miss you guys."

Allison glared at me with tears in her eyes as she walked out of the room. I knew she was hurting, and so was I. Everyone else walked over and gave me a hug while wishing me well. After everyone was gone, I decided to stay after and lock up. I walked around the shop thinking about all the great memories I had there. I cried knowing that I had to give it all up, not because I wanted to, because I had to. I walked into the kitchen thinking about my current situation and became angry. I saw a pipe sitting by the door, and I picked it up and started smashing everything in sight. I couldn't stop crying. I felt betrayed by life and cheated out of a future. I continued to smash anything I could find. Then my eyes caught sight of my blue mixer, and I stopped. I looked at the mixer and dropped the pipe. My mother inspired me with that mixer. There was no way I could destroy it. I looked around the room and it was a mess. In sadness, I took the mixer and left. I called Nikki and told her to inform everyone that the shop would be closed tomorrow for repairs. Then I called a cleaning and repair service to fix the kitchen I had just destroyed.

Life was anything but fair. I was the good girl who did everything right. Yet I was cursed to have witness the wrath of the Foster men. All I wanted was to be loved, but I abandoned all of my morals for the sake of companionship. I felt like my life was over and had no one to blame but myself. I was pregnant with a baby who may or may not have a plausible future. Sometimes in life we're tested, and hopefully we're able to make the right decisions. As for me, that wasn't the case. I failed, and may have destroyed any chances of having a happily ever after.

Part
III

New Beginnings

Prologue

Making a relationship work in the conventional sense was hard, but being in a relationship with me could prove to be problematic. I always found myself in one unpredictable romance after another, and my so-called track record with men was about as understandable as my comprehension of relativity. For the most part, all I ever wanted out of life was to be happy, but in reality what I was really searching for was my happily ever after. The successful business, the loving husband, and the adoring kids were all that I ever wanted. That was my goal, but instead I was a single parent, coping with HIV, and falling for a guy whom I was afraid to give my heart.

The fear of being alone always clouded my judgement. Now, with my illness lurking in the background, I've often wondered what I could possibly offer someone in a relationship. My contribution would always fall short whenever it came to sex and no matter what my heart felt, I could never give a man 100% of myself. The entire situation felt like a cruel joke, but I was done mourning over the issue. I could either fall victim to my own circumstances or I could figure out a way to do something about it.

Wanting to move forward, on the other hand, was hard.

Sometimes I felt like I was self-sabotaging. I would seek out the worst in a situation, instead of trying to figure out a way to make things work. I've always allowed myself to see the horror in everything and I chose to block out any possibility of what could be. But through time my heart has changed, and I no longer wanted to live in fear. I wanted to seek out my possibilities to see where they would lead. I didn't want to push love away any longer. I didn't know how I was going to make a relationship work, but I needed it to work because, in the end, I was willing to put my heart on the line...one...last...time.

Chapter 15

From Scratch

Sometimes in life you have to own up to your mistakes, but accepting the consequences can be quite hard. I never thought life would betray me, but it did. I had imagined myself with a family, maybe two or three kids; but instead I was taking a daily regimen of medications and carrying a baby who was possibly HIV positive. What kind of life could I give my baby if I decided to keep it? The harsh realities regarding my baby's future were starting to quickly sink in. The thought of keeping the baby scared me, and getting rid of it frightened me even more. So, I decided I wouldn't make any rash decisions until I was settled in Colorado.

Then one day, while I was at home packing some moving boxes, my doorbell rang. I answered and it was Matt.

"Hey, so what brings you by?"

"I have your finalized contract. You'll have more paperwork to sign later on, but this is the one that gets the ball rolling."

Matt handed me the contract and I looked it over. When I saw the offer I almost gasped.

"What's this?"

"That's your new offer. I went back to Jackson & Murray, reviewed your annual profits, and pushed for a better deal. If you're going to give up your livelihood, then the least we can do is pay you accordingly.

"But, Matt this is a lot of money." I stared at the number listed in bold print; $75 million. I knew my bakeries were worth a lot to me, but never in a million years would I have thought they'd be worth 75 million. "Is this number real?"

"No, it's not." I gave Matt a confused look.

"So, what is this?" I stopped flipping through the documents. "Where is the real contract?"

"You're holding it, but that number doesn't become real until you sign it." Matt and I started to laugh.

"You are so wrong." I placed the contract in my briefcase. "Well, everything looks good. Once Kyle reviews it, we should have a deal."

Matt walked over and sat down on the couch.

"Can we talk?"

"We are talking."

I began to pace around the room.

"No, seriously. Can we talk?"

"Sure. What do you want to talk about?"

"I want you to be honest with me. Why are you really doing this?"

I sat on the couch next to Matt, and as much as I wanted to tell him the truth, I couldn't.

"Because it's time. A lot has happened and I need a fresh start."

"So, you think selling your shops is a good idea? You worked so hard to make Davenport Sweet Cakes a success, and now you're giving it all up because you need a fresh start. I'm not buying it."

"Well it's the truth. I am emotionally drained and I need a change of scenery."

"But Colorado?"

"I know it seems crazy, but I need to get away. No one knows me there, and I can create a new business from scratch."

"So, you're really doing this? You're giving up everything and running away."

"I'm not running away. I'm starting over. I wish I could give you all the details, but I can't. Just know that what I'm doing is what's best for me."

"If you feel this is what you need to do, then I wish you the best. But know, if you ever need anything, I'm only a phone call away."

"Thanks, Matt. You are a true friend."

Matt kissed me on the cheek and then he left. I got dressed and I went to my parents' gravesites. I laid down between my mother and father's grave, and I explained to them that I was moving to Colorado. Even though my parents were gone, I still felt embarrassed over the entire situation. I went home and prepared myself a drink. I looked at the moving boxes and I couldn't stop crying, so I poured myself another drink. The doorbell rang. I looked through the peep hole, and saw it was Julian.

"Go away."

"I can't. I miss you."

"I don't care. Go home and leave me alone."

"I'm not going anywhere. Not until we talk."

"Then stay outside. I'm going to bed."

I turned off the lights and headed for bed. Maybe it was the wine, but I slept like a baby. When I woke up the next morning to get the newspaper, I opened the door, and Julian's body fell at my feet. I couldn't believe he slept outside the entire night. I stepped over his body as I reached for the paper, and without warning, he grabbed hold of my right leg.

"Let go of me."

"Not until we talk."

Julian got up and walked inside the house.

"Get out now or I'm calling the cops."

Julian seemed too distracted by the moving boxes to hear anything I had to say.

"You're moving? Why?"

"You really need to ask that question?" I scanned the boxes lying around the room hoping my forwarding address wasn't listed on any of them.

"So, where are you moving to?"

"I'm moving out of this house. That's all you need to know. Now get out."

"Maya, why are you doing this? You know I love you."

"Love. Really. I'm sorry Julian, but you don't know what love is. You asked me while I was in mourning to give you another chance, and like a fool I did. I wanted to believe you had changed, but deep down I knew you hadn't. So, I took a gamble by being with you, and now I'm paying the ultimate price."

"I'm paying that price too so don't act like you're in this alone."

"I am alone! I loved and trusted you, but that didn't stop you from cheating on me with Regina! Regina!" I threw a vase at Julian's head. "She tried to have me killed; and thanks to you, she succeeded."

"Maya, I messed up and I get that. I wasn't thinking straight and I'm sorry."

"You damn right you're sorry." I tried to calm myself down. "No, I'm not doing this with you! I've had plenty of time to think about everything that happened and I forgive you."

"Maya…"

"No, let me finish. I forgive you for being who you really are. I was the one who didn't know any better, and for that reason alone, I can't blame anyone but myself." I pushed Julian aside and began to pack. "So, if you'll excuse me, I have to finish up here. I have a lot of stuff to do and a short time to do it in."

"You're right. I screwed up your life and I was a reckless with your heart. I've apologized to you over and over again, but that doesn't make up for what I did to you. So, I'll go." As Julian began to walk off, he noticed all the empty wine bottles sitting on the floor. "You've been drinking?"

"I'm a grown woman. I'm allowed to have a drink."

"And what about the baby?"

"Like I told you before, there is no baby."

Julian began to tear up.

"Why would you do that? Why would you get rid of our baby?"

"That baby was nothing but a mistake just like you. Now leave."

Julian seemed distraught.

"And go where? I have nothing. I've lost you and now our baby. So tell me, Maya, what am I supposed to do? Where am I supposed to go?"

"Home, Julian. You need to go home."

Julian was in tears.

"I'm sorry, Maya. I'm so sorry."

"I know you are."

Julian hugged me, and as much as I hated him, I decided to hug him back. The two of us shared a long cry, then he left.

By the end of the week the house was empty. I walked through the house one last time then left. I flew to Colorado to embark on my new life. I was so nervous. What if I didn't like it there? Unfortunately, at this point, it was too late for second thoughts. As I drove up to the new house, part of me felt at peace while the other half of me wanted to run back to Atlanta. I walked into the house. It was empty but somehow it instantly felt like home. I started a fire, and then I drove to the store to pick up some necessities while I waited on my furniture to arrive. When I returned home, the moving truck were in the driveway. It took a couple of days to get my house in order, but once everything was in place, I was finally able to relax. After learning about my illness, I didn't give myself time to grieve over the situation. I kept myself preoccupied, so I wouldn't have to think about it. With no friends and no family around, I was now in a position where I had nothing but time to think, and once my reality set in, all I could do was cry. I fell into a deep depression and isolated myself for a couple of weeks.

Then one day while I was going to the bathroom, I felt a sharp stabbing pain in my stomach. I didn't know what was causing it, and I became afraid. So, I got dressed and drove myself to the hospital. While the doctors were examining me, I explained my medical history and current diagnosis. After several test, the doctors concluded the baby was in distress. I was advised to take better care of myself by eating well, taking my prenatal vitamins, and getting plenty of rest. One doctor then asked me how I felt about my pregnancy, and I explained to him how I had mixed feelings regarding keeping the baby. The doctor then explained that babies can sometimes sense our emotions. He also advised if I didn't want to keep the baby, then I needed to make a decision as soon as possible. After my examination, it was discovered that I was further along than expected, and the option to abort would no longer be feasible.

So, I went home and I thought about the doctor's suggestions. In reality, I hadn't given my baby a fair chance. I was drinking when I knew it could harm the baby. Furthermore, I wasn't taking proper care of myself. I walked into the living room and turned on some music. I poured myself a cup of warm milk and relaxed by the fire. I rubbed my stomach and the baby kicked. At that moment, I broke down in tears. I couldn't believe how horrible I had been towards my baby. I became very emotional. My baby was innocent, and I had neglected it due to my own selfishness. So, I decided I would keep the baby. I promised myself, from that day forward, I would take better care of us both and to love my baby unconditionally.

While I was sitting on the couch enjoying my milk, the doorbell rang. I went to answer, and there was a couple standing at my door holding a basket of muffins. The woman was young with long blonde hair and a petite body. The man was tall with salt & pepper hair and a nice trimmed beard.

"Hi, neighbor! We're the Hughes and we live next door." The woman had a huge smile plastered on her face.

"Hi. Come on in. I'm sorry I haven't had a chance to introduce myself to everyone."

"Oh it's okay. I'm April and this is my husband Gary."

"I'm Maya, and it's nice to meet you both."

"Oh, and these are for you. They're my grandmother's recipe."

"Thank you."

I placed the muffins on the table and escorted the Hughes to the living room where we sat by the fire.

"You have a lovely home," said Gary.

"Thank you. I was drawn in by its staircase."

"Yes, very nice." April looked around the house, and then she focused her attention onto me. "Well, let me tell you a little bit about us. Gary and I have been living here for the past 12 years, and we know everything about everyone in the neighborhood. We have three beautiful kids; two boys and a girl named Aden, Alex, and Victoria. So, what about you? Are you married? Do you have any kids?"

I could see this couple wasn't going anywhere any time soon. So, I decided I would be up front with them regarding my situation; and if it bothered them, then I wouldn't have to worry about them coming around anymore.

"Well, I'm not married and I don't have any kids, but I am pregnant. The baby's father gave me HIV, and now I'm trying to figure out how to start over and raise this baby alone."

I looked at the couple and I waited for them to freak out and leave.

"Okay, well I'm sorry to hear that and congratulations…"

I looked at April and Gary and started to laugh, and they joined in.

"I know and thank you."

"So, how far along are you?"

"I'm at four and a half months. It's scary because I don't know what to do, and I'm afraid I may have already made some really bad choices."

"I know it can be scary and if you ever need anything, just let us know."

"Thanks."

"Oh, and if it's okay, I can come over later and we can discuss some healthy choices regarding you and the baby…and ways to cope with HIV." I gave April a disconcerting stare. "I'm a nurse at University Hospital and would love to help if you'd like."

"I would love that."

"And Gary here is a great handy man; so if you ever need anything done around the house, just let us know."

"And if you ever get lonely sitting in this big lovely house, then you're more than welcomed to come over and hang out with us. The kids are a little much sometimes, but they'll keep your spirits lifted." Gary seemed so sincere and I became teary eyed over their generosity. I tried to stop crying, but I couldn't.

"It's okay, Maya. We know this is probably a hard time for you, but know that you're not alone, and we're here for you whenever you need us."

"Thank you so much."

The Hughes left and I couldn't stop crying, but this time I actually felt relief. I felt like God was angry with me for my mistakes and I was being punished because of it. However, at that particular moment, I knew He was watching over me and that everything would be okay.

April came over as promised, and she recommended a variety of doctors who could assist me during my pregnancy. Her upbeat spirit and unwavering generosity gave me the strength I needed to move forward with my life. She and Gary kept their word, by dragging me out of the house and getting me involved in community activities. Their kids were also a joy to be around. They kept me laughing and constantly on my toes. I was starting to feel like my old self again.

Then one day, unexpectedly, I went into the kitchen and pulled out my blue mixer. I hadn't used it since the day I found out about my diagnosis. I pulled out my iPod and turned up the music. I began to bake relentlessly. The baby started kicking which made me smile. I took the desserts over to the Hughes. They were surprised I made something so delicious. Their kids couldn't stop eating them. I explained to them that I use to own a bakery in Atlanta. April then suggested I sell my desserts at the annual county festival, but I refused. I explained to her that I didn't want people to feel betrayed if they ever discovered I was HIV positive. April then proposed that I inform people about my illness. There was no way I could publicly expose myself. I didn't need strangers weighing in on my shortcomings.

Time went on and I thought about what April suggested regarding my illness. Considering if I was ever hurt in any way, I would want people to know how to handle and treat my injuries. So, I decided to give my testimony at church and I revealed to everyone that I was HIV positive. I figured some people wouldn't take it as well as others, but it felt good to finally get it off my chest. After service was over, part of the congregation came over to applaud my courage and offered their assistance in case I'd ever need it. It was nice to know there were people who weren't frightened of me because of my disease.

Then one day while I was out in the garage looking for some supplies, I stumbled across one of the boxes that came from my father's house. I took the box inside and started to ramble through it. I laughed at some of the photos of me when I was younger, and then I saw one that I had never seen before of my mother and me. She was so beautiful, and I wished I had the chance to know her better before she passed. I continued to search through the box and found a photo album with my name on it. I opened the book and the first picture I saw was of me when I was a baby with my mother and my father close by. I stared at my father and he seemed so happy. I continued to flip the pages and there were pictures of me when I was in elementary school all the way through high school. There were also pictures of me from college, and it tickled me to see how my hairstyles had changed over the years. I flipped another page, and there were newspaper clippings of me from all of my bakery openings. My father seldomly attended my openings, but he had clippings that dated back to my very first one. I continued flipping, and when I came across the last page, I broke down in tears. It was a Polaroid picture of me and my father dancing at the opening of Charlie's. One way or another, my father tried to hold on to his memories of me and for that reason alone, I would always love him.

Time passed, and I was now six months along in my pregnancy. I could no longer walk as fast as I use to, so April offered to escort me to all of my doctor's appointments. As we made our way into the exam room, I looked down at my belly and it had grown so big. I couldn't believe how fast I was transitioning through my trimesters. Before long there was a knock at the door, and Dr. Peterson walked into the room to begin my examination.

"So, Ms. Davenport, how are you feeling today?"

"I'm running out of clothes to wear, but other than that I'm feeling pretty good."

"Well, that's good to hear. So are you ready to see your baby?"

"Yes. I'm ready."

The doctor squirted cold gel on my belly and began his examination. Within seconds I heard the baby's heartbeat.

"You hear that? That's a strong heartbeat." I began to smile. "I know I've asked you this several times before, but would you like to know the sex of your baby?"

I looked at April and she shook her head yes.

"Sure, why not."

"Congratulations, Ms. Davenport, it's a boy."

"A boy!" I was so excited and afraid at the same time. My laughter soon turned into tears. If I was having a little girl, then I knew what I would tell her. I'd warn her to stay away from men like her father, but having a little boy was a different story. There wasn't a male presence in my life that could help teach my son how to be a man.

"Ms. Davenport, are you okay?"

"Yes, I'm fine. I'm having a little boy."

"Yes, you are, and now that you're entering your last trimester, we need to make sure you have your affairs in order."

"Affairs? Like what?"

"Well, considering your circumstances, it's best you schedule a cesarean. If not, you'll run the risk of having a vaginal birth which increases the chances of you passing the disease onto your baby, assuming he doesn't already have it."

"I understand the risks and I would like to go ahead and schedule the cesarean. I don't want to cause any further harm to my baby."

"I think you're making the right decision. After your appointment is over, we'll have Nurse Johnson schedule your surgery. Okay."

"Okay."

I scheduled the surgery and then we left. I was nervous about having a cesarean, but I knew it was the only way I could protect my child at this point. Since I knew the sex of the baby, April and I decided to go shopping for the nursery. It felt good to finally be able to put the baby's room together. I stood in the doorway for hours gazing at the nursery and thinking about the life that would one day fill it.

I knew that keeping the baby was a selfish choice, but regardless of my decision, it was too late to change my mind. I was choosing to have my baby alone. The more I thought about the baby, the more I thought about Julian. He was going to be a father and didn't know it. I felt as though my decision was reckless, but I honestly didn't know what else to do. I was still angry with Julian, so I wrestled with the thought of telling him the truth about the baby. In time I knew I would eventually tell him everything, but that time had yet to arrive. In life you're given a choice, and regardless if I made the right decision or not, I prayed that God overlooked my most recent discretions and allowed me to have a healthy baby boy.

Chapter 16

Not Now

Time was flying, and I was now nine months along and three days away from my scheduled cesarean. My bags were packed and I was set for the big day. I didn't know what to expect but I was so ready to have this baby. My back was aching and my feet were swollen. It took me forever to go to the bathroom; and if I lay on the couch, it was almost impossible for me to get back up. April tried to help by getting me a two-way radio. That was her creative way of keeping me from getting bored. I explained to her that's what texting is for but she didn't want to hear it.

Then one day while I was lying down on the couch watching television, my cell phone began to ring. I tried to get up and answer it, but I missed the call. I looked down at the phone and it was Matt. I thought about calling him back, but I didn't. I figured if it were important, he'd call back. So, I placed the phone on the counter and went to the bathroom. As I was walking out, I felt a sharp pain in my stomach that was so strong my knees buckled and I fell to the floor. I tried to get up but the pain was unbearable. I laid on the floor screaming for help. I was afraid that I might be in labor. I saw the two-way radio sitting on the couch and I tried to make my way to it, but I couldn't force myself to stand up. I was on the floor on all four limbs trying to figure out a way to get help.

"Come on, baby. Not now. You're too early. Please."

I tried to plea with the baby but the contractions were constant and the pain was unbearable. I needed the pain to stop long enough for me to make it to the phone. There was a period of relief when I tried to crawl towards the counter; but as soon as I started to move, I had another contraction. I was in tears. I couldn't risk having a vaginal birth. I needed to get to the hospital quickly.

I tried to fight through the pain, but it was hard. I screamed while dragging myself towards the phone and then my water broke. Where were my neighbors when I needed them? Out of nowhere, I heard the doorbell ring? Hopefully someone had heard my screams.

"Help…someone please help me!"

"Maya?"

It was Matt. What was he doing here?

"Matt, is that you?"

"Yes. What's going on?"

"I need your help. I need you to call an ambulance now."

"Maya, are you okay? Open the door!" I screamed out in pain and Matt broke the glass panel and opened the door. He saw me lying on the floor in a puddle of water. "Maya, are you okay…" Matt was shocked when he saw me. "You're pregnant?"

"Yes! I'm pregnant and I need you to call an ambulance now."

Matt called for help and the attendee tried to walk him through the steps of assisting me until the ambulance arrived. The operator wanted him to check me, but I refused to let him touch me.

"Maya, I'm trying to help you."

"Then go into the kitchen and get a pair of gloves. I keep them under the sink." I screamed out in pain.

"I don't have time for this. I need to check you now."

I slapped Matt's hand.

"Not until you put on some gloves."

"We don't have time for this. Now move your hands."

"Matt, I'm HIV positive so please go and get the damn gloves." Matt looked at me in shock. He walked into the kitchen and got the gloves from under the sink. "Tell them to notify Dr. Peterson and let him know that I'm in labor."

Within minutes the paramedics rushed through the door. They put me on a stretcher and Matt offered to ride along with me. When we arrived at the hospital, Dr. Peterson scheduled an emergency cesarean. They wheeled me into the operating room and the nurse advised Matt that he could suit up and come into the room with me. I was so afraid, but Matt never let go of my hand. Dr. Peterson also ensured me that everything would be okay. I laid on the operating table in shock. I couldn't believe what was happening. I was having a baby. I was so nervous, but before my mind had time to wonder, I heard a cry.

"Okay, Ms. Davenport. Get ready to meet your baby boy." One of the nurses brought the baby over towards me. I looked at him and broke down in tears. He was so beautiful. I wanted to hold him but the nurse took him away.

"My baby. Where are you taking him?"

"We're going to clean him up. Once the doctor is done taking care of you, then we'll bring him back."

"Okay…" Matt tried to wipe away my tears but I couldn't stop crying.

The entire day felt unreal, and I was so exhausted that I fell asleep. When I woke up, I noticed Matt sitting in a chair next to my bed. He looked at me and smiled.

"You had a baby."

"I had a baby." I looked around the room for him. "Where is he?"

"He's in the nursery." The expression on Matt's face instantly changed. He seemed serious about what he had to say next. "So, why didn't you tell me?"

"Because I was ashamed."

"Ashamed of what?"

"Not what. Who?"

"What are you talking about?"

"I'm talking about Julian."

At that moment, Matt's eyes began to water.

"No."

"Yes."

"But why?"

"Because I was lonely and I needed someone. And he was there."

"Why didn't you call me?"

"Because you're my friend, and I didn't want to run the risk of losing you."

"But you did lose me."

"What are you talking about?"

"I offered to be there for you over and over again, but you never wanted to be with me in that way. You made up excuse after excuse as to why we shouldn't be together. But low and behold, the one guy who made your life a living hell, you found a way to make time for him. So, was it worth it, Maya? Did he give you everything you were looking for?"

"Matt, that's not fair."

"No, what's not fair is the way you've treated me. I've always been there for you, and even know I'm still here supporting you, but no more. I love you, Maya, and I always will, but this is where our friendship ends."

"Matt. Please don't do this."

"I'm sorry."

Matt left and I broke down in tears. He was the only guy whose friendship I truly valued, and now he was gone. A few minutes later, the nurse brought in the baby and placed him in my arms. I looked at his little face and I melted. Even though my heart was heavy, he lifted my spirits.

"Hey there little guy. How are you doing?"

I looked at him and he was so precious. It's funny how reality has a way of changing your perspective. Months ago, I was ready to abort him, but now I couldn't image my life without him.

"Have you decided on a name?" The nurse asked as she wheeled the baby's cart next to the bed.

"No, not yet."

"Okay. Well, I'm going to leave some forms here for you to fill out while you try to think of a name for that handsome fellow."

"I will and thank you."

I stared at my baby trying to figure out who he resembled. Even though it was too early to tell, I could still pin point some of my features in his face; and once he opened his eyes, I almost cried. At that point, all I could see was Julian. He definitely had his father's eyes. Before long, Dr. Peterson came walking into the room.

"Good morning. Well, I'm glad to see you bonding with the baby. So how are you feeling?"

"I'm okay. A little sore, but that's to be expected." I looked at my son and I was so grateful. "And I would like to thank you because I don't know where I would be right now if it wasn't for your support."

"It was my pleasure. And I came to let you know we ran some test on your son and..."

"And?"

"And he doesn't have HIV. It's not uncommon for this to happen, but consider yourself lucky. If your friend wouldn't have gotten you here in time, then this conversation would have been completely different." Dr. Peterson began to gaze around the room. "So, where is your friend?"

"He had to leave."

"Well, next time you see him, thank him on my behalf." Dr. Peterson looked over at the baby. "Have you decided on a name?"

Even though Matt was mad with me, if it wasn't for him, then my baby's fate would've been totally different.

"Yes, I have. His name is Matthew."

"Matthew. I like it."

"So do I."

"Well, I wish you the best and you enjoy Matthew, okay."

"I will."

Dr. Peterson walked out and I couldn't stop smiling. I was ecstatic that my baby wasn't sick. I kissed my son on the forehead and I asked him to forgive me for all the wrong choices I made while I was pregnant with him.

Later on, I called April to inform her of the baby's birth. She and Gary immediately came to visit us. I waited for Matt to return, but he didn't. I was so crushed. I tried not to let it bother me, but it did. I didn't want our friendship to be over, and yet it was. I filled out the baby's birth certificate naming him Matthew J. Davenport and listed Julian as the father. Even though I hated Julian for what he had done to me, he was still Matthew's father. I debated on a nickname for the baby as well. Even though I was grateful to Matt for his help, his name needed a little flare. So, I decided to call the baby, Mattie for short.

Three days passed and it was checkout time. I was so thrilled to be going home. April was there to assist me. I don't know what I would have done without her. I gathered Mattie and his belonging, and then the nurse wheeled us out to April's car. When I arrived at home, I tried to settle in and get some rest while Mattie was asleep. I was still sore and was advised not to walk up and down the stairs, so I decided to camp out in the living room. Later on while I was feeding Mattie, the doorbell rang. I answered and it was Matt.

"Hey."

"Hi. Can I come in?"

"Sure." I opened the door and Matt walked in. We sat down on the couch and there was an awkward silence between the two of us.

"I'm sorry. I was angry. I lashed out at you and I was wrong. You just gave birth and I abandoned you because my feelings were hurt. It wasn't fair of me to react that way and I hope you can forgive me."

"I'm sorry, but I can't." Matt looked disappointed. "Not until you promise to never do anything like that again."

"I promise."

"Then, I forgive you."

Mattie woke up and he tried to open his little eyes.

"Do you mind?"

"No, not at all." I placed Mattie in Matt's arms and he looked like a natural holding the baby. "He likes you."

"For now."

"So, tell me something. Why were you at my house on the day I went into labor?"

"Because I received a letter in the mail from your lawyer giving me ownership of Charlie's. I tried to call you but you wouldn't answer; so I decided to come and see you instead. So, why did you do it? Why did you leave me Charlie's?"

"One day while I was flipping through some pictures, I came across the restaurant, and I realized I had forgotten all about it. I didn't want to keep it for the same reasons I didn't want to keep the bakeries. So, I thought about who I wanted to give it to and I thought of you."

"But, why not Allison? She's your best friend."

"I left Allison a gift that's going to keep her preoccupied for a while. Besides, I knew who I wanted to leave Charlie's to…I wanted to leave it to you. I wanted you to have a piece of me, and that was the only way I knew how to make that happen."

"Maya." Matt grabbed my hand. "It was a sweet gift, but I don't know the first thing about running a restaurant."

"And you don't have to. That's what Tina is for. You'll be the owner, but Tina runs that place." Both of us started to laugh. "So, you can keep it or sell it. It doesn't really matter because it's yours to do with as you please."

"Well, thank you for the gift."

"You're welcome."

Matt began to look around the house.

"So what are you planning on doing with the rest of your life?"

"I don't have any plans other than being a mother to my son."

"You're not going to try and start up a new business while you're here?"

"No. I thought about it, but I'm sick, and I don't know how this virus is going to treat my body. So, I want to spend as much time as I can with my son."

"I know I may be overstepping a little, but did Julian know he was sick when he infected you?"

"No. He didn't know, but Regina did. You warned me about her, and I didn't listen."

"Regina? What does she have to do with this?"

"She was the one who carried the disease. She slept with Julian *knowing* she was sick. Then she broke into his house and poked holes into all of his condoms."

"I told you that chick was crazy."

"Yes, she is, but I made my peace with it. I'm just happy my baby is healthy and her selfish actions didn't affect him in any way."

"So, what are you saying? He's not infected with the virus?"

"Yes, that's correct. He was given a clean bill of health. God was watching over him even when I wasn't."

"Maya, that's great news." Matt looked down at the baby. "So, does this little guy have a name?"

"Yes. His name is Matthew." Matt was stunned.

"Matthew? Why would you name your baby after me?"

"Who said I named the baby after you?"

"Really? And how many other Matthews do you know?"

"Just one who's a very good friend. And if it wasn't for him, my baby's fate would've been totally different."

"Okay, but what is Julian going to think when he finds out you named your baby after me?"

"I don't know. He's a big boy, so he'll be alright."

"Are you sure about that?"

"No, but what is done is done."

"So when do you plan on telling him about the baby?"

"I don't know. I'm afraid to tell him anything because I can't trust Regina. I don't know what scheme she'd think of to cause harm if she found out about Matthew. And if she harmed my son in any way, I'd kill her. I mean literally kill her."

"I understand, but as much as I don't like the guy, you should still tell him about the baby. Remember, you're not the only injured party in this situation."

"You're right. I'll figure something out, but right now, I want to enjoy my time with you. So, when do you go back?"

"That depends on you."

"On me? Why?"

"Well, I felt so guilty for the way I behaved at the hospital that I took some time off from work to help you with the baby…that's if you accept my help of course."

"You took off? For how long?"

"For however long you need me." I started to tear up.

"Are you serious?"

"Yes. Once you feel you're up to speed then I'll leave."

"Thank you!"

I gave Matt a hug as I tried to dry my eyes. He went out to his car and bought in his luggage which was placed in the guest room. Later on that evening while Matt and I were playing with the baby, the doorbell rang. Matt jumped up and answered the door.

"Hi."

"Hello, and you are?" Matt seemed confused.

"I'm April, Maya's next door neighbor. Is she home?"

I could hear April at the door.

"Matt, it's okay. You can let her in!" April walked in and Matt closed the door behind her. "April, this is my friend Matthew and Matthew, this is April."

"So, you're Matthew. I've heard a lot about you, but Maya never mentioned how handsome you were."

"Okay, April. If you want to stay, then stop."

"Stop what? I'm not doing anything."

I glared at April but she couldn't stop smiling. She stayed over for a while and we chatted the night away. A couple of days passed and Matt's timing couldn't have been more perfect. It was hard trying to get around. His assistance with taking care of Mattie gave me more time to focus on myself. April and Gary had us over for dinner on several occasions; and I started to feel normal again which sadden me because nothing about my life was normal. I was grateful to Matt for what he was doing for us, but his presence only reminded me of what I would never have…a real family.

Then one night while sitting on floor with Mattie, I looked at him and wondered about the life he would have. Matt came downstairs and decided to join us on the floor.

"He's perfect, you know that?" Mattie gave me a joy that I never thought I could have again.

"He's greedy, that's what I know." Matt and I started to laugh.

"I don't know how I could ever repay you for what you've done for me and Mattie. You didn't have to stay, but you did, and all I can say is Thank You."

"You know I would do anything for you."

"And that scares me."

"Why?"

"Because as nice as this is, you're going to leave, then I'm going to be all alone again."

"But you don't have to be alone. There are plenty guys out there who would love to meet you."

"See, now you're being mean."

"Why?"

"Come on, Matt! Can you picture me dating? Hey, I'm Maya, I love to bake, I'm a single parent, and oh by the way, I'm HIV positive."

"Look, Maya, dating isn't like it used to be. There are several couples out there where one of the partners is HIV positive."

"Yeah, but not by choice, so forgive me for fearing rejection. As much as I don't want to be alone, I think I'm cool with it being just me and Mattie for a while."

I walked upstairs and prepared Mattie for bed. As I laid him down in his crib, Matt walked into the room.

"He's out for tonight, so I think I'm going to turn in as well." I turned to walk out of the room then stopped. "And, Matt."

"Yeah."

"I'm okay now, so you can leave whenever you're ready."

"You sure?"

"Yes. I'm sure."

Matt walked towards me and gently embraced me with a kiss. It felt nice considering I haven't been kissed in a while.

"Why are you doing this to me?"

"Because you did it to me first."

"But I'm sick, Matt, and can't nothing good can come from this."

"We'll see." Matt kissed me on the forehead then walked into his room.

I went into my room, laid across the bed, and cried. I heard my door open, and Matt walked into the room, and laid down beside me.

"What are you doing?"

"Nothing. If you want to cry then cry, but I'm not going anywhere. Not right now." I cried as Matt held me in his arms. He reassured me that everything would be okay even if I knew it was a lie.

A couple of days later, Matt finally left. I knew this day would eventually come, but it felt weird being in the house without him. I had to start over and figure out a new routine, not only for me, but for Mattie as well. Matt had us spoiled and I was going to miss him.

I looked at Mattie and wanted nothing but the best for him. The way I imagined my life was completely different than the way it turned out. And even though Regina had set out to hurt me, instead I was blessed with the greatest gift of all...Mattie.

Chapter 17

I'm Sorry

I was learning how to live alone with just Mattie and me, and it wasn't as bad as I thought it would be. April and Gary kept us busy with daily activities, but it was my time alone with Mattie that I enjoyed the most. He was getting so big and his laughter would fill the room. I didn't think that I could be this happy.

Then one day while I was in the kitchen cooking dinner, the doorbell rang. I went to answer and it was Brandon. I didn't know what to do. I quickly scanned the room for anything that belonged to Mattie, and then I opened the door.

"Brandon."

"Hi, Maya, how are you?"

"I'm good. So, why are you here?"

"I need your help. Can I come in?" I looked around the room and Mattie's intercom was sitting on the table. I prayed he stayed asleep until Brandon was gone.

"Sure. So how did you find me? I didn't leave a forwarding

address." I walked into the kitchen to turn off the stove, and I hid Mattie's intercom behind the cookbooks.

"I have my ways."

"Sure you do. So, what can I help you with?"

"It's Julian."

"It's always Julian. What now?"

"He's not well and I wanted to know if you would talk to him."

"No! Now what else can I do for you?"

"Come on, Maya. Please! I wouldn't be here if it wasn't important. I've never seen my brother like this before and I don't know what else to do."

"Take him to church. It works wonders."

"Church? I'm being serious while you're joking. You don't care about Julian at all, do you?"

"No. I cared too much and that's the problem. That's why I'm in the predicament I'm in now."

"I know he hurt you, but can you please have some compassion for my brother and go and see him."

"Compassion." I laughed. "Where was the compassion when your brother cheated on me with Regina? Where was the compassion when he infected me with HIV? I lost everything because of Julian, and now you want me to show him some compassion?" I was furious. "I think it's time for you to go."

"I get it, you're hurting. But my brother is a victim in this as well."

"Victim? Did you really just say victim? He willfully slept with Regina. She didn't put a gun to his head. He did it all on his own. Now you're here asking me for sympathy. Well, I don't have any to give."

"That's cold, Maya, even for you." Brandon seemed uneasy. "You claimed to have loved me once, so where is your compassion for me?"

"It left when you walked out on me. Now is there anything else I can do for you?"

At that exact moment, Mattie's cry sirened through the intercom and I almost had a heart attack.

"What was that?"

"A baby. You've never heard a baby cry before?" I tried to cover myself as quickly as I could.

"A baby?"

"Yes, I'm babysitting. Now is there anything else I can do for you?"

Brandon became quiet as he scanned the room.

"Babysitting?"

"Yes, and what are you looking for?"

"Not for, at."

"What are you talking about?"

The only pictures I see in here are of you and a baby. And look, there's one with Matt as well. What's going on here, Maya? You told Julian you got rid of the baby."

"And I did."

"Well, it doesn't look that way to me. It looks like you lied to him."

Mattie's cry grew louder and louder.

"Excuse me."

I went upstairs to take care of Mattie, and while I was calming him down, Brandon walked into his room.

"You lair! You kept the baby and you lied to my brother about it."

"And for good reason."

"What reason is there to keep a father from his child?"

"Oh, so we need to go down *that* road again?"

"Maya, this is wrong and you know it."

"No, what would be wrong is you opening your mouth and

saying something about this. I kept quiet to protect my son and I suggest you do the same."

"But Julian deserves to know."

"Yeah, but once Julian finds about the baby, Regina would to. Look at the situation she put me and Julian in. Who knows what she'll try to do to hurt my son…and I'd do anything to protect him. So, I need you to keep this to yourself. Okay?"

"Maya, Regina is no longer a threat."

"What? How can you be so sure? That chick is crazy."

"Because she's dead."

I was shocked…and somewhat relived at the same time.

"She's dead? How? What happened?"

"She committed suicide. It was all over the news."

"I can't believe her. She went around ruining people's lives, and then she takes the easy way out by killing herself. Unreal."

"So, you see. There's no reason why you shouldn't be able to tell Julian about the baby."

Mattie became fussy.

"Look, Brandon, let me put Mattie back to sleep, and then we can finish our conversation downstairs."

"Okay." Brandon sat in a chair across from mine as I rocked Mattie to sleep. "His name is Mattie?"

"Yes and no. His name is Matthew but I call him Mattie for short."

"Matthew. You know Julian is going to flip when he finds out you named his son after Matt. Why would you do that?"

"Look, I don't have to explain my decision to you. His name is Matthew. Case closed."

I was finally able to put Mattie back to sleep, then Brandon and I went downstairs to finish our conversation.

"So, will you do it? Will you go and talk to Julian?"

"Look Brandon, I know where you're coming from, and I get it; but I don't have anything else to say to Julian. He hurt me in the worse way, so I don't know how I could possibly help him."

"Just talk to him, Maya. Tell him anything. I don't care. I just need him to see you're okay and that he can be okay as well."

I looked at Brandon and felt sorry for him because of what he was going through, but there was too much animosity in my heart to help Julian.

"I don't think I can do it. I'm sorry." I turned to walk away and Brandon stopped me.

"She shot herself in front of him! You get that! She killed herself in front of my brother and it broke him. Now I get that he hurt you, but my brother is broken and I don't know how to fix him." Brandon was in tears. "He doesn't eat, he barley sleeps, and he's about to lose his job. To be honest, I don't think he's taking his medication either. So you see, you may be his last hope because I don't know what else to do."

Tears ran down my face as I tried to comprehend the urgency in Brandon's request.

"You're asking me to put myself in an uncomfortable situation."

"And yet I'm the one here begging you for help."

I tussled with my decision. I knew I would regret going to see Julian, but I didn't know what else to do.

"Fine, I'll go, but I'm not telling him about Mattie. Not yet. Julian needs to get his act together before I can bring my son into the picture."

"Thank you, Maya. Thank you, thank you." Brandon was so excited, but I was terrified of going back.

"So when do you head back?"

"Tomorrow."

"And where are you staying?"

"Downtown. My wife booked a hotel near the airport."

"Wife? So, you finally made Angela an honest woman?"

"No. Too much had happened between us to make it work; but I met Veronica over a year ago and we clicked. The rest is history."

"Well, I'm happy for you."

"You know, it's crazy because she reminds me of you." I could see the sincerity in Brandon's eyes. "But, Maya, can I ask you a question?"

"Sure. What is it?"

"Why did you go back to Julian? Did you ever consider that being with him would hurt me?"

"I considered it, but I was grieving and was in a bad place. I just needed someone to take the pain away."

"So why didn't you call me? You know I would have come."

"No, you wouldn't. You chose Julian over me, remember."

"Yes, I chose my brother, but when I heard you and Julian were back together, it broke my heart."

"Brandon…"

"No, I figured I had it coming, but I really did love you."

"And I loved you too."

Brandon gave me a long and endearing hug.

"Thank you for agreeing to talk to Julian and I hope to see you soon in Atlanta."

"Same here. Good-bye."

Brandon left and I felt flushed. What was I going to say to Julian? I didn't know how to help him. Part of me was still angry at him for what he had done to me. I went into my bedroom and prayed. I was lost and desperately needed God's guidance to help me through this situation.

The next day, I called April and informed her of my visit to Atlanta. I asked if she and Gary would keep an eye on the house while I was away. She agreed and I began to pack. I looked at Mattie and prayed I was making the right decision. The next day, we flew out on the first available flight to Atlanta. When we landed, it felt weird being back in town. I checked into a local hotel and I began to make my rounds, but there was one stop I needed to make before going to see Julian. I pulled up to Mayhem's and smiled. I took Mattie out the car and placed him in a stroller. I opened the door and I couldn't stop smiling. The shop was so classy. There were stylish clothes and jewelry everywhere. I walked towards the register. Allison was standing at the front counter with her back facing me. I placed Mattie's stroller beside the counter so she couldn't see him.

"Excuse me. I was once told that I was fashionably challenged, and I wanted to know if you had anything in here that would fit me."

Allison turned around and I could see the shock in her eyes.

"I'm sorry, but we don't have clothes for synclinal disingenuous traitors. Fashionably challenged or not."

"Really? Because I thought those were your only clients."

"You got some nerve! You don't get it do you. I'm mad at you. How could you leave town without saying goodbye, and then you throw this business on me without any warning?"

"I told you at the meeting that I was leaving town, but you didn't want to hear it. I had a lot going on in my life, and there was no way I could continue to live in Atlanta."

"So, why didn't you come and talk to me? You were my best friend. You know I would've done anything for you."

"I didn't say anything because I was embarrassed and didn't want a lecture from you or anyone else. I was going through a traumatic situation and all I wanted was to be alone."

"What was so traumatic that you couldn't talk to me about it?"

"I don't want to get into it in here, but I'll stop by your place later and tell you all about it. Okay."

"Sure. So, how are you doing? I haven't seen you in over a year."
Allison was observing my body. "And I see you put on a little weight as well. It looks good on you."

"Yeah. Having a baby tends to do that to you."

"Baby? Are you serious? You had a baby?"

I stepped aside and took Mattie out of the stroller.

"Allison, I want you to meet Mattie."

"Oh, Maya, he's gorgeous. How could you keep this from me?"

"I didn't want to, but after the way you treated me when you discovered I was back with Julian, I didn't want to say anything."

"I'm sorry about that. I was so mad because I didn't want you to get hurt again."

"I know, but I really needed you that day."

"And I hate that I didn't stick around. I'm sorry, Maya. I'm truly sorry." Allison began to play with Mattie. "So, is Julian the father?"

"Yes, but it's complicated. Like I said before, I'll tell you all about it later."

"So where are you staying?"

"I'm at the W."

"You know you can always stay with me."

"I know, and I may take you up on your offer later. So how is the shop?"

"I hate to admit it but I love it. I was so angry with you for leaving; and I wanted to quit, but I didn't. Not only did you leave me a shop, but you left me employees who became my family. So, thank you, Maya. Thank you for never giving up on me."

"You know I could never do that. Besides you're my family and I'll always have your back."

I gave Allison a hug and was glad everything had worked out for her.

"So what do you have planned for today?"

"I have some more stops I need to make, but after that, I'm free to do whatever."

"Okay, well call me later so we can meet up."

"Will do."

I left the shop and debated on how I wanted to approach Julian. I didn't want to take Mattie with me, so I decided to call the only person I knew I could always depend on…Mary. I parked on the curve. It felt strange being back at my childhood home. I rang the doorbell and Mary answered.

"Maya! Oh my goodness it's so nice to see you."

"It's good to see you too."

"Come in." I clutched Mattie in his carrier as we walked inside the house. "Wait a minute. Who is this handsome fellow?"

"Mary, meet my son, Mattie."

"Son! Oh Maya, I didn't know you had a baby."

"I know. I intentionally kept it a secret from everyone, but I'm here because I need a favor."

"Sure, anything for you. What do you need?"

"Can you watch Mattie for a while? I have an errand to run and I can't take him with me."

"Oh sure, it would be my pleasure to watch him."

"Thank you, Mary. I have his bag in the car and I promise not to be long."

"Take your time. It's been a while since I've had a little person in my presence."

"Thank you! You're a life saver."

As I was about to leave, I noticed the house had been redecorated but I could still see my past playing out in each room.

I left Mattie with Mary while I debated on what I should say to Julian. I didn't know how I would react to seeing him again. So much had happened between us; and even though I hated him for what he had done to me, part of me still loved him. I wanted to move forward with my life, and the only way I could do that was by telling Julian the truth about Mattie. If something happened to him before he found out about his son, it would kill me. In my eyes, I've always played Julian out to be the monster, but keeping Mattie away from him was turning me into the real villain.

Chapter 18

You're Not Dead

I drove around for a couple of hours contemplating on whether or not I should follow through with my plan to see Julian. I parked my car outside of his house and sat there too afraid to move. I didn't know his current state of mind, and I didn't want to upset him by saying the wrong thing. So, I looked in the mirror, gave myself a pep talk, and decided to get out. My mind was racing, but I knew there was no turning back at this point. I ringed the doorbell, but there was no answer. Brandon ensured me Julian was home, so I continued to ring the doorbell until someone answered.

"What!"

Julian answered the door angry and upset. He had a patchy beard, matted hair, and an awful body odor.

"Julian, it's me. Maya."

Once Julian realized who I was, he calmed down and invited me in.

"I'm sorry, I didn't know it was you." I walked in and realized

Brandon's account of Julian's lifestyle was accurate. His house was a mess, and he looked and smelled terrible.

"How are you doing?"

"You know. I'm okay considering the obvious. How about you? You look good."

"I'm fine."

"Good. So, why are you here? Was it Brandon? Did he send you?"

"Yes, he did. So what's going on Julian? What's all of this?"

I looked around the room at the filth Julian was living in, and as much as I hated him, it shattered my heart to see him broken and defeated.

"It's nothing. I'm okay."

"Really? Because you look a mess. So what's really going on?"

"Like I said before, it's nothing. And why do you care? I ruined your life, remember?"

"And how could I forget? But that's not an excuse to let myself go. Look around. What is this?"

I pointed out the trash and dirty dishes Julian had lying around the house.

"It's me facing reality. My life is over, Maya, and I did this to myself. You get that? I have no one to blame here but me."

"Yeah, I understand you're giving up. You're faced with a horrible disease and you want to throw in the towel. But guess what, Julian? You may be sick but you're not dead."

"Well, I may as well be because there's no cure for this disease. So, why are you here trying to sell me on hope? Because I don't have any."

"I'm not trying to sell you on anything! Do you think I'm breezing through this disease on some type of fairy dust? Well I'm not. I'm dealing with this virus day by day and sometimes it takes everything in me to get up. But guess what? I get up. I'm alive, and as long as I'm living, I'm going to fight to be here."

"Well, I'm happy for you, Maya. I truly am."

Julian sat on his couch and faded out. I looked at him and it reminded me of how I use to be. I walked into his bathroom and turned on the shower. I knew I couldn't carry him, but I was determined to snap him out of the hopelessness he was stuck in.

"Come with me."

"What are you talking about?"

"Stand up and come with me."

"Maya, I don't have time for this."

"Sure you do. Look around you. You have nothing but time."

I grabbed Julian's hand and he snatched it away from me.

"I told you to leave me alone."

"And I told you to get your ass up!" Julian was shocked by my reaction. "You don't get it! You did this! You did this to yourself! So don't expect any pity from me. Now I said get up and let's go."

"Fine." I took Julian's hand and I guided him to the shower. He saw the water running and he began to cry. "Maya. . ."

"I know."

I walked him into the shower until he was underneath the showerhead. I took his shirt off, and Julian held me in his arms as the water ran over us.

"I'm sorry, Maya. I'm so sorry for what I did to you."

"I don't want you to be sorry. I want you to get better. You stay here. And when you come out, I want you to have shaved and put on some clean clothes. Okay?"

"Okay."

I dried off, and then went into the living room and began to clean up. I thought about the time Julian helped me when I felt hopeless, so the least I could do was return the favor. While I was vacuuming, I heard a loud thump. I raced to the bathroom and Julian was lying on the floor.

"Julian! Julian, are you alright?"

"I'm fine. Just a little lightheaded, but I'll be okay."

"Are you sure you're okay? Did you take your medicine today?"

"No. I forgot."

"Okay, where is it?"

"In the top drawer."

I reached into the drawer and pulled out Julian's pills. I could easily tell he wasn't taking his daily regimen. I poured a cup of water and handfed Julian his medication.

"Swallow. Come on. You have to take all of this." I could sense he was weak and I was trying my best to hold back my tears, but it was hard. I tried to get up, but Julian held on to me.

"Don't go."

"I'm not going anywhere." I eased back down as I ran my hand over Julian's head. "Have you eaten anything today?"

"No, not yet."

I tried to wipe away my tears as I held Julian in my arms on the floor. He was broken, and I didn't know if there was anything I could do to help him. "Better now?"

"Yeah, I'm good."

"Okay. I'm going to the kitchen to make you something to eat. If you need anything, let me know."

"I will."

I went into the kitchen, but there was nothing in his refrigerator to cook. I wanted to go to the grocery store, but I was too afraid to leave Julian alone. So, I decided to call for takeout. When Julian walked out of his room, he looked like his old self again.

"How do you feel?"

"Better." Julian walked over to the couch and sat down. "I don't get it."

"Get what?"

"Why are you here and why are you helping me?"

"Because you needed help and that's all to it." I walked over and sat down beside Julian on the couch. "Oh, and I ordered some takeout which should be here soon."

"Okay." Julian reached over and grabbed my hand. "Thank you, Maya, for what you're doing. I know you don't have to be here, but you are. So, thank you."

"You're welcome." I looked at Julian and my heart went out to him. "So, tell me something."

"Sure. What would you like to know?"

"How did you get to this point? I mean you're a strong person, so what happened?" I knew the answer, but I wanted to hear Julian's response.

"It was you."

That wasn't the response I was looking for.

"Me? What did I do?"

"You killed our baby and then you left." I was so stunned that I let go of Julian's hand. "You took everything away from me including your love, and I was left with nothing."

Tears ran down my face as I tried to compose myself. I wanted to tell Julian about Mattie, but I wasn't sure if the timing was right.

"You were left with nothing. Really! I agreed to be your wife, but you chose to betray me with another woman. I had to give up everything I had ever worked for because I didn't want this disease to tarnish the reputation of my business. So, you see, you may have been left with nothing, but I was forced to give up everything."

"It was a mistake, Maya! A huge mistake! Trust me, I didn't want any of this to happen."

"Then why did you sleep with her?" I became very emotional. "Why would you throw away what we had over Regina? Why?"

"Because I wasn't thinking. You were right about everything, and I'm sorry."

"Sorry. You know sorry can't excuse the damage that you've caused. Nothing in my life will ever be the same because of you." I grabbed my purse and headed towards the door.

"So, you're leaving now?"

"No. I'm not leaving. I'm stepping out for some air. I'll be back."

I went outside, sat in my car, and cried. I was doing everything I promised myself I wouldn't do. I was there to try and help Julian, but instead I felt like I was making matters worse. I had to put my feelings aside, go back in, and try to work something out. As I walked inside, Julian was nowhere to be seen.

"Julian! Julian." I tried to open his bedroom door but it was locked. "Julian! Open the door! Julian." I beat on the door until he opened it.

"Why are you yelling?"

"Why is your door lock? I told you I was coming back."

"Well, I didn't believe you."

"Okay, fine you didn't believe me. Now open the door."

"Why?" I could smell weed coming from the room. "Are you getting high?"

"Maybe."

"Really." I walked over to the couch and Julian opened the door. "I thought you were about to..." I thought about Regina but didn't want to mention her name unless Julian was ready to talk about her.

"You thought I was about to what? Come on, Maya. What's on your mind?"

"It's nothing. You're fine."

"It's okay. I get it. You thought I was going to hurt myself like Regina did?"

"I don't know. The thought may have crossed my mind. I just don't want to see you hurt. Okay?"

"I understand, but you don't have to worry. I wouldn't do anything to hurt myself." Julian pulled the blunt from behind his back and walked over towards the couch. "You want some?"

"No, I'm good."

"You sure? It's medicinal so you're safe." I stared at Julian as he handed me the blunt. I took a puff and handed it back. "Yeah, I knew you wanted some."

"Whatever. So, how are you taking it?"

"Oh you know...maybe one or two a day."

"I can't with you! I'm not talking about the weed. I'm talking about Regina. How are you dealing with her...you know?"

"Oh, I don't know. I try not to think about it."

"Do you want to talk about it?"

"I do and I don't."

Julian passed the blunt back to me. I took a couple of puffs and passed it back.

"Good, huh?"

"Yeah." We started to laugh. I looked at Julian and I didn't want to push the issue, but I did want him to talk about what happened, hoping it would help him in some way. "Well, I'm here if you ever want to talk about it."

"Okay." We sat around and smoked the blunt in silence. "Tell me something. Why are you being so nice to me?"

"I'm not being nice. I'm being empathetic."

"Call it what you want, but I'm grateful you're here." Our food finally arrived and we sat down at the table and ate. It was the weirdest thing ever, but it felt normal in some way. "This is nice."

"It's something."

Julian smiled at me and I couldn't help but to smile back.

"She came over begging for me to take her back."

"What?" I was taken off guard.

"Regina. She came over that day begging me to take her back, but I couldn't. I confessed my love for you, and then she pulled out a gun. I thought she was going to shoot me, but then she turned the gun on herself."

"Julian…"

"I tried to talk her down. I even told her that we could get back together, but she said she didn't believe me, and then she shot herself." Tears ran down Julian's face. "I can't believe she pulled the trigger."

I tried to wipe his tears away, but he grabbed my hand and kissed it. "Promise me you won't ever leave me."

"I'm not going anywhere." Julian leaned over and kissed me. "Julian, it's not like that."

"I'm sorry. I got caught up in the moment."

"I understand."

"So, where do we go from here?"

"I don't know. We try to heal and move on."

"But I don't want to move on with anyone else but you."

"Julian, we can't. As much as I love you, I don't trust you. In a relationship, I have to feel as though I'm number one. Not second or third, but first in your life, and I don't."

"But you are."

"No, I'm not because if I was, then you would have never slept with Regina. Regardless of what happened between the two of you, she was still number one in your heart."

"She wasn't number one, she was just familiar. Part of me felt guilty because I was never able to love her in the way that I loved you. I'm not saying that justifies what I did, but it's the truth."

Julian was throwing on the charm but I couldn't fall for it. Not again.

"I'm sorry but I can't." I didn't want to keep leading Julian on, so I decided it was time I told him about Mattie.

"Just think about it. Before you turn me down cold, just take a moment and think about us."

"Julian..."

"Please, Maya, just think about it."

"I'm not making any promises, but there is something I need to tell you."

"Okay, what is it?"

"It's the real reason why I'm here."

"And what reason is that?"

"Just promise me you won't get upset."

"Well, that depends on what you have to say. So, what's going on, Maya?"

I was so nervous, but it was time Julian knew the truth about Mattie.

"Remember when I told you I was ending my pregnancy?"

"Yes."

"Well, I lied. I kept the baby." I was uncertain of how Julian would react. He stared at me in silence. "Julian, did you hear me?"

"Yeah, I heard you but I don't believe you."

"Well, it's the truth. I was afraid to keep the baby, but I couldn't force myself to get rid of it either."

"So, you're not lying. We have a baby?"

"Yes. We have a baby."

I thought Julian was excited but then he became angry.

"Why would keep this from me?"

"Come on Julian. You know why. After everything you and Regina put me through, there was no way in hell I could risk the welfare of my son."

"Son. So, I have a son?"

"Yes."

Tears ran down Julian's face. I felt horrible for what I had done, but I knew I had made the right decision.

"So where is he? When can I see him?"

"See, that's the thing. I'm not allowing you to see him until you get better. That's why I've been so worried about you. I want you to be a part of your son's life, but I can't bring him over here with your place looking like this."

"You won't allow me! He's my son too, Maya."

"Yeah, and just a minute ago you looked like you were at death's door. Come on, Julian. I'm trying to work with you here. Our son is a happy little boy, and I need you to be in your right mind if you want him to be a part of your life."

"I can't believe this. I want to see him."

"The best I can do is show you a picture, but I'm not taking you to see our son. Not yet."

"A picture. I don't want to see a damn picture! I want to see my son."

"No! Picture first. I have to be able to trust you before I can let you see Mattie."

"Mattie. So that's his name?"

"Yes and no. His name is Matthew, but I call him Mattie for short."

"Matthew. You got to be kidding me. You named my son after Matt?"

"Yes I did."

"What the hell were you thinking? We're changing his name as soon as possible."

"No we're not. Long story short, if it weren't for Matt, then our son would be sick like us. So, his name will stay Matthew."

"Wait, so he doesn't have the virus?"

I started to smile.

"No. He's not infected."

"But how?"

"I don't know. Call it a miracle. I'm just happy he's healthy."

Julian couldn't stop smiling.

"We have a son and he's not sick. This is cause for a celebration." Julian went into his kitchen and poured a glass of wine. "Drink with me."

"Oh, so now you're using my line?"

"Yes. Drink with me." I picked up the glass and Julian and I toasted to having a healthy baby boy. "Okay, I'm ready to see that picture now." I pulled out my phone and showed Julian several pictures of Mattie. "He's beautiful."

"Yes he is. So, here's the deal. I'll take you to see Mattie, but you have to promise to take your medication every day."

"I promise, Maya. I'll take it every day."

"And I know this part may seem hard, but I need you to claim your life back because once you meet Mattie, you're going to want to be around him all the time; and you can't do that if you don't have your life together."

"I understand."

"And before we go, I have to say this. I'm sorry. I know it may not mean much, but I am. Mattie is your son, and I should've told you about him sooner. I did what I thought was best, and I am sorry for shutting you out."

"I'll accept your apology if you allow me one kiss."

"Julian. I told you I can't go there with you again."

"I know, but all I'm asking for is one kiss. One kiss to feel normal again. One kiss to say I'm sorry for all the bullshit I put you through. Please." I sympathized with Julian and I thought about the kiss Matt gave me which made me feel somewhat normal. "Please, Maya, just one kiss." Even though I knew I was making a mistake I decided to allow Julian to kiss me.

"Fine."

Julian leaned in to kiss me and I was so nervous. I was always vulnerable around him and didn't want to get caught up again. He kissed me. At first it felt like a normal kiss, but then the kiss intensified, so I quickly pulled back. I couldn't allow myself to go there again.

"Okay, we have to stop."

Julian continued to kiss me.

"I missed you."

"Okay you missed me. That's nice but we're over, remember? I gave you a kiss. Now let's go."

"So, you're not going to give me another chance? Are you?"

"No. You had a second chance to make it right and you blew it. I've moved on. I have Mattie and I'm happy. So all we can ever be is friends."

"Friends? Really."

"Yes. I love you, Julian, and it would be convenient for us to be together, but I can't. Your betrayal didn't just hurt me, it cost me. So, in my eyes, the only thing we could ever be is friends."

"I understand." As we walked out the house, Julian grabbed my hand. "One day I will win you back."

"No, one day you'll move on and learn how to live without me, as I've learned how to live without you."

I smiled and I took Julian to see Mattie. As he walked into the room, he appeared very nervous. I picked Mattie up and I placed him in Julian's arm. The smile on his face warmed my heart. Julian was so happy, and I was content that he was finally able to meet his son. A lot had happened between us, and with the three of us being together, we almost felt like a family; but I didn't want to mislead myself. Our love for each other could not erase the past. We had been through too much, and for the first time in my life I was happy being alone with just me and my son. In life we have to learn how to forgive and forget. And even though Julian's betrayal was unforgivable, the love we had for our son proved to be the most powerful absolution in the world.

Chapter 19

Happiness Does Exist

It was getting late and I decided to head over to Allison's before I called it a night. I was happy Julian was able to meet Mattie, and I prayed he stayed healthy for our son's sake. I looked at Mattie and he was so innocent in all of this. I wanted to protect his happiness, but I knew that was out of my control.

Once I arrived at Allison's, I ringed the doorbell, and she yelled for me to come in. As I walked through the door, there was a loud scream.

"Surprise!"

I was so shocked that I almost dropped Mattie. I looked around the room and the entire gang was there. Nikki, Tina, and even Matt.

"You guys almost gave me a heart attack."

I took Mattie out of the carrier and Nikki was first to take him out of my arms.

"Maya, Maya, Maya. I see you have been a very busy woman. So, who is this little guy?" Nikki was making faces at Mattie.

"This is my son, Mattie."

"Well I don't believe it. Maya's a mother." Tina cut her eyes at me and then she smiled.

"I know it's kind of crazy right, but I'm a mom."

"Well, I'm happy for you." Tina gave me a hug.

"Me too," Nikki said smiling.

All of us sat around and laughed for hours. I saw Matt talking with Tina and I decided to join in on the conversation.

"Hey, Tina, I meant to ask you how was the restaurant doing?"

"It's good. My new boss here gave me free reign to do whatever I want." Tina smirked as she referred to Matt.

"Yeah, and then I had to pull reins back a little."

I started laughing because I knew Tina.

"So, what did she do?"

"I didn't do anything." Tina was defensive.

"Yeah right. I came in one day and I thought I was in Rio at Carnival. There were men and women walking around half naked, and so was this one. Strutting around in nothing but a leotard and feathers! I didn't know what was going on."

I couldn't stop laughing.

"Feathers, Tina! Really?"

"I was going for a theme night. You know, to bring in some young and hip customers."

"You're not fooling anybody, but I still love you." I couldn't stop laughing.

"Whatever. I looked good and we had a great time. Didn't we, Matt!"

"Yeah, it was fun but it'll be a while before we can do that again."

"Why the wait? If it was a hit, then why can't you guys do it again?"

"Tina, please explain to Maya why we can't do it again?"

"Long story short, Carnival turned into a street party, and we closed Peachtree Street down."

"What's bad about that?"

"We didn't have the permit to do so."

"Plus the party got a little out of control, and we had to shut it down, which sucks because we made a killing that night."

"We sure did." Tina gave Matt a high five.

"But in Tina's defense, it was a good idea, only next time we'll have to plan it better."

"Next time? So, you're saying you may let me do it again?" Tina seemed excited.

"We'll see."

"Oh Matt, you're the best." Tina winked at me. "He's a keeper."

"I bet he is." I smiled at Matt. "So, did you guys take some pictures? I want to see how it turned out."

"Oh you know I did." Tina pulled out her phone and showed me pictures from Carnival.

"Tina, you look gorgeous. You think you can do that to my eyebrows?"

"I don't know. You are a work in progress." Both of us started to laugh. "I've missed you, Maya."

"I've missed you too." I hugged Tina and gave her a kiss on the cheek. Allison looked over at me and smiled. I missed the gang so much, and it made my heart heavy to think about having to leave them again.

Mattie became fussy and I tried to put him to sleep. It was way past his bedtime, and he was probably tired and exhausted from being up so late.

"Okay guys, it's been fun but it's late. Maya has had a long day and her and the baby need to rest." Allison ended the party, and everyone walked over to give me a hug and a kiss goodnight.

I went to lay Mattie down. When I came out of the room, Matt was helping Allison clean up.

"Hey, you're still here?"

"Yeah, I decided to help Allison out so you two can catch up."

"Oh, you don't have to do that. I can clean this up later."

"No, I insist. You two go and catch up, and I'll take care of this. Besides, I don't have anywhere to be." Matt reached behind the counter. "Here's a bottle of wine, and I'll see you two later."

Allison and I looked at each and decided to go into the living room to relax. She poured us a glass of wine, and we stretched out on the couch.

"So, are you finally going to tell me why you left?"

"Yes. Just know that I always wanted to tell you the truth, but I was too embarrassed to say anything."

"Okay, so what happened?"

"The day you left me at the hospital, the doctor did more than inform me about my pregnancy." I felt mortified to continue on.

"So, what else did he tell you?"

"That I was HIV positive."

Allison's mouth dropped open.

"HIV! Are you serious? That damn Julian. How could he!" Allison realized that she was loud with her response. "I'm sorry. I forgot Matt was in the kitchen. Does he know?"

"Yeah, he knows." I looked at Matt in the kitchen and then I looked at Allison. "I hate myself sometimes because everyone warned me to stay away from him, but I didn't listen. Then I thought about the business and I didn't want my illness to sabotage it, so I sold it and left."

"Oh my goodness. Mattie. Is he?"

"No, he's good. By the grace of God he's not infected."

"So, Regina. Is that why she?"

"Who knows, but she's the reason why we were infected in the first place."

"Regina. How?"

"You ready for this? She was infected, and she wanted to hurt Julian in any way that she could. So she got back at him by poking holes in his condoms, and the rest is history."

"That chick was truly crazy."

"Yes she was."

"So, how are you dealing with all of this?"

"To be honest, I don't know. There were times when I wanted to give up, but then I thought about Mattie. God knew what I needed when he blessed me with that little boy." Tears ran down my face and I quickly wiped them away. "He saved my life, and I don't know what I would do without him."

Allison was in tears.

"Maya, I'm so sorry you had to go through that alone."

"It's not your fault. I chose to be alone. Besides, you've always been there for me, but this time I had to learn how to cope on my own. You're my best friend and I didn't want to burden you with any more of my problems." I was starting to feel sentimental. "I've done that to you too many times over the years and for that, I'm sorry..."

"No, I'm the one who should be sorry. I..."

"No, you've done a lot. You've always been my voice of reason and I don't know what I would do without you. I love you Allison."

"I love you too."

Allison gave me a hug and then Matt walked in.

"Am I interrupting anything?"

Allison and I began to laugh.

"No, we're good."

"Well, the kitchen is cleaned and I'm going to leave you ladies to it."

"You know, it is late. So, thank you for the surprise party, but I think it's time we headed out as well."

"You sure? You know you are more than welcomed to stay."

"Thanks, but Mattie's formula and my medication are back at the hotel. But don't worry, I'll be in town for a while, so there will be plenty opportunities for us to sleep over."

"I guess…" Allison and I smiled at each other. It felt good hanging out with her again.

"I can give you a ride if you want." Matt suggested as he was getting his coat.

"No, we're good. Besides, it's late. We'll be okay."

"But I don't mind. Plus, it'll give me more time to hang out with you guys."

"That's nice, but…"

"No buts. I told you I don't mind."

"Oh for Pete's sake take the ride." Allison interjected.

"And what about my car? I drove here."

"Then I'll enforce bar rules." Matt held out his hand. "Keys please."

I smiled as I handed over my keys to Matt. I gathered Mattie's belongings and we left. Once we arrived at the hotel, Matt helped me carry everything into the room.

"Thanks." I tried to lay Mattie down but he was fussy.

"Let me hold him."

"No, you don't have to do that. It's late, and…"

"And I want to. It's been a while since I hung out with my buddy. So, you go and do whatever you need to do, and I'll take care of Mattie."

"You sure?"

"Yes. I'm sure."

As I put everything away I peeped in on Matt and he was a

natural. While he was feeding Mattie, I decided to take a shower. It had been a long day. Dealing with Julian and then the surprise party. I was exhausted. When I went to check on Matt, him and Mattie were both asleep. I attempted to take Mattie out of Matt's arms, and he woke up.

"Hey, I'm going to lay him down."

"Okay.'

After I laid Mattie down in his crib, I went to say goodnight to Matt, but he was fast asleep on the couch. So I took a blanket, laid it over him, and went to bed. When I woke up the next day, Matt was still asleep on the couch. I tried to be quiet as I prepped a bottle for Mattie. Once he was fed and back asleep, I decided to get dress. When I came out the room, Matt was awake.

"Morning. So how did you sleep?"

"It was okay. I didn't mean to impose. I didn't know I was that tired."

"You could never impose on me."

"So, what do you have planned for today?"

"Well, first thing first, I'm going to the cemetery to visit my parent's grave, and after that I may take Mattie to see Julian."

"So, you told him about Mattie."

"Yep."

"And how did he take it?"

"He was surprised and then excited. I want him to do better for Mattie's sake, but I think this entire incident has taken its toll on him."

"So, are you guys going to try and work it out?"

"You know I thought about it, and it would be convenient for Mattie to have his mother and father living together, but I don't know if I could do it. Julian claimed he loved me, and then he slept with Regina. How can I forgive that?"

"I don't know, but you have to do what you feel is best for you and Mattie, and no one including me can tell you what that is. I want you to be happy, Maya, even if it's with Julian."

"You don't mean that."

"You're right, I don't." Matt and I started to laugh. "But if he makes you happy, then I do. I love you, and I want you and Mattie to be happy."

"Believe it or not, I am happy. That little boy brightens my day and I'm truly blessed to have him in my life."

"Then whatever you decide I'm behind you all the way."

"Thanks, Matt."

"Hey, can I use your bathroom?"

"Sure."

While Matt was in the bathroom, I decided to pack Mattie's diaper bag. I thought about what he said about me and Julian getting back together. And as much as I wanted to embrace the idea, I couldn't. Julian didn't just cheat on me; he cheated on me with the one person whose ultimate goal was to destroy my life. Maybe in the future I could truly forgive him, but for now my heart was still healing.

Matt came out of the bathroom and he looked beat. "Well, let me get out of your hair so you can get a start on your day."

"And what do you have planned for today?"

"Nothing at all! Wait! I may take a nap later."

"Are you serious? That's it?"

"Yeah. I've had a long week and I need to relax. So, if you and Mattie get bored, you're more than welcomed to come over because I'll be at home doing absolutely nothing."

"Well, we may take you up on that. And, Matt…"

"Yeah."

"Thank you. Your friendship means the world to me. I know

I've made a lot of bad decisions in the past, but you never gave up on me. So, thank you."

Matt gave me a hug and I rested my head on his chest. I missed him, but I knew I had to let him go as well. As I pulled away, our eyes met and Matt embraced me with a kiss. I felt wrong for what I was feeling and I quickly pushed him away.

"What's wrong?"

"This. This is wrong."

"Maya, you know how I feel about you, so why do you keep pushing me away."

"Because this it's healthy, Matt, and you know it."

"No. Hiding how I truly feel about you isn't healthy. You know I love you, and I never knew how much I cared about you until the day you left town."

"But why love me when there are thousands of women out there for you to choose from."

"And yet I choose you."

"This isn't right and you know it."

"How can me loving you be wrong?"

"Because I'm sick Matt, and there's no way around it. So how could we have a possible future together? We can't. But Julian, on the other hand is sick as well; and maybe in time I could find a way to forgive him, and we could be a family."

"So, you're willing to be with Julian because you're both sick instead of following your heart and being with me?"

"Matt, that's not fair."

"No, what's not fair is the fact that you're constantly not giving me a chance. I get it. I'm the white boy in this situation, and you feel as though we don't have anything in common, but we do. We love each other and that's all that matters."

"Matt, your race doesn't have anything to do with my decision.

It's me. If I gave you HIV, I wouldn't be able to live with myself. I don't want to do anything to hurt you."

"Maya, I'm a grown man; and if that was to happen, then it would be on me, not you. I'm not stupid. I know what I'm getting myself into. Because when you love someone, you love them completely, and I love you with all my heart."

I was in tears. How could I love Matt the way he needed to be loved? He deserved better.

"Matt, you know I love you, but I don't want to hurt you."

"Then stop pushing me away. Let me love you, and we'll figure this out as we go."

"I can't love you the way you needed to be loved. We could never be spontaneous, and we'll always have to be careful. What kind of life would that be for you? It's not fair of me to put you in a subjective relationship. So, I can't."

"Why do you keep making decisions for me? You don't think I know what it entails to be with you? I've done my research and thought this through. Nothing has changed. I love you and I want to be with you and only you." I looked at Matt and I couldn't stop crying. I loved him but I was so afraid of hurting him. Matt walked me over to the bed and sat me down. He wiped away my tears, and then grabbed my hands. "I love you Maya, and nothing is going to change that. Not even HIV. So if you want to be with Julian, then be with Julian because you love him and not because you feel obligated due to your illness; because you do have options, Maya, and I'm one of them."

"It's not fair, Matt. It's just not fair."

"I know."

Matt continued to wipe away my tears and then he kissed me. "Matt..."

"Just let me have this moment."

Matt kissed me, and at that moment, it felt like home. I thought about Colorado, and our time there together was perfect. I was afraid of what I was feeling, but I was so tired of turning Matt away.

"Let me love you."

"I don't want you to resent me, and I know that one day you will."

"Maya, the only thing I resent is that I didn't go back for you and Mattie weeks ago. So, let me love you, and I promise I'll never leave you."

I leaned in towards Matt and he embraced me with a passionate kiss. Our kissing intensified, and before I knew it, we were taking each other's clothes off. I almost forgot that I was sick and then I stopped.

"We can't."

"Yes we can. Like I said. I know what I need to do in order to be with you. So, let me love you. Okay?"

"Matt, I'm afraid. If I was to…"

"Don't think about it. Just close your eyes and let me love you."

I closed my eyes and I couldn't believe the way Matt was making me feel. We made love; and it blew my mind that he knew exactly what to do and how to handle the situation. I didn't think that being with someone who wasn't infected was possible, but Matt showed me that it was. Why he loved me, I didn't know; but I was grateful that he did. Would our relationship last? I didn't know, but making a relationship work in the conventional sense was hard, but being in a relationship with me could prove to be problematic. I always found myself in one unpredictable romance after another, and my so-called track record with men was about as understandable as my comprehension of relativity. For the most part, all I ever wanted out of life was to be happy, but in reality what I was really searching for was my happily ever after. The successful business, the loving husband, and the adoring kids were all that I ever wanted. That was my goal, but instead I was a single parent, coping with HIV, and falling for a guy whom I was afraid to give my heart.

The fear of being alone always clouded my judgement. Now, with my illness lurking in the background, I've often wondered what I could possibly offer someone in a relationship. My contribution would always fall short whenever it came to sex and no matter what my heart felt, I could never give a man 100% of myself. The entire situation felt like a cruel joke, but I was done mourning over the issue. I could either fall victim to my own circumstances or I could figure out a way to do something about it.

Wanting to move forward, on the other hand, was hard. Sometimes I felt like I was self-sabotaging. I would seek out the worst in a situation, instead of trying to figure out a way to make things work. I've always allowed myself to see the horror in everything and I chose to block out any possibility of what could be. But through time my heart has changed, and I no longer wanted to live in fear. I wanted to seek out my possibilities to see where they would lead. I didn't want to push love away any longer. I didn't know how I was going to make a relationship work, but I needed it to work because, in the end, I was willing to put my heart on the line…one…last…time.

Chapter 20

Endless Possibilities

During my time in Georgia, I visited my parents' grave every chance I got. I told them about Matt and his willingness to be with me. I didn't understand his logic, but I felt blessed for his love and understanding. Julian and I made amends, and I decided to be up front with him about my relationship with Matt. He was heartbroken at first, but he understood that his betrayal destroyed any hopes of us ever being together again. He wished for me to be with someone else other than Matt, but he knew that Matt would love and take care of Mattie like his own.

As time passed my way of thinking changed, and due to our illness I didn't want Julian to miss any more moments in Mattie's life. I made a proposition to support him financially, so he would have time to spend with his son. He denied my request at first, but then he realized it was the best thing to do. Our disease didn't guarantee us anything but a certain death, and I wanted to do what was right even if I didn't feel comfortable in doing so.

The more time Julian spent with Mattie, the more I thought

about where I wanted to live. I loved everything about Denver, but Julian's family was in Atlanta; and going back and forth between Colorado and Georgia was becoming exhausting. I needed to make a decision on where I wanted to live, and fast.

Whenever I would visit Atlanta, I would stay with Matt in his condo. If we were going to declare our love for each other, than it only made sense that we lived together. Then one day, while I was sitting in the living room watching television, the thought of where to live entered my head once again. I wanted to ask Julian to move to Colorado, but that didn't seem fair to him or his family. I, on the other hand, didn't want to move back to Atlanta. I loved Colorado. It was the only place that truly felt like home. I heard the door slam and I snapped out of my trace. Matt walked into the room and kissed me on the cheek.

"Hey, so how was your day?"

"Confusing."

"Confusing? How?"

"I need to figure out where I want to live. It's hard because I grew up in Atlanta, but I love Denver."

"Okay, so what does your heart say?"

"Who cares what my heart says? You're in Atlanta. Julian's in Atlanta. So it only makes sense for me to move back to Atlanta."

Matt hugged me and then he gave me a kiss.

"I want you to be happy, so it doesn't matter where you live as long as we're together."

"So, if I decided I wanted to stay in Colorado, then you're willing to uproot your life here in Atlanta, and move back with me?"

"Yes. I don't know about you, but I remember our time in Colorado, and we were happy."

"And that may be the case but what would your family say?"

"I don't know, but you can ask them tonight over dinner."

"Tonight? What are you talking about?"

"Well, as you know I'm pretty close to my parents, and since we're practically living together they wanted to meet you."

"Matt, in the time that I've known you I have never heard you talk about your parents."

"And why would I? There was never a reason to bring them up until now. They really want to meet you, and I think that it's only fair to give them the opportunity to do so."

"And you're sure you want to do this?"

"Yes, I love you Maya, and if this is going to work then I want you to meet my family."

"Then let's get dressed."

I was so nervous. What was I to wear and my hair; I didn't know what to do to it. I had never been in this stage of a relationship before. I asked Matt to watch Mattie while I ran an errand. I raced over to Allison so she could help me figure out what to wear, and Tina came over to do my hair. After they finished, I couldn't recognize myself. I was so grateful for their help. When I returned back to the condo, Matt was surprised by my look.

"You look great."

"Thanks, I needed a little help. I didn't know what to wear."

"Maya, they're my parents not the Kennedys, so you would look great in anything you put on."

"You're so sweet."

I gave Matt a kiss, then we grabbed Mattie and left. I didn't know if Matt's parents would like me or not, but I was curious to know if they knew about my illness. Before long we pulled up to a grand two story mansion on the outskirts of town. I went from being nervous to morbidly petrified. We got out of the car and I couldn't stop my hands from shaking. Matt grabbed my hands and started to caress them.

"You're going to be fine."

"I don't know. I don't feel so good."

"It's okay. Calm down. You got this."

Matt ringed the doorbell and an older gentleman answered.

"Mattie! It's good to see you son!"

"Mattie," I said under my breath. Was he serious? His nickname is Mattie. I looked at Matt and he gave me a sly smile.

"Dad, I want you to meet Jeremiah Davenport." Matt's father shook my hand as I tried to regain my composure.

"It's Maya."

"Well, Maya, I'm Richard and it's nice to finally meet you. Come on in." Richard looked down and saw Mattie. "Oh, and who do we have here?"

"This is my son, Matthew."

"Matthew huh? So, son is there something you would like to tell me?"

"Oh no, they just share the same name." I was baffled at trying to get my words out.

"I'm only kidding. I know all about Matthew. You guys come on in and make yourself at home." I looked at Matt and I was about to pass out. My nerves were about to get the best of me.

I went inside the house and it was beautifully decorated throughout. Matt escorted me to a bedroom where I could lay Mattie down, and there was a crib in the room, which shocked me.

"Does someone here have a baby?"

"No. I told my parents about Mattie, so they went out and bought a crib when I told you were coming over for dinner."

"So, they bought a crib just for tonight?"

"Yes."

"And you don't think that's a bit much?"

"No. They wanted Mattie to be comfortable while he's here.

Besides, I would feel better knowing he's in a crib verses lying on the bed."

"Yeah. Maybe you're right."

"You know I'm right."

Once I was able to get Mattie settled, I then turned my sights towards Matt.

"Okay, I have to say something before we go back downstairs."

"Sure, what's on your mind?"

"Your nickname is Mattie. Are you kidding me? Why didn't you ever say anything?"

"Because I thought it was cute. Besides, it was nice to hear someone else being called Mattie other than me."

"Cute! Really. You're not slick! Mattie is not your mini me."

Matt couldn't stop laughing. He kissed me on the forehead and then we walked out. Matt's mother met us in the dining room. She was petite and her hair was styled in a short bob. His father however offset her with his height. As we all sat down at the dinner table, I knew it was only a matter of time before his parents would start questioning me.

"Maya, this is my mom, Diane."

I shook her hand.

"It's nice to meet you."

"I'm sure."

I looked at Matt because I didn't know how to take her response.

"So, Maya, Matthew tells us that you owned several bakeries at once upon a time. How did you get into baking?" His father seemed very curious.

"My mother. She gave me my first mixer when I was eleven, and the rest is history."

"And what did your mother do?"

"She was a stay at home mom."

"And your father?"

"He was a District Court Judge."

Matt's father was asking a lot of questions but his mother remained quiet. She seemed withdrawn from the conversation.

"So, how did you and Matthew meet?"

"In a very unorthodox way. His firm wanted to buy me out, and he came around every month trying to persuade me to sell."

"Really." Richard was smiling at Matt. "Maya, can I let you in on a little secret?"

"Sure."

"Dad." Matt seemed embarrassed at what his father was about to say.

"Come on, son. She deserves to know the truth."

"The truth about what?"

"Your company...it was always under the radar at Mattie's firm. He only came around every month because he wanted to, not because he had to. It wasn't until you decided to sell, that your company became a hot commodity."

"Are you serious?"

I was shocked. I looked at Matt and he smiled while shrugging his shoulders.

"Sorry son."

"Sure you are."

I couldn't help but laugh. Even though Richard seemed to enjoy teasing Matt, that didn't divert his attention away from me.

"So, Maya, back to the topic at hand. Since I know it wasn't my son's persuasiveness that caused you to sell, do you wish to elaborate on what did?

"Dad." Matt seemed uncomfortable regarding his father's line of questioning.

"Well, it's a fair question, son. I'm just curious to know why she sold her business."

"It's okay. I don't mind. I sold it because it seemed like the right thing to do. A lot had happened in my life, so it was time for a change."

"Change." Diane laughed under her breath as she ate.

"Mom. Really?"

"What? I didn't say anything."

"Please excuse my wife. She can be very cynical over Matthew. He's our only child, and we only want the best for him."

"I understand." I felt so inadequate at that moment. I was ready for this experience to be over as I sat and ate my dinner in silence. I looked at Matt and I felt as though I was holding him back. His family seemed propionate in the community, and I was probably the black stain that would tarnish their reputation…in more ways than one.

"Why are you with our son?" I knew his mother was probably holding that question in from the moment I stepped through the door.

"Mom! Why would you ask her that?"

"It's only a fair question, right."

"Right. I'm with Matt because I love him. It took a while for me to finally come around; but when I did, he grabbed my hand and he never let go."

"And do you feel as though you're worthy of his love? I mean, I heard you strung him along for years and you didn't give my son a chance until you became damaged goods."

"Diane, that's enough!" Richard seemed displeased by Diane's unwarranted criticism.

I felt so hurt at that moment. I loved Matt, but maybe his mother was right. Maybe I was with him out of convenience. I could feel my eyes as they began to water, but I refused to cry. Diane had every right to be protective of her son, and if I was in her shoes, I would feel the same way about Mattie.

"No, it's okay. You're right. I am damaged, but that wasn't my reasoning for being with Matt."

"Maya, you don't have to do this." Matt was outraged.

"No, I do. If you must know, I went my whole life looking for Mr. Right, and I thought this other guy was the one. He claimed he loved me and wanted to spend the rest of his life with me, and I believed him. So, I put all my trust in him, but in return he hurt me in the worst way possible. So, long story short, I didn't think that I could love again until Matt showed me I could."

"Well isn't that nice. Our son's charity reaches beyond the courtroom."

"She's not a charity case. I love her, and if you can't get on board with that, then we have nothing else to talk about. Today or any other day."

"Mattie you don't mean that." Diane seemed stirred by Matt's response.

"Wait, there's something I want to say." Richard decided to jump back into the conversation.

"No, dad, I'm done."

"I know, but I have to say this." Richard turned his attention towards me. "Maya, what you don't understand is that Matt and I didn't become close until he got older. It felt nice to be able to talk with my son about anything, and over the years he's always talked about you." I looked at Matt in disbelief. "I remember when he first met you, he talked about this strong, independent woman who was out changing the world one shop at a time. He told me how you chose your employees, and I was impressed and yet skeptical at the same time. It was unconventional what you were doing, but it worked. He then told me about the softball games, and how much fun you guys had together. Even when he was with Amy and Samantha, I always caught him talking about you. Then he told me you met this guy named Julian, and he was so heartbroken."

"Dad…"

"No, let me finish. Just so you know, he couldn't stand the guy; and when the two of you broke up, he lit up with excitement. He told me about the dates the two of you went on and from my understanding they were pretend to you, but they were real to my son. Then later on he told me about your father's death, and that you pushed him away. For months we barley had anything to talk about expect work. I could see the sadness in his eyes, and there was nothing I could do to change it. Then you up and moved away, and so did my son's spirit."

"Matt, I'm so sorry." My heart was so heavy.

"I know." Matt's eyes were watery. I could tell he was trying to stay strong during his father's remarks, but it was hard.

"Then one day he received some important documents in the mail, and he was off to Colorado. He was gone for a while; and when he returned home, he didn't seem the same. I tried to get him to talk, but instead he broke down in tears. I've never seen my son like that before. That's when he told me about Matthew and your illness." Matt was in tears and so was I. I didn't know the depth of Matt's love until that moment. I felt so stupid for pushing him away all those years and now that we're together, I feel as though I've cheated him out of a real relationship. "So understand why my wife is so defensive when it comes to Matt. His happiness means the world to us, and we've discovered that his happiness revolves around you."

"He loves you, Maya, and I don't want to see my son get hurt. He's all I've got and his happiness means the world to me." That was the first pleasant comment Diane had made the entire night.

"And I love him too. I pushed Matt away for years, because I didn't want to lose his friendship. Usually, when my relationships are over, so is the friendship. So I depended on Matt's friendship more than he knew. He always wanted more, but I was afraid to give it to him. And when he found out about my illness, I felt like he was going to turn his back on me, but he didn't. He was committed to being with me, and I was tired of turning him away."

"Well as long as Mattie is happy, then so am I." Diane wiped Matt's tears away, and I truly understood the love that she had for her son.

"I'm happy mom. I'm truly happy."

"Will you please excuse me for a moment?"

I went into the bathroom and cried like a baby. I was so busy holding on to one love, that I didn't see real love when it was staring me in the face. Maybe I wouldn't have known the depths of Matt's love without first being tested by Julian. I believed everything happens for a reason, but I wished God would have opened my eyes sooner, before I had given Julian a second chance. He may have been the worst mistake in my life, but I wouldn't have my Mattie if it wasn't for him. Life can be very strange, and as for me, I finally understood the complexity of my situation.

While I was freshening my make-up, there was a knock at the bathroom door. I opened it, and it was Matt.

"Hey, are you okay?"

"Yeah, I'm fine." In my heart, I truly didn't know how to feel. My emotions were all over the place. "So, tell me something."

"Sure."

"Why didn't you ever tell me how you truly felt about me?"

"Because I wanted you to come around on your own. I love you and I wanted to be with you, but I didn't want to force it."

"You know your mother is right. I don't deserve you."

"And I could say the same thing about you. You are an amazing woman and I love you."

"I love you, too." Matt kissed me and I melted in his arms. There was no question that he loved me, and I was so blessed to have him in my life. "I'm sorry."

"Sorry for what?"

"For not seeing your love sooner. I hate that I pushed you away all those years, and I'm grateful that you still love me."

"Maya, I fell in love with you years ago, and that's why it never worked out with anyone else. I tried to move on but I couldn't. It was you. It was always you." Matt and I kissed and we enjoyed the rest of the night with his family.

The next day, I thought about my decision and realized I had been selfish long enough. I decided to move back to Atlanta so Julian and I could easily share custody of Mattie. Brandon was his uncle and he wanted to be a part of Mattie's life as well. I told Matt I wanted us to find a house together, so we could make a home for Mattie. So we decided it was time to go house hunting. While we were out, we passed by the bakery and Matt pulled over. It had been a while since I had stepped foot in Davenport Sweet Cakes. I walked in and the scent brought back so many memories. Nikki spotted me and raced to the counter.

"Maya, it's so good to see you."

"Thanks, it's good to see you too." I looked around at all the customers in the bakery. "I see the shop is still booming. So what do you have that's new?"

"Funny you should ask." Nikki went in the back and came out with a beautifully decorated cupcake.

"And what is this?"

"I call it Journey. It's a chocolate cupcake with a vanilla cream center, but the taste of cherry is infused throughout the cake. It's a spin on your chocolate cherry cake."

"Well it looks delicious."

"Great! Now try it, and tell me what you think."

I looked at Matt and smiled.

"You want some?"

"I don't know. You taste it first. We are talking about Nikki remember."

"Whatever, Matt."

We all laughed as I bit into the cupcake, and without warning my tooth hit something hard. As I pulled it out of my mouth, I noticed it was a ring. I looked over at Matt who was down on one knee.

"Maya…"

"Matt what are you doing?" Everyone in the shop was looking at us, and Tina and Allison came walking out of the kitchen.

"Maya, I knew a long time ago that I wanted you to be a part of my life. Even though we took an unconventional route to get here, we made it; and I wouldn't change it for anything in the world. I love you and Mattie, and I want to know if you'll marry me?"

I couldn't stop the tears from flowing. Part of me was afraid to say yes because I didn't want to cheat Matt out of a future but I also knew that running away wouldn't solve anything. I looked at all of my friends and it felt like my heart was about to explode.

"Yes. I will marry you." Matt placed the ring on my finger then kissed me. I was so happy, and I prayed that nothing went wrong.

Once Diane got news of the engagement, she was all over throwing me the wedding of the century. She and Richard pulled out all the stops when it came to the preparation of the wedding. I was overjoyed with excitement, but that joy was soon cut short when I realized I had to tell Julian about the wedding. Dating Matt was one thing, but marrying him was another. I didn't know how Julian would feel about Matt being Mattie's stepfather. So one day, I decided to go and see Julian to tell him about the wedding; but when I rang the doorbell, there was no answer. So, I decided to use the spare key he gave me to let myself in. I called out for Julian, but there was still no answer. So, I opened his bedroom door, and to my surprise I caught him having sex.

"Oh, I'm so sorry!" I closed the door as quickly as I could and rushed towards the front door.

"Maya, wait. What's going on?"

"It's nothing. I came over to tell you something but it can wait."

"No, don't go anywhere. Give me a minute and I'll be out."

Julian went back into his room, and when he came out, he was holding hands with a pretty young woman with long brown hair, who looked like she was in her mid-thirties.

"Maya, I want you to meet Felicia. I met her at a support meeting. And as you can see, we hit it off."

"I'll say." I looked at Felicia and smiled. "It's nice to meet you."

"Same here."

"She's helped me a lot, and I don't want you to think that this is some random hookup because it's not. She's truly special to me."

"Well, I'm happy for you."

"So, what's up? Why are you here?"

"I almost forgot." We all started to laugh. "I'm here to tell you that Matt asked me to marry him and I said yes." I held up my hand and flashed my ring.

"I'm happy for you."

"Thanks, and the only reason I wanted to tell you was because of Mattie. Once Matt and I are married, he'll be Mattie's stepfather; and I didn't want you to think that I was trying to replace you in any way."

"I know you wouldn't do that, and thank you for being considerate of my feelings. I know how you feel about Matt, and even though I don't care for the guy, I know he'll be a great stepfather to Mattie. Now with all of that being said, I do have one question for you."

"Okay, what?"

"Once you're married, are you moving back to Colorado?"

"No, I've decided that it's in Mattie's best interest to be able to spend as much time as he could with both of his parents. And the only way that can happen is by us moving back to Atlanta."

"Really! You're moving back? You don't know what this means to me to be able to spend more time with Mattie! So thank you."

"Don't thank me just yet. You know the condition of our agreement, right?"

"Yes, and Felicia has been helping me stay on track."

I looked at Felicia and smiled.

"Thank you for what you're doing for him. Even though it didn't work out between us, I still want Julian to be healthy and happy."

"I understand. Our illness can be very tricky at times."

"Oh, so you're..."

"Yes. I'm HIV positive as well."

"So, are you guys being safe? I mean, how does that work with you both being positive?"

"I know it would seem convenient since we're both positive, but we still use protection. We're still learning about this disease and we want to be around for each other. So, we're being precautious because I want to spend as much time as I can with my son."

"Well I'm glad to hear that. And believe it or not, I'm really proud of you."

"I'm proud of me too." We all laughed as I proceeded to the

door. "And, Maya, I want you to know that I'm really happy for you and I wish you best...even if it's with Matt."

"Thanks, Julian that means a lot." A thought came to my head and I wanted to dismiss it, but I asked anyway. "You know, if you guys don't have anything to do on the 12th of next month, then you're more than welcomed to attend my wedding."

Julian seemed shocked.

"You would invite me to your wedding? Why?"

"To show you and Felicia what you have to look forward to. When people say HIV, the only thing that follows is doom and gloom. So, why not have something *positive* to look forward to instead of defeat."

"You know you're right. But, Felicia, if we go, don't be getting any ideas." We all started to laugh.

"I just have to say this. I love you guy's relationship. It's so beautiful to see the support that you two have for each other," Felicia said, as she held on to Julian's hand.

"Trust me, it wasn't always this great. It took time; and in the end, we discovered it was no longer about us, but about the love and support we have for our son. We want him to have the best memories possible, and he can't have that if his parents are constantly mad and angry at each other. So, we made peace with the situation and we decided to be each other's keeper. Even though we're sick, I refuse to allow our illness to defeat us because we deserve to be happy too."

"Yes we do." Julian walked me to the door, gave me a kiss on the cheek, and then I left.

The twelfth finally rolled around and I had my dream wedding. Richard walked me down the aisle and Allison, Tina, and Nikki were my bridesmaids. Mattie was the ring bearer and he stumbled the entire way. He was so cute and we couldn't help but to laugh every time he fell. I looked out into the audience and saw Charlie and Thad as well as April, Gary, and the kids. I continued to look around and spotted Julian and Felicia. And to my surprise, Brandon and Veronica showed up as well.

To some it would seem strange to have your ex-lover at your wedding; but for me, it was the total opposite. We'd learned how to support each other and how to be a witness for hope and not defeat. My wedding wasn't just about bringing me and Matt together, but bringing my unconventional family together as a whole. As the wedding commenced, it felt like a fairytale and I was overcome with happiness. Matt and I said our vows, but when I closed my eyes to kiss him, I fell into complete darkness.

I began to panic. I didn't know what was happening to me. I felt an intense chill quiver up my spine. I tried to open my eyes, but couldn't. Finally, I could see a glimmer of light peering through the crevice of my eyelids. It was the strangest feeling. One much like I was waking from a long deep sleep. As my vison came into focus, I sat up in disbelief. Were my eyes deceiving me? I scanned the room in utter shock. I was afraid to move. I continued to observe my surroundings. I felt like I was losing my mind. I tried to move but a sharp abrupt pain penetrated my neck. While massaging my upper body, I thought about Mattie. I raced to my bedroom but he wasn't there. Anxiety took over, then fear. I searched every room, but still no Mattie. My worst nightmare was coming true.

"Mattie! Mattie, baby, where are you? Mattie!" I reached for my cell phone to call the police. As my hand brushed the screen, August 2, 2015 appeared on the screensaver. I dropped the phone in complete horror. The year was 2017, not 2015. I couldn't make sense of what was happening. It felt like the room was spinning. I picked up the phone and the screensaver showed a picture of me and my father. I decided to check my call history. The last person I had spoken to was Mary. I scanned my phone and there were no pictures of Mattie…none of me and Matt…not even Julian. I wanted to call someone but didn't want to sound like a crazy person. I needed to make sense of what was happening. I sat on the couch contemplating what to do next. As I shifted in the chair, out the corner of my eye, I caught a glimpse of the sleeping pills sitting on the table.

"No way!"

I picked up the bottle to research the medication. "Impairment! Unusual dreams! Do not take with alcohol as combining them can cause extreme sleepiness or difficulty waking up." I looked over at the wine glass sitting on the table. I was surprised I didn't put myself into a coma. I was devastated. If everything I read was true, I had hallucinated two years of my life. Tears fell as I threw the medication in the trash. There was no Mattie. He wasn't real. I sat and began to mourn the loss of a child who never existed. I could still see his face…and hear his voice. It felt like a cruel joke. First my father and now Mattie. All I could do was scream! In the midst of my breakdown, I realized if there was no Mattie, then I wasn't HIV positive either. My tears of sadness suddenly turned into a hysterical laugh. I wasn't sick. This newfound revelation gave me an optimistic spirit. I wiped away my tears and I felt like I was given an unconventional second chance. I got up, cleaned the house, took a shower and debated how to proceed next. I could do anything I wanted but didn't have the slightest clue what that entailed. While sitting in perpetual thought, my doorbell rang. I was curious as to who it could be.

"Who is it?"

"It's Julian."

Julian? Was I ready to deal with him again? He put me through a ring of emotions, although they were all in my head. I didn't know how I wanted to handle the situation. Even though the experience wasn't real, my emotions were. I opened the door.

"Hi, Julian."

"Maya. Can I come in?"

"Sure." I waved Julian in the house. He seemed surprised I let him in. "So, what do you want?"

"To talk."

"Okay. Let's talk." I sat on the couch and Julian sat next to me. "What do you want to talk about?"

"Us. But first, I want you to know I'm sorry for your loss. I know you were very close to your father."

"I was. Thank you."

"With that being said, I miss you. I know I messed up when I didn't tell you about Regina. But honestly, we were over. I get that I hurt you but I want you back."

I looked at Julian and debated if I should tell him about my dream. In my heart, I would always care about him, but I wasn't willing to give him a second chance.

"Julian."

"Yes."

"Can I be honest with you? I mean completely honest?"

"Sure."

"What we had was special. I felt it and I know you felt it too."

"I did."

"But, we don't belong together."

"Maya…"

"Wait. Hear me out. Yes, there was something there." I thought about the feelings I had for Julian in my dreams and how I had to learn how to love him. The same was true with Matt. I had to learn how to love him after my fiasco with Julian. Both relationships were based off of acquired feelings instead of genuine, unwavering love. "But whatever we had went away the day I fell in love with Brandon. I know this isn't what you wanted to hear, but it's the truth."

"But why, Maya? Why him? He's my brother. Why would you do this to me?"

"I don't think either one of us planned for it to happen. It just did. But I'm not saying I want to be with Brandon. I'm not saying I want to be with anyone right now. I just know that I can't be with you."

"Maya, please. I'm not a bad guy. I promise you."

At that point, I decided I would divulge some of the dream I had with Julian, hoping he would see part of my perspective on things.

"I'm going to share something with you and I need you to keep an open mind."

"Okay."

"I took some medication that put me in a lucid dream state. Everything that happened within this dream felt real…as real as you and I sitting on this couch having a conversation right now. And in that dream, we got back together, got engaged, then I found out I was pregnant with your child and you had infected me with HIV."

"I what?!!"

"Yes. You had sympathy sex with Regina who intentionally infected you to get back at me. Long story short, you failed me. Even in my dreams you found a way to screw things up. I fell in love with you. I agreed to be your wife and you still cheated on me…with Regina. Let me emphasize that again…Regina! My dream ended with me falling in love with and marrying Matt."

"Maya. As crazy as that sounds, it still doesn't change the fact, that it was just a dream. It wasn't real."

"But it felt real. I woke up a few hours ago mourning the loss of a child who never existed. That's how compelling this dream was. So, yes, none of it was real however the actions that took place were very convincing."

"Don't do this."

"I'm not trying to hurt you. Trust me. I'm not. But we can't be together."

"Maya…"

"We can't." Tears fell from my eyes. Dream or not, the emotions were still raw, but hopefully in time I would find a way to release the false memories and replace them with real ones.

"I understand. I don't like it and I'm not sure what just happened here, but I'll respect your wishes and walk away."

"Thank you. Oh, and Julian, promise me one thing."

"Anything."

"Stay away from Regina. Something isn't right with her and I'd hate for her to hurt you in any way."

"I promise. And I need you to promise me something as well."

"Anything."

"Throw your medication away. Flush it down the toilet. Wash it down the sink. Just find a way to get rid of it. We don't need you having any more crazy dreams."

Both of us started laughing.

"I'm already ahead of you."

Julian stood up, headed towards the door, and then stopped.

"You know I'll always care about you, right?"

"I know."

"Take care."

"I will. And stay Regina free! I mean it."

"Noted." Julian gave me a kiss on the cheek and left.

I closed the door feeling like a new woman. I didn't know what the future had in store for me but I was willing and optimistic for whatever's to come. I readied myself to go out, but then Mattie's face entered my mind. It hurt because he was my heart and now he was gone. Thinking about Mattie forced me to think about Matt. I was marrying him just before I woke up. Was he the guy God wanted me to be with? Or was there someone new out there for me? I was so confused. So, I decided to be proactive and send Matt a text to see what he was up to. He texted me back informing me he was on a date; and quote unquote, she may be the one. It couldn't get more obvious than that.

So, to take my mind off things, I decided to go to the one place that made me happy…the farmers market. I walked around and it felt like home. The simple things I missed felt new again. It's crazy how the mind is able to fabricate time. It felt like ages since I was last there. I picked up some fresh fruit and berries as I made my way around the market. As I stood in line for yogurt, a sunflower peered over my shoulder. I turned around and it was Brandon.

"Brandon."

"Hi. This is for you." Brandon handed me the sunflower.

"Thank you. So, what are you doing here?"

"Doing some last-minute shopping. What about you? What brings you out this way?"

"Believe it or not, this is my favorite place to come and clear my head."

"Mine too. I know I'm late saying this but I'm sorry about your father. I know he meant a lot to you."

"Thanks. He did. So, how are things with you and Angela? She still has a veil over you?" I teased Brandon as I sniffed my sunflower.

"No, she doesn't. We're no longer together."

"Sorry to hear that."

"No you're not."

"Let's pretend I am." Both of us started to laugh. "Well, it was good seeing you."

"It was good seeing you too." I turned to walk away. "Maya, wait."

"Yes."

"I need you to know why things didn't work out between me and Angela."

"No. I don't need to know. It took time, but I was finally able to let go of the pain I felt when you left me. So, no. You can hold on to your truth because I don't need it."

"But I need you to know why."

"Brandon…"

"Hear me out. After our relationship went public, my actions following were out of fear, not dishonesty. I didn't want to leave you but I was afraid of hurting everyone else. And despite what Julian thinks, Angela didn't have a hold on me. You did."

"No. I can't do this with you."

"And why not? I know you still care about me. Every time we're near each other I can feel it. I know you've felt it too."

"You know what I've felt? Heartbreak. That's what I've felt. I loved you and you broke my heart. But I've had time to reevaluate my life. At first I wasn't sure what I wanted, but now I do."

"And what do you want?"

"I want a family. I want a man who loves me unconditionally without doubt or hesitation. I want certainty, and I can't get that from you. My father once told me his greatest achievement in life, was *me*. I want to know that feeling. I want kids. And I know you're not capable of giving me any of that." I became emotional. Tears fell as I thought about Mattie. Brandon whipped away my tears, looked into my eyes, then he kissed me ever so softly. I was stunned by his action.

"But I am. In time you'll see that. I know it's hard to trust me right now, but like you, I had an epiphany too. And you know what I discovered?"

"What?"

"That I am the man you're seeking and I will give you what

you're asking for and more." Brandon walked off smiling. "You'll see." He yelled back to me. I turned to walk away. My mind was in overload. I wasn't sure how to feel about Brandon. Nothing at that moment made sense.

I stopped by the shop on my way home to check in with everyone. When I walked through the door, I almost teared up knowing that I was still the sole proprietor of all of my establishments. Everyone was excited to see me. I walked over to Allison and gave her a long hug.

"Maya, are you alright?"

"Yes. I'm fine. I'm just glad to have you ladies in my life."

The rest of the gang walked over and we shared one big bear hug. Everything in the world was right again. After our heartfelt moment, we sat around and gossiped for hours. Before long I decided to head home. Once I made it in, I put away the groceries and cooked myself something to eat. I sat on the couch and the house felt so lonely. As I was flipping through the television channels, the doorbell rang.

"Who is it?"

"It's Brandon."

Brandon? I opened the door.

"Hi."

"Hi. Can I come in?"

"Sure." Brandon walked in and we sat down on the couch. "What's on your mind?"

"To prove to you that I meant every word I said earlier, I went and spoke to Julian about us."

"Why would you do that?"

"Because I needed him to be on board with us getting back together."

"But we're not getting back together. I told you, Brandon, I don't trust you..."

"And I get that. But hear me out. Every action leading up to this moment happened for a reason. I don't know why it took me so long to fight for what I wanted; but one thing rings true, and that's my love for you."

"And as sweet as that is, I don't know what I'm feeling any more. I know Julian probably mentioned it to you, but I recently woke from a really crazy dream that put all of my emotions into a tailspin. I'm not in a good head space right now and it wouldn't be fair of me to mislead you in any way."

"Let me ask you this. Do you want the family you were talking about? Because I'm here offering it to you. All you have to do is say yes."

"You know I do, but…"

"No buts. Based off what Julian told me, you were married to Matt in your dream. Why marry him? Why make a family with him? It was something about him that made you say yes?"

"Matt was always a constant in my life. He never let me down and he loved me no matter what. And in my dream, I had HIV and he still wanted to be with me. That's love."

"So, what was my role in your dream?"

"You didn't really have one."

"So, my brother and Matt were the only love interests in your dream. Doesn't that sound off to you? When we dated, I was the only constant in your life and I loved you unconditionally."

"But you left me."

"Because I was stupid and that's probably why you blocked your feelings for me in your dream. What my brother did to you was wrong, but I cut you deeply. So, I guess the only thing I could ever be to you in your dream was nothing."

Brandon was right. In my dream I only saw and spoke to him in passing. He had no valid role whatsoever. I hid my relationship with

Julian in the same matter I did with Brandon. I gave my heart to Matt the same way I did to Brandon. The only memorable moment regarding Brandon was when I saw him in Colorado and he told me his wife reminded him of me. Maybe Brandon was right. Maybe I had suppressed my feelings for him because I was afraid to face them…because they hurt so much.

"You're right. What you did to me hurt and it still hurts."

"So let me make it right. No replacing me with other people. No blocking me out. Let's face our feelings here and now."

"I can't!"

"Why not?"

"Because I don't want to feel that pain ever again."

"And you won't. I promise. No hiding. No secrets. No lies. No masking your hurt in dreams. No imaginary babies. Just me and you. Doing it right this time. There's nothing stopping us but you."

I looked at Brandon and he was right. I took all my hurt and masked it into a nightmare. I replaced him with everyone instead of confronting my true feelings.

"You're right. I'm the creator of my own pain and as much as I want to give us another chance, I don't know you anymore."

"And I'm willing to work on that. What we have is still there. It never left. You placed a veil over your heart and with time I'm willing to help you remove it if you give me another chance. Please, Maya. Will you take me back?"

I was afraid to say yes, but seeing how my dreams had masked my feelings into a paradox, I knew I needed to push past the fear and give love a second chance.

"If I say yes, we start from scratch. You and I know the love is still there, but as you stated, I need to remove the veil from my heart. So, if you're willing to take it slow, then my answer is yes."

"Thank you." Brandon kissed me and I allowed myself to enjoy it…before I pushed him away.

"Slow, remember?"

"You're right. But before we slow it down can I ask you for one favor?"

"It depends on what it is."

Brandon pulled a DVD from behind his back. "I figured if things worked out we were going to need something new to talk about. So, are you up for a movie?"

I started to smile. "Sure. What do you have in mind?"

My life had been a rollercoaster for years and I didn't feel like I deserved to be happy. I had abandoned the values I treasured so deeply because I didn't want to be alone. But in the end, I had to learn how to stop blocking my blessings and to be open to what life had in store for me. I felt like I didn't deserve a second chance, but I was given an unconventional one. I thought about all my iniquities, misfortunes, and somehow I was still amazed at how God found cause to not ABANDON ME.

The End

Feedback at: catalystic2002@yahoo.com

Printed in the United States
By Bookmasters